The Girl Who Walked on Ice

Joseph Lewis

BAYNAM BOOKS PRESS

For Mom and Dad.

Heaven restores you in life.

CONTENTS

"For in their interflowing aggregate, those grand freshwater seas of ours—Erie, and Ontario, and Huron, and Superior, and Michigan—possess an ocean-like expansiveness, with many of the ocean's noblest traits. They are swept by Borean and dismasting blasts as direful as any that lash the salted wave; they know what shipwrecks are, for out of sight of land, however inland, they have drowned many a midnight ship with all its shrieking crew."

— Herman Melville, Moby-Dick

Part One

Dead Calm

BAYNAM BOOKS PRESS

Chapter One

T his was the time on the island when everyone slept—the brief, still hours before the first person awoke. The winds blew snowdrifts down desolate roads, and wind chimes played songs that no one would ever hear. As the island slept, all footprints were scattered and erased by the wind, all traces of human activity wiped clean for the night. Barren tree limbs danced and swayed in the breeze that swept in off the lake, illuminated in the last of the moonlight, just before the brilliance of dawn. Out over the lake, no one would hear the shifting of the ice, its low moaning and cracking as it inched ever nearer to the shores of a slumbering Sandy Stone. Here, against the breaking of the night, all the animals on the island were restless and stirred within the deepest shadows of the woods, beyond the rows of cottages and hotels. For just a moment, as the first light touched the island, a whisper-like sigh passed through the trees, like a voice caught and carried in the wind—a voice that left no trace, disappearing as quickly as it had come. As the subtle burning of dawn crawled up into the eastern skies, and the deep blue of early morning slowly gave the isle light and form, the island, in return, gave a collective breath of relief, as though something unseen had retreated into the night. And as the first person awoke, the world returned to normal.

CHAPTER TWO

Sarah had begun her run later than she would have liked, as she had overslept for a good part of the morning. The sky was a brilliant, cloudless blue, and she was disappointed that she had missed most of a clear morning. It was cold, even colder than the previous few days, but the sun had helped to distract her and remind her of better days to come, which lifted her spirits.

The path she ran followed the perimeter of the island, and today she had planned to run as far as the limestone quarry, if her legs would carry her that far. She would run past the disused lighthouse—the antiquated beacon that rested quietly on the northernmost point of the island—past the dock that was packed full of people in the summer, now deserted save for the seagulls hoping to find a meal somewhere on the frozen lake. She wanted to run the loneliness out of herself. Classical music had begun to play over the loudspeakers, signaling high noon. Wagner's *Tristan and Isolde: Prelude to Act 1* played out over the island, and Sarah was always very comforted by this; she turned off her own music, pulled off her headphones, and ran to the sad symphony Mark had chosen to play today. Her lungs filled with cold air as she ran. She felt better already, and inside, she felt ready for the long run.

Sarah was struck by the unusual of all the places that came alive during the summer as she ran through the downtown area: the dollar movie cinema that played films which were at least five years old, where the projectionist always had to change the reel halfway through, eliciting a groan from the audience, and Classic Custard's Last Stand, where the chocolate was always scooped down to the very bottom of the quart, but the real secret gem of the place was the pistachio, her favorite. Just past that were the empty, skeletal rails of the bike rack where Dan had his shop and always overcharged the tourists for rentals. Last summer, Dan, Amy, and Sarah had gotten drunk and taken a golf cart to the old chapel in the woods just past midnight, smoking cigarettes and taking a rare break from the seasonal insanity that summer always brought.

She had woken up today to find a few messages waiting for her on her phone. Most of them were from Nathan, the young man she had met while bartending at Mickey's last summer. He was a few years younger and had spent a long weekend on the island over the 4th of July. He had come up with some friends, but they had gotten drunk early, and he grew bored with them and visited a few bars until he stopped at hers. He was charming and left a generous tip with his phone number. Sarah ended up surprised to find him still awake after her shift had ended. From then on, he occasionally visited her on the island for the rest of the summer. By the end of August, he had gone, and she'd barely heard a word from him since. Now and then, she'd get a drunken sext from him late in the night, and if he was really wasted, an amorous phone call. She didn't mind any of these; she had received many before and liked to hear from non-islander men during the off seasons. It reminded her of more to come: new loves, exciting flings, and more men to flirt with at the bar during the summer months. It reminded her that she was not alone and was still desired and not forgotten. She archived his messages, just as she had with all the others. She replayed them and reread them on the loneliest of nights.

She had also received a strange text from her sister, whom she hadn't heard from in three months, and did not want to spoil her good mood by thinking about it. *Alice can wait*, she thought. *She's made me wait three months.* She felt her skin grow flush with anger and began to run faster and harder, as if she would leave it behind. *Dad would have given you so much shit if he was still alive,* she thought. She had said that more times to her sister than she cared to remember.

Already she was planning what she would do with the rest of her day; she would stop by Mary's house, where a full English breakfast (Cleveland style), replete with scrambled eggs, kielbasa, perogies and a rich coffee stout, would be waiting to undo all the calories she burned on the run. Then she would go back to the B&B where she stayed for the winter and shower, respond to any emails she had received, and then head out to the bar to get it ready for tonight. She felt like opening earlier, just like last night—only tonight she would drink, get nice and drunk with the others, and play some of her favorite tunes at the bar.

Suddenly, her day was full, full of things that would tide her over until the next one. It was her way of coping, to fill these winter days as best she could. She imagined how much easier it must be off the island, for people to get on with their lives during the long winter months, but here, one's options were limited, so the islanders—the ones who "chose" to stay—had to dig deep into their creative wells. Each day was carefully planned, and any moment of "dead time" was to be avoided at all costs. The islanders often socialized during these months, and for most of the season, felt like a family: the holiday celebrations, the potlucks, the winter hikes, movie nights, and of course, The Fat Crab, where many of them came even on nights they hadn't planned on venturing out. Very rarely did she stay alone if she could help it.

Further down the road, away from the other hotels and bars, stood the historic Sandy Stone hotel, built long before even her grandmother was born, but able to withstand the brutal winds and storms that often visited the island throughout the year's various seasons. It stood large, still, and empty as it looked out over the lake, the huge water fountain in front empty for the season, coins frozen at the bottom. Cory had worked at the front desk last summer, and on some of the hottest nights, let her sleep in the vacant rooms facing the lake. The hotel had no air conditioning, but the breeze from the lake was cool, and it was a much more welcome sleep than the workers' dormitory she stayed in during peak season. But that had its charm, too. It was cheap. All these places were relics now, abandoned monuments from better and brighter times. She tried not to let it make her sad; Mark had made a good point during their last conversation: *Every single day of every single month can't be like the 4th of July, or you'll lose your fucking mind. You need time to decompress, to sit back and reflect, and enjoy the things you just did. It could* *be worse. You could be stuck in Florida or Vegas, where it's nice all year round and the fucking tourists never leave.*

She had never been to either of those places, but Mark had been everywhere, so she believed him. She picked up her pace until she had gone through all of downtown, past the rows of tourist cabins, and farther still, past the houses where many of the islanders lived. She felt relieved to leave all that behind her today.

As she continued along the path, she could see the limestone quarry to the right, now abandoned like most other places during the winter season. Huge piles of broken rocks extended beyond her line of sight. It looked small now, but had seemed so large and endless when she and Alice were young and played there until it grew dark. They would pack snacks and lunches and then head out, finding small man-made ponds to swim in and caves to hide in. As she ran past, she remembered one instance when she and her family were walking down this very same path, and Sarah had run ahead of them into the quarry. It was a summer evening, back when the days were long and fireflies flashed brightly along the path, guiding them as it grew dark. It was here she hid within a cave. She and Alice had found this spot before, a small cave easy to see out into the world but difficult to see into from the outside. Here she felt the thrill of being alone, of being able to watch without being watched, and she saw her father frantically looking for her. They must have looked for some time. To this day, she never understood why she hid from him when she knew they were all so worried. She remembered her father calling her name, and the comfort she felt, being desperately wanted and needed back then. Years after her father passed away, she looked back upon this memory with an almost overwhelming sadness, and she was now disappointed that it had resurfaced during an otherwise fulfilling run. Sarah frowned as she ran. She had made him worry needlessly, and he already had so much on his mind that she never knew about. But the memory faded as quickly as it had come, and she was back on track, running faster, her calves sore, her heart pounding, her body warm despite the cold air.

Dad. In her mind, Sarah already knew which length of the path she would turn around for the stretch back. She never ran by the northern end of the island. Not since she lost her father. *Where they found him,* she thought. Then she picked up her pace to keep the memory from darkening what was left of her day. *Oh, Dad,* she thought. *I wish you were here to help get me out of this place.* She would never say those words out loud, not around the others. They worshipped the island and never wanted to leave. But Sarah did not share their sentiment, and she couldn't leave, though she had tried to so many times.

Up ahead, a stretch of path lay blanketed in darkness under a cathedral of red pines; it went on for nearly half a mile. The light dissipated substantially as she entered the forest, the trees all wearing a blanket of snow and ice. Everything was still; even the wind seemed unable to penetrate the thick darkness, and as she looked up, she could see only a thin, lonely sliver of blue. Sarah could barely hear the music playing from the loudspeakers. It seemed miles away, almost as if it was coming from another island. The silence of it all made her uneasy, and again she picked up her pace, but the faster she ran, the longer the arms of pine seemed to reach out and block out all light. She began to hear a rustling sound not far off the path, and stopped briefly to listen. The sound was farther away than she thought, but seemed to be getting closer. She could hear twigs snapping and breaking beyond her line of sight. First a few, then more and more. And now it was getting louder. She started running again, even faster this time. The stretch of pines seemed to go on forever. More twigs snapped. The breaking of limbs. Footsteps? She ran harder, nearly slipping several times on the path, which had grown icy and treacherous.

She could not yet tell which direction the sounds came from, as they seemed to surround her. Yet the pines were motionless, and their limbs barely swayed. She stopped again. The sounds continued to grow louder this time. Multiple footsteps. It sounded like more—almost an army. Hundreds of footsteps, moving fast. More branches were breaking. Now she could see something—the rustling of pine branches. And out they came, a large herd of deer led by the biggest buck she'd ever seen, rampaging through the forest, tearing branches from limbs, colliding with trees, and running as fast as they could. But from what? Her legs froze as she saw them stampeding toward her, their eyes frantic. She ran too, trying to find a spot where she would not be trampled. She had merely seconds left as they approached.

Just off the path was a large oak that had died long ago and been torn in two by a storm. Sarah dove behind it and felt the rage of the herd storm by her, the ground thundering. Ten, maybe more. She had shielded her tiny body behind the massive trunk, and the animals jumped and stomped all around it. She closed her eyes and put her hands over her ears, hoping that if she were very still, the storm would pass...

The boat is at the mercy of the waves, and they are the largest the girls have ever seen. They suddenly realize they are being taken away from the island, taken to some remote part of the lake where she fears they will never be found, and if they don't drown, they will surely starve. Alice says they should swim back, but Sarah can hardly hear over the sound of the rain and the thunder. The waves mock their efforts to bail water out with their hands, and it fills the bottom of the boat, coming very close to the rim. Where's Dad?

...Silence. Hoofprints all around her, leading off into the abyss of red pines. Her heart raced, and she couldn't hear anything except the blood pumping through her ears. There was nothing to hear. In all her years on the island, she had never heard or seen anything quite like that. The world had returned to normal. There was no one else around, no one to witness this incredible, terrifying migration. Where were they going? She knew that on the other side of those woods was the frozen lake. She followed their footprints into the forest, and here, far off the trail, the overhead patches of sun became less frequent. No winds swept through these pines, no noise except the sound of unseen crows hidden high in the branches, watching her small figure make its way through the thick trees. She walked past broken limbs, seeing some with fresh blood on them.

Through a clearing in the branches, Sarah saw an endless whiteness: the ice-covered lake stretched out as far as the eye could see in all directions. She reached the clearing and saw the hoofprints leading out onto the ice. In the distance, the herd was silhouetted against the blue horizon and then gone. The wind ripped off the shores of the island as branches, leaves, and debris blew about over the jagged, uneven surface. Even birds—the ones that had stayed for the winter—seemed to be leaving as well, fleeing from the island in every direction. It was as if the island were trying to escape itself, inch by inch, removing itself from the lake. Retreating. The sun's glare off the ice was almost blinding, and at that moment, she felt no comfort from the clear blue sky above. Far across the lake, she could barely make out a strange bank of dark clouds, eclipsing all light beneath them. Instead of moving toward the island or in any particular direction, it simply hovered there, waiting. Could a patch of lake effect snow clouds? An unforeseen clipper making its way south? Nothing like that in the forecast, but those storms did pop up from time to time.

She was cold now and did not want to go back into the forest. For some time, she waited and listened, for what exactly she didn't know. What else was roaming the forest now, she wondered. In the summertime, joggers, bicyclists, and hikers would be there, as well as boats on the lake and people asleep on towels on the beach, enjoying the sun. But they were all gone now, and the path on which she ran suddenly felt alien. She resolved to walk alongside the beach where land met ice and make her way back home. As she walked back, hugging herself against the arctic winds, she found herself feeling horribly alone, and for the first time in ages, she felt as if she was the only one on the island.

Sarah took the phone from her pocket. There were five more missed calls from Alice. Still shaking from the adrenaline, she tried to call Alice back. No signal. *There's never a signal here when you need one.* She looked back out over the lake. *I'm sure if it was serious, she'd just leave a message.* Sarah was grateful that everyone would be coming out tonight for their weekly get-together at the Fat Crab. The day, which had barely just begun for her, now seemed late, and the sun was already low in the blue winter sky. She picked up her pace and jogged back on the snow-covered sand, back towards the civilization she had left behind.

Chapter Three

Outside the bar, no one could hear the Thompsons' dog barking at the northern wind that came off the lake. It howled through old window frames, and the swings at the playground near the city center swung madly back and forth, their rusted bolts and chains screeching angrily. Large icicles dangled from them like dragons' teeth. In the center of Main Street, one of the grocery carts had escaped from the store lot and had guided itself slowly down the street alone, banging into curbs and parked cars as its wheels squeaked. The world without people on the island had come alive, unwitnessed. The sole, warm glow of light came from a small pub, nestled snug on the corner of Main Street where asphalt ended and brick began, where on warm summer nights one could hear the clop-clopping of touristy carriage wagons making their way down the road. But not tonight.

On a lonely path that followed the serpentine perimeter of the island, Sarah walked alone, carrying what looked like a scarecrow on a pole over her shoulder, except the scarecrow was dressed in Santa gear. Sarah wore a Santa hat as she walked against the howling winds that came off Lake Erie. She labored against both the weight of the scarecrow and the wind and fell to one knee a few times until finally she reached The Fat Crab's bar—not her bar, but hers to run for the winter. Outside, she could see the snowmobiles (and Mary's cross-country ski set) parked up against the southern wall of the bar, away from the snow drifts and all things falling. Through the windows, she could see the golden flicker from the fire, its trance-like beams dancing on the snow outside. For the first time that week, she did not feel like the last human being on earth. At times, she wished she lived closer to the others. Living on the opposite end of the island from everyone provided the privacy and quiet that she needed at times, but it left her feeling alone at others. Alone, but not unsafe. Never unsafe. Still, she was the only person on this side of the island, and she tried to push out unwelcome thoughts, thoughts of how long it would take others to get to her if something did happen. In her pocket, she could feel her phone vibrating. It was the third time since Sarah's walk back to the bar that her sister, Alice, had tried to call her, but she would deal with that later. Tonight would be a happy night. She felt good about so many people coming to her side of the island for a change. The island felt alive again, if only for a night. Sarah opened the door and carried her Christmas scarecrow inside.

Her patrons had already polished off most of the mulled wine, and backup cocktails were being made, right next to the food that everyone brought. As Sarah entered, everyone cheered when they saw what she had: The scarecrow from the front of the B&B where Sarah stayed for the winter. She set it up against the wall, then made her way back behind the bar. Sarah continued to make drinks, and her heart was full knowing that once again the bar was replete with loud, drunken patrons, and for a quick moment, she felt like it was summertime again. All the mess—the cans, the cigarette butts, the empty plastic cups—would have to be cleaned tomorrow, but this part she did not mind. As long as it meant more gatherings were to come, she would gladly spend her long, empty days cleaning up afterwards. Sarah didn't feel like telling the others about the strange incident during her run earlier. She wanted to leave it behind in the forest, just as the deer left their tracks in their wake.

Fat Christmas lights and cheap tinsel lined every inch of the bar, while *It's a Wonderful Life* played on the old-school TV with rabbit ears as The Moonglow's "Just a Lonely Christmas" wistfully played on the old speakers at each corner of the bar. On the wall, half-assed tinsel dangled over the year-round décor: Ohio State flags, a giant Sturgeon that every local swore their father had caught (but nobody really knew how it ended up there), and a large, stone carved face of the Lake Erie Monster—Sarah called him Larry—with his own Santa hat placed upon his horned head as his inanimate eyes gazed out upon the inebriated crowd. A giant "Goodbye Christmas" sign with the "mas" torn off swung like a childish pendulum over the crowd as they took no notice of it. The holiday was already past, and the group had devised a way to rid themselves of the bountiful leftovers from the real Christmas dinner they'd had just days ago.

As she surveyed the crowded bar around her, Mark again ran behind it to make his own drink—of course—and after the third time, Sarah had given up kicking him out of her territory. Although technically not an islander by birth, Mark had lived on Sandy Stone since Sarah was a child. Lived on and off, she reminded herself. But the past few years, as he had gotten older and closer to retirement, he had been more on than off. He made Sarah laugh, and during the long periods on the island between the moments of real life, that meant a lot to her. He had been friends with her father, and now he possessed a similar role to her, although that never stopped his friendly advances.

In his mind, he was still the free spirit wandering the world, not stuck here like everyone else. He seemed to be immune to the cold, and, having lived in all the farthest reaches of the world, he brought those strange places back to Sarah, and she liked that, too.

He spent most of his free time on the island during the winter months painting, and as Sarah looked around the walls, she could see some of his works that she had hung for decoration. Mark always hoped to sell his paintings, but once winter came, he never did. And so, he passed the time running a small arts and crafts shop that showcased the works from traveling artists, and, on occasion, would sneak one of his own pieces into the shows. He grabbed a whiskey glass and poured himself a generous fill of Black Label, and she could see the missing ring finger on his right hand, which he had lost in a logging accident back in his twenties. He used it in any number of his gags, including shoving it up his nose, amongst other places. When he smiled at her, she could see some of the missing teeth he had not bothered to replace as he aged. With his unkempt gray hair and secondhand attire, he could easily pass for a bum in any other setting. But here, he was just Mark.

Philip, the one everyone dubbed "The Mayor" (though he was not the mayor of the island now, nor had he ever been), was passed out at the bar, his head down and resting on his own Santa hat. He was covered in bottle caps and party favors that the others had been flicking his way when they got bored. It had become a game for a brief time, but when they got tired of it, he was forgotten. Mark pushed past Sarah and grabbed The Mayor's wrist. "Still alive," he confirmed, after checking his pulse.

Sarah laughed, then shook her head. The Mayor had grown up on the island and, though he had no educational background in history, had nonetheless become the Sandy Stone historian and ran the local historical society museum, which Mark had dubbed "The most fucking boring place on earth." Truth be told, he had lived there long enough—he too was in his 60s now—that he knew pretty much everything about the island, and thus someone, at some point in time, dubbed him "The Mayor." The real mayor was off the island and would be, for the next few weeks, though hardly anyone noticed. During the summer days, he would lead his historical walks, invite guests to speak at his museum, or brag about being asked to consult with Erie historians and geographers, something he was always happy to share with anyone within shouting distance. But during the winters on the island, he spent the long, cold days like he did tonight, passed out, alone, and dreaming of the warmer months still so far away. All days of the year, he pranced around in historical costumes, something tourists and locals alike found both charming and odd.

Sarah looked beyond the Mayor and spied Mary sitting alone at a table. Bopping her head slightly to the music, she never let the thick smoke and drunken camaraderie get under her skin, though this scene was not hers and hadn't been for years. Mary liked Sarah and appreciated the company, especially during the holidays. She had brought pasta shells stuffed with ricotta and mozzarella, an island favorite, and was pleased to be able to contribute to the festivities, though the hour was late, and she did not want to walk back alone. She would wait for Mark to leave and help guide him home to prevent him from passing out somewhere in the cold of the night. Sarah smiled, filled a clean glass with soda water and a lime, then walked over and handed it to Mary. Mary ran her mom's psychic-reading shop in the summers, the kind that offered every psychic cliché—tarot cards, incense, ambient music—and although the tourists loved it as a lark, it never seemed to make Mary happy.

Mary looked at Mark, who was tapping the slumbering Mayor on the head with a plastic wiffle ball bat. "He just keeps going and going, doesn't he?" Mary asked.

"Yeah, I think he thinks if he acts young enough, he'll outlive us all."

Mary laughed. "I keep waiting for him to keel over, but he never does. Is that bad?"

Sarah shook her head. "No, I think we all watch him like a car crash. How's your mom doing?"

Mary coughed a bit on her drink. "Oh, sorry, I wasn't expecting the lime. She's ok. Fine, I think. I think she'll feel better when the weather warms up and I can take her outside."

Sarah wiped the spilled drink from Mary's glass. "We'll all feel better once the nice weather comes back. I'll go let Mark know you're waiting on him."

"Oh no, please don't say that. I don't want him doing jumping jacks all around me. I'll just wait here." Sarah nodded and walked back to the bar, nearly knocking Amy off her stool.

Amy sat at the end of the bar, talking to Dan, the heat melting the makeup from her face, causing her to look like a demonic Kris Kringle with the Santa hat she wore. Dan and Amy never left each other's side. For their fifth wedding anniversary, they planned to take a trip to somewhere they had never been before, and on the advice of some friends, they traveled to the island in May. They had fallen in love with the island and never wanted to part with it or each other. Together, they ran a large Ohio sports-themed pizzeria that was a favorite of tourists, with signed frames of famous Ohio athletes adorning their wooden walls. The profits were enough to let them live comfortably in the offseason until they came out of hibernation to do it all over again in the spring.

Jack, already drunk well before the festivities began, eyed his glass of bourbon and swayed in his seat as the others moved around him. He was happy to leave his wife and son behind for a night. Unlike some of the others in the room, he did not live alone, nor did he possess the freedom or finances to come and go as he pleased. In the warmer months, he was a manager at the limestone quarry, but in the dead months of winter, he, like everyone else, waited for the island to come alive again. For extra money, he moonlighted as a maintenance man in the dead season, though many on the island had never really seen him fix much of anything. He had told his wife that he'd be home by midnight, but it was already well past his "curfew," and he had not received a concerned or angry text from her yet. He rarely did these days. Sarah loved his son, Bill, and had often thought that raising a deaf and mute boy would be hard, especially on this island, but Bill had turned out to be a bright child, and Jack was a good father to him.

Tonight, Jack did not think of his wife or his son. Here, away from all of that, he found his mind wandering off to other, younger places as he watched Sarah make her cocktails on the other side of the bar. She looked up and caught him staring, and the liquor had made him too slow to react. All he could do was smile.

Sarah rolled her eyes and smiled back. Although the people here felt more like family than the strangers who came in during peak, she was still used to the wandering eyes of men. Sometimes she missed the attention. As Sarah poured another round of shots, Mark collided with her while making his concoctions. She watched him from the corner of her eye while trying not to spill the shots she was pouring. "Why the hell do you keep coming back here?"

"Don't worry about me, I'll work around you," he began, grabbing random bottles from the shelf, pouring and shaking them in the mixer, and spilling their contents everywhere in the process.

Sarah laughed. "If you told me what you wanted, I could make it for you." Mark snuck up close and whispered in her ear, "If I told you what I wanted, you'd kick me out of here and lock the doors." He tickled her, laughed, and then spun away as she reached out to slap him, laughing even harder when she missed.

"You're driving me crazy. You're worse than those little college brats that come in here during peak."

Amy ashed her cigarette in an empty beer bottle. "Oh, for Christ's sake, Mark, would you please stop groping every woman that walks through the door?"

Sarah looked past Amy over to where Mary was sitting and smiled. She slid up next to Mark as he continued to make his drink.

"Looks like someone's waiting over there for you." As she elbowed him, he began to spill even more of his drink. "Do you even know what you're making?"

"Don't break my concentration. I made this ages ago in here, and if it's as good as I remember, you'll thank me for it."

Mary, her drink empty and her spirits restless, grabbed a broom and began to sweep up the leftover merriment on the floor.

"Mary, you don't have to do that," Sarah protested over the noise. She had reached the perfect pitch over the years, and her voice was always heard in any bar she tended, no matter how chaotic, but Mary just smiled without even looking up.

The night was beginning to wind down, and most of the crowd had already left. The wind outside began to pick up, and static snow played on all the TV screens after the film had ended. Mark had finished his drink and was starting on another when Sarah stopped him.

"You'll regret it tomorrow morning if you drink that last one."

"I'm already at the point of no return." He winked at her. "Might as well go down with the boat."

That last line chilled her, and suddenly she felt tired and drained all at once and wanted the night to be over. She rarely called these gatherings, but the hour was late, and she was contemplating whether to clean tonight or let the ruin wait until tomorrow, when she would most likely be nursing a hangover (and perhaps chasing a little hair of the dog with a Bloody Mary for herself and Mark).

The lights began to flicker, then they all went out, and everyone stood or sat in darkness as the wind continued to howl.

"Looks like we're sleeping here tonight, Sarah," Mark laughed.

She hated it when the island blacked out, and it frequently did during heavy winds and storms. In the summer months, the transformers would overload due to all the air conditioning units, but there were always plenty of repairmen on site. Chris, the one-eyed (whom Mark called Captain Ahab, which he hated) island maintenance guru during the winter seasons, had departed earlier in the evening and left his companion-in-drinks, Jack, alone and passed out at the bar.

"Anyone sleeping here has to clean this shit up for me by tomorrow morning."

The group sat surrounded in darkness, with only the outside moonlight silhouetting them. No one moved or spoke, and for a moment, all Sarah could hear was the low moaning of the wind through the old windows in the bar.

Mark shattered the silence. "Ok, everybody start touching each other's junk. Sarah's got mine already!"

Sarah laughed as well, then said, "Jack, go out and fix that fucking transformer."

In the darkness, Jack found his drink and mumbled something about things always fixing themselves around here, then lit a cigarette.

Everyone laughed and fumbled for their drinks. Sarah took out some old candles and placed them along the sticky bar. Mary lit them one by one with her lighter, and then with the last candle, she lit her own cigarette. This marked the hour when the last of the crowd began to shuffle out slowly, and the patrons said their goodbyes, collecting some leftovers and drinks for the road on their way out.

The lights had finally come back on, and the wintry dawn was just a few hours away. Dan and Amy helped the Mayor from his chair and back into his winter clothes, then led him outside. As each person left, a gust of arctic air burst through the door, filled the room, and then left as quickly as it had come.

Mark looked up at the lights. "If Jack ever finally decides to retire and the generator goes out, we're fucked."

Sarah shrugged. "Jack showed Luke how to work the generator."

"Like I said, we'd be fucked."

Sarah had wrapped herself in her sweater, unaware that Mark had used it earlier to wipe up a spilled drink. Mary was cleaning too, grabbing empty cups and tossing them into the overflowing wastebasket.

'Mary, you don't have to stay."

"I'm not leaving you here with this deviant."

"What about your mom?"

"She's sleeping now. She'll be all right. The wind helps her sleep."

After half an hour of cleaning, the three of them sat at the bar. Mark held out his arm in a wrestling invitation to Mary.

Sarah took the phone from her pocket and saw seven missed calls from her sister, Alice. *What the hell does she want at this hour?* she thought. Sarah looked through the texts she had missed throughout the night, only half listening to what Mark and Mary were saying. Her heart jumped as she scrolled down and came across a text that Alice had sent hours earlier. All it read was:

Please call me as soon as you can.

"Hey," Mark yelled. "Stop ogling those dick pics your boyfriends sent you and get back to work."

Sarah looked at the other two, busy with their drunken cleanup. "Guys, I'll be right back. Don't burn the place down while I'm gone." Sarah hurried to the door, pushed it open against the raw force of the arctic wind, then stepped outside in only a sweater. She dialed Alice and paced quickly back and forth to keep warm. The wind howled in her ear, and she tried to muffle the sounds. No answer, just Alice's recorded voice on the voicemail. She tried again. And again. She could feel the cold seeping through her light sweater, her exposed extremities stinging, and then becoming numb. At last, she settled on leaving a message: "Hey, it's me. Sorry, just got your text. Just want to know if everything is alright. I'll be up for at least a few hours. Please give me a call back when you get this." She hung up. Neither of them ever said "Love you" in their messages, but this time, for some reason, she wished she had. She stared at her phone, half expecting it to light back up with Alice's name on it, but it remained dark. She shivered as the chill continued its firm grip on her. *Well,* she thought, *I'm not going to die out here waiting for you. I'm guessing it's trouble with yet another boyfriend.*

When Sarah pushed her way back inside, she saw Mark trying to arm wrestle Mary while she attempted to wrestle her arm away from him.

Sarah stomped the snow off her feet and felt her body soak up the instant warmth of the place. "Are you guys seriously arm wrestling?"

Mary laughed. "No, I'm trying to read the jackass's palm here, but he insists on screwing around."

"Tell me how many beautiful women are going to come into my life within the next year, Mary."

Mary exhaled slowly, tilted her head back, and smiled, revealing the pagoda tattoo on her neck. "I could tell you that without looking at your palms."

Mark smiled, quite drunk. He enjoyed flirting with every female member of the island. It occupied his idleness until a fresh flock of tourists came each spring. "That's fine. Then read Sarah's."

"You want your palms read?" Mary took another deep puff. "I think it turns Mark on."

"I think everything turns Mark on. That's ok, Mary. I'll pass."

"No really, I don't mind. I'm not very good. I never had the gift like my mom, but I knew how to sell it like she did. I won't sell you the bullshit I sell my customers. It'll be honest."

"Let me just finish up here."

"Come on, Cinderella, it will only take a minute."

Sarah smiled. "Ok, but no bad news or omens. I'm maxed out on bad news."

Mary looked at Sarah and smiled. "Let me see what you got, lady." She began to softly mumble the words to *"Lay Lady Lay"* by Bob Dylan, which was playing on the jukebox. All the TVs played static, and the air was thick with candlelight and cigarette smoke.

Sarah downed her mulled wine and held out her palm to Mary, who slowly began to examine it. "Don't you use tarot cards?"

"Nah, that's just for the tourists. A psychic—a true seer—knows even before they put the cards on the table. Mom would have taken one good look at you and given you your next forty years." She looked over Sarah's small hands, all the little scars and burns acquired over many long, warm summers and dark winters. Mary read the history of the woman whose hand she held, sketching her finger across the creases of her palms, seeing both history and future far apart and all at once, all paths both clear and uncertain. They unraveled themselves before her, and she closed her eyes. A cold chill passed through the room, then left as quickly as it had come.

"Someone right now loves you very much."

Sarah laughed. "Well, I know you aren't talking about my sister."

Mark put his arm around her shoulder and kissed her cheek. "I coulda told you that without reading your palm."

"Mark, go find something good on TV for us, huh?" Mary smiled. Mark saluted, grabbed his drink, and marched over to the television set.

"Good boy," Mary said, and her smile faded quickly. "No, it is family."

Sarah thought of her sister's missed texts and calls, and her heart sank. What if it was something serious? she thought. She tried to shake the thought away like dust from a rug. "What else?"

"I know why you stay on the island and never leave."

"Everyone knows that."

"There's something else." Her eyes were shut tight, almost as if she were wincing in pain. "I see you as a child. A child here."

"I grew up here. Everybody knows that, too. Come on, Mary, I'm waiting for you to blow my fucking mind."

Mary smiled a bit, her eyes still closed. She held Sarah's hands tighter, focusing on something deeper within, places that the other two could not see or hear. "I see you walking on ice. A whole ocean of ice, alone."

Sarah's heart began to beat faster. "On the island?"

"No, not on land. Not at all. Far from any shores I can see. You're walking alone. You're frightened. But no one can see you. Yes, there you are, all alone, except..."

Mark sat down next to Mary, with three piping hot cups of mulled wine for each. The fire in the corner had faded to a whimper, with only a sporadic crackle of bursting embers. Outside, the winds roared on, and the old wood moaned and swayed in the night. Mary plucked Mark's cigar from his mouth and put it out in someone's abandoned drink.

Mark laughed. "Hope I don't get too drunk and accidentally drink that."

Mary exhaled her smoke and coughed a bit. "Why do you think I did it?"

The lights flickered on and off again. But there was no wind outside, just a sudden stillness. This time, Mark didn't say anything to break the mood. Sarah looked at the two of them as her eyes grew heavy. "I should really close up now, guys."

As Sarah took their drinks behind the bar, she noticed that the clock on the wall had stopped at two thirty. It was still plugged in. *Is that thing broken now, too?*

Sarah, Mark, and Mary walked out of the bar, arm-in-arm. Mark stumbled a bit as the two women helped steer him down the lighted path toward Main Street. Mary had had the good sense to bring her car, and Sarah was grateful not to have to walk the longer distance to drop him off. Sometimes she did miss living near all the others, and both her bar and the bed and breakfast were here on the other side of the island—the tourist side—and all the locals lived as far away as possible from it. But she took comfort in knowing that one was never too far away on the island at any given moment. The rest of the world—Ohio, at least—was nearly 10 miles away, and the ferries had stopped running long before the ice swept over the surface of the lake.

As she began to lose herself in thought, Mark grabbed her by the arm. "Look, look out there!" he yelled, pointing at the lake. "That ice is so damn thick right now, I could take you for a drive in Mary's car clean across the way to Sandusky on the other side."

Sarah laughed. "Have you ever driven on that thing?"

Mark began to pull her off the path, closer to the ice shoals and the barriers at the lake. "Oh yeah, you could drive a fucking tank on that thing and not even have it crack the surface."

Mary shook her head and hugged herself in the cold. "Mark, no one's driving my car or anything else on that lake tonight. We're taking you home."

But Mark persisted, tugging Sarah along with him as they got closer to the beach, once sand and stone, now covered in snow. There was no discernible overlap between land and lake now; they had become one, enjoined under the snow. Mark pulled her closer to it. "I wanna go ice skating."

Sarah laughed nervously as they approached the lake. She began to pull back now. "Mark, Mary's really tired and needs to get you home." She could feel her heart pounding. Rarely did she let herself get this close to the edge, even after a long night of drinking. She could not pull away from Mark's grip, and he was completely oblivious to her struggle. They were getting closer.

"No, just the two of us. Let's skate! I'll show you." He pulled harder, unaware of his strong grip. Sarah's heart began to pound faster, and she found that she did not have the strength to push away.

"Mark, please stop..."

But he could not hear her over his own loud, drunken rantings. "We can howl at the moon when we see it out on the ice. Howl with me, Sarah!" He began howling, and then he was on the lake, and as he pulled Sarah onto its icy surface, she began to breathe faster and faster, but the air didn't seem to be going to her lungs.

"Mark, I have to go back!" The words barely left her mouth. But Mark did not hear her. Instead, he pounded his foot on the hard ice.

"See?" he said. "Harder than steel right now!"

Sarah could feel her body go numb and could hear her heartbeat in her ears. And then she screamed.

Mary ran down from the path and grabbed onto Sarah, pulled her away from Mark, and, more importantly, off the frozen surface of the lake. Sarah shook and cried in Mary's arms as she looked at Mark with scornful eyes.

"You damn idiot, you know she can't leave the island."

Mark took off his oversized ushanka hat and held it with both hands, his head lowered like a shamed child. "I'm sorry, Sarah. I was just having a bit of fun."

Mary held Sarah and shushed her as she trembled. "It's ok. You're back on the island now. It's ok. Come on, I'll walk you home."

Sarah wiped her eyes and pulled away. "No, really, it's ok. I'm fine. It's stupid, really."

Mark remained where he was on the iced-over lake. "Sarah, I'm sorry. I'm really sorry."

She looked over and smiled through her tears. "I know. I know, Mark. I'm going to walk home on my own."

"Are you sure?" Mary asked.

"Yeah. I think we've all had too much to drink tonight. I'm going to walk it off before I get to bed."

Mary smiled. "We can come with you."

"No. No, I'd rather go it alone. I'll be ok. I'll be fine."

"I hate that you live so far away from the rest of us."

"Honestly, Mary, I'll be ok. Please."

Mark stuck his hands in his pockets. "I'm really sorry, Sarah. I just got a bit carried away." Sarah nodded. She didn't want this moment to linger any longer. She wanted instead to maintain the warm memories of good company she'd had tonight.

"It's ok, Mark. Really. I'll be fine."

Mary gave her a goodnight hug, and then she walked off into the darkness without saying goodbye to Mark.

On her walk home, Sarah could see the silhouettes of ice shoves, monolithic figures rising out of the shoreline along the path she took to get home. In the moonlight, they almost seemed to be reaching up toward the dark heavens, the star-filled skies without a trace of cloud. Sarah walked beside them, the snow crunching beneath her feet. It had been a cold winter—the worst in years—and the frigid winds had swept over the frozen tundra of Lake Erie day after day. Although she had endured many a miserable winter on the island, she had found it particularly hard to stay warm this season.

Under the winter stars, she walked alone along the path, now buried in snow, and she found comfort in the footprints of others—including her own—reminding her that she was not the only one on the island, that the world had not abandoned her on Sandy Stone. Sometimes the winter nights grew so dark that she could see the flickering lights of the mainland far across the lake, and though she knew that she would never leave the island, she was happy knowing that civilization was just a ferry ride away once the ice had cleared over the waters.

The owner of The Fat Crab, now living in his summer home in Thailand, liked to have someone keep the place open during the winter, someone to make sure the pipes didn't burst or the ceiling didn't collapse from the weight of the snow. She had asked him 5 years ago if she could bartend there during the wintertime, and he had happily taken her on. During the summer months, money was not hard to come by at all; tourist season seemed to start earlier and earlier every year, a fact that pleased her and dismayed much of the island's population. But tourist season, along with the warmer months, was now only a distant dream. The barren tree limbs blew in the wind, and as she walked, she closed her eyes and imagined the way they looked when green and full in the summer breeze, the way the late summer evenings cast long shadows of the trees. These remembered moments seemed sad, and so she went over the evening's events in her mind instead. The lampposts that guided her home were dimly lit to conserve energy, but tonight they seemed even dimmer than usual, and she found herself in a deep bout of sadness, which she vowed to get over by the time she reached the Sandy Shell, her bed and breakfast. These bouts of melancholy were frequent during the winter season, and she had worked hard the past few years to find her own remedies to battle them. In the morning, she would have a mug of strong French roast coffee, then go for her daily run along the lakeside path. It would be sunny tomorrow, and the feel of the sun on her face during a run was already something she looked forward to. The sun would not rise for a few more hours, and though she had enjoyed a great many sunrises over the lake while standing on the southern pier, tonight she was tired and welcomed a good night's sleep.

At The Fat Crab, she always played hits from the previous summer on the jukebox until the customers came in, and they would tamper with it until a kaleidoscope of every musical genre blasted through the speakers. She had opened the bar early at four, even though The Fat Crab wasn't supposed to be open until six. The owner wasn't here, and Sarah grew restless in the long hours before people started to arrive. Here, every night was slow, and those who did drag themselves from their winter hibernation were happily greeted by blue and yellow floodlights, a crackling fireplace, and warm mulled wine, which Sarah only made in the wintertime for the locals and herself. Many a night she had stumbled back to the bed and breakfast drunk, but tonight she did not indulge in shots with the customers. Mark had practically stumbled in the moment she unlocked the door, and from then on, he would talk to her until she decided to close the bar, or he would pass out. She had few regulars during the wintertime, but Mark was by far her most devoted patron.

Up ahead, the B&B stood still against the darkness of the night, and Sarah could hear the wind chimes playing their tune in the cold breeze. Already in her mind's eye, she could envision the streets filled with tourists, and '50s rock would play over the loudspeakers that dotted the island. Last summer had remained with her like a warm companion throughout these cold days. During the summer months, she would return to work at Mickey's, where the younger, well-to-do crowd frequented and the tips were enough to last her for the rest of the year. The other bartenders would, of course, return to their corners of the world, but she would remain here. She never felt lonely here during the summer months, when the island came alive and frozen lakes were just a dream. The air smelled like meat on the spitfires, suntan lotion, and honeysuckles that grew everywhere on the island. People came from all over Ohio and even beyond; last summer, she had met a group of men from Ireland touring through the Midwest, a couple visiting from Japan, and tourists from every corner of the states. Although it had been since her early 20s that she first (and last) ventured off the island, these people would bring the rest of the world here to her, with their stories, their culture, and their history. She saw the rest of the world through their eyes, and thus she told herself she had no reason to ever leave the island, if only she could endure the long months of winter.

The inside of the B&B was dark and unlit, but she had wandered these halls and rooms so many times she could

map out the interior in total darkness. Her father had
told her this was a wonderful exercise against dementia, to
map out rooms in one's mind and find them in the dark.
The inside smelled like musty old carpet and wallpaper,
and in the darkness, she could hear the hiss from the
steam radiators keeping the place warm for her when she
was away. In the summertime, all six rooms would be
rented out for top dollar, but now everyone was gone,
including Miss Paskert, the B&B's owner, who overcame
the long winters by lounging on the beaches somewhere in
southern Greece. Sarah would hear all about it when she
returned—all the rich young men who bought her drinks
and asked her questions about the island, then invited her
on their yachts. Sarah sometimes wondered if these things
really happened to Miss Paskert at all. Maybe she didn't
go to all those places; she might have spent the winters
with her nephew in Dayton, staring out the window
and watching him shovel the driveways. But she had told
herself she would not be cynical. She would believe the
stories that everyone who came to the island had told her.
She would, of course, have loved to see Greece, Thailand,
and all the other places that people spoke of. She would
love to backpack all over Europe or ride a motorbike
through the rice-paddy-laden countryside of Vietnam to
meet strange, handsome men at hostels and make friends

all over the world. She would have loved all of that. But she knew she would never leave the island—could not leave it—and that she was destined forever to live vicariously through the well-traveled souls who came through her small life on her small island. Her virtual therapy sessions had not cleansed her phobia, and no amount of alcohol or sedatives could give her the strength to cross the waters of Erie. And so it was.

Here, she chose not the largest of the guest bedrooms but the one with the best view of the lake. In the dark, she could not see it, only hear the frigid winds roaring across the icy surface and making their way through the smallest crevices of the B&B. The old house whistled all day long, and though the radiators were always at full blast, she could never seem to get warm there. But that was how she preferred it when she slept. It was the one thing about winters here that she loved, and her slumbers were deep. Tonight, she continued her usual ritual just before bed: She opened both windows just a crack until the cool air spilled in and flooded the room with winter, then grabbed all three bed comforters she had taken from storage and bundled herself up.

On her bedside table was an old picture of herself, her father, and Alice, down by the lake and smiling on a sunny day. *Alice*, she thought. She would call her back tomorrow.

She looked at the picture for a while longer. *Goodnight, Dad.* Dawn was just a few hours away, and Sarah felt comforted that when she awoke, the sun would be out, and the world would return to normal until once again the sun set beyond the lake.

The room was especially cold tonight, and the wind howled and whistled as Sarah shut her eyes to begin her personal method of meditation, one that took her far off the island. There were many scenarios that she would play out in her head, but tonight, she chose one where she was alone in a tent somewhere in the mountains of the Himalayas, and a great storm would descend bringing fierce winds and blinding snow, yet within the tent she was warm and safe, and as long as she kept the zipper shut, no cold air could penetrate her space. Within the tent and her cocoon of blankets, her eyes grew heavy, and slowly she drifted out of this world and into another, one beyond the island and past the snow-capped mountains, where the sun and the moon both shared the sky and summers never ended.

Chapter Four

Off in the distance, Luke could just make out the outline of the mainland. Even on a clear day, the wind was merciless as it swept across the frozen lake, kicking up snow and obscuring everything in every direction. But he felt comforted knowing it was there, knowing that the surface of the lake was solid and thus traversable if one needed to get to the mainland. His patrol car rounded the serpentine road that followed the jagged coast for nearly three miles. The island was shaped like a fist, and as he rounded the bend of the thumb, he recalled seeing an aerial photo and thinking the name of the island, Sandy Stone, was all wrong. But now the name had stuck, and it was known all over the state of Ohio as a prime summer tourist destination. In the summertime, these roads would be bumper to bumper with traffic, the white sands of the beaches virtually invisible as tourists swarmed the coastline, and the sparkling waters dotted with boats. The skies would be clear, and the nights would be warm.

But that season was a long way off, and the long stretch of winter seemed unending. As his thoughts drifted toward warmer days ahead, they were quickly interrupted by the static hiss of his radio.

Luke took a side road that led to the village on the far side of the island. Overlooking the lake, he could see the ghostly shell of the ancient Sandy Stone Hotel, a historical trek for older tourists and an eyesore to him. The paint was peeling, the screens on the outdoor dining area were torn, and the owner never seemed to put much money into the place. Luke hated the outdated look, the old 50s-looking tackiness of it, and would stand on his car and celebrate the day the hotel was bulldozed. He felt that way about a lot of places on the island, and while the tourists said they felt like they were being taken back in time, he only saw a group of greedy, lazy owners who had allowed the island to rot while they lined their pockets. But the people who lived on the island year-round were a special lot. *Everyone thinks this place is deserted for six months*, he thought. *If only they knew*. No, the islanders were special indeed: misfits, loners, storeowners-in-hibernation, and too cheap to live somewhere saner for the winter. That was this place, he thought. And in their isolation, they brought their strangeness everywhere they went. They almost made a game of it. Yoga, potlucks, and costume parties. It seemed to Luke that the winters here were far more interesting than the summers. Tourists were boring. These folks belonged on a safari ride.

His father had told him many times that he was lucky to patrol such a safe area where cats stuck in trees and the occasional drunk driver were the zenith of danger, while in the big cities, law enforcement was far more dangerous. His job was cushy and stable, and enviable for his locale. Besides breaking up a few drunken brawls and arresting underage teens for drinking on the beach, his job required very little of him. Luke grimaced as he realized that his father thought that this job was the best possible thing that he could achieve. And he truly despised every minute of it.

His mother had thought differently. She had told him as much. 'You'll waste all your time there on that island, waiting on that girl, and then you'll wake up one day and realize you missed out on the rest of the world. And you'll still be alone." He had failed to convince her many times that he wasn't staying on the island for Sarah, until they eventually stopped talking about it. It became the unspoken thing at the dinner table before they had left the island, leaving Luke behind.

The bends in the road were slick and treacherous, and even though he had driven these roads his entire life, his heart skipped a beat with every slip. He loathed the winters the most because he had to stay on the island—someone did anyway—to watch over the lonely few of Sandy Stone. The island was far from the Ohio shoreline of the mainland. It felt much further away in the winter. He turned the bend that looked out on the frozen lake, and something white and fast ran across his line of sight, nearly blending into the whiteness. Luke slammed on his brakes. "Shit!" he screamed. The car swerved and refused to stop, nearing the edge of the bend where a flimsy rail was the only protection against a certain fall—and death—into the ice below. "Please don't let me die here," he said aloud to no one. Then the car slowed, losing momentum as he neared the rail. He sat there a minute, watching his breath before him. Luke stepped out of the car, tracing the snowy landscape for any signs of the object. Then he saw it.

It was a white fox—just as white as the snow—blending in seamlessly save for the yellow eyes and dark streaks near the tail of the small beast. It looked at him, disinterested in the chaos it had just created. The fox watched Luke as it crossed to the other side of the street and disappeared into the dark forest of pine. He leaned against the car to catch his breath. His face reddened from the shame, and he felt like a child again. He could remember his father cheering him on as he had failed to excel on all his sports teams as a young boy. Even through his father's cheers,

Luke could hear the disappointment. He remembered asking his father not to come to any more of his games. Luke never told him why, and his father had never asked, and so he stopped going. And now his father was gone. The memory cut him deep, and it felt strange to him to have such a painful recollection resurface now, of all times. He calmed himself and looked deep into the forest. For some reason unbeknownst to him, Luke had wanted to follow the white fox into the woods. But Luke chased away the thought quickly, got back into his car, and left much slower than he had come.

As he pulled into the gravel parking lot, he could see that Mary had placed a new outfit on the life-sized skeleton named Hank. He sat in the folding chair all year round. This one had a Santa jacket and sunglasses on as it sat there, grinning and motionless. Luke parked his car next to hers and sighed. He could feel a headache coming on.

Mary stepped outside in her bathrobe and snow boots, curlers still in her hair, and a cup of coffee in both hands. "Morning, Luke!"

Luke opened the door and was met by a harsh breeze that crept in from off the lake. He shook his head. No matter where you were on the island, you could never escape the wind. "Morning, Mary. You're up early. I thought you guys were out late last night."

Mary smiled. "We were. I just don't think any of us went to bed."

Luke took the coffee, sipped it, and smiled. "Wow. How do you keep from bouncing off the walls in there after drinking this?"

Mary shrugged. "Mom keeps me plenty busy. I need it."

Luke nodded. "How's she doing, anyway? You two getting by okay this winter?"

Mary cleared her throat. "You know Mom. She's stubborn. She's hanging in there. Not much she can do. I know she misses coming to town to see all of you."

"Well, we all have her in our thoughts," Luke said.

Mary squinted at Luke. "What's wrong, Luke? You look weird."

Luke grimaced. "I almost hit a fox on the way here. Nearly went off the edge of the road."

"A fox?"

"Yeah, a white one."

"No white foxes on this island. No white foxes this far south of Canada."

"I know. But I still saw one."

"Maybe it was covered in snow."

"Maybe." Luke took another generous sip of coffee and felt his heart skip a few beats from the strength of it. He looked at her Chevy. "What happened? Did you forget to turn the lights off when you got home?"

Mary sheepishly scratched the back of her head. "Actually, yeah, I did."

"I thought you didn't drink."

"I don't. I was just tired. Really tired." She laughed.

Luke looked over her tired face. The bags under her eyes did not lie. "Don't you have that old yellow Beetle in the garage? The one you drive in the July 4th parade every summer. That thing still works, doesn't it?"

"It's an antique, Luke. Not meant for the snowy roads of the Midwest."

"Fair enough," he said. "Hold this." He handed her his cup of coffee, then walked over to his patrol car, where he pulled some jumper cables from his trunk.

Mary looked him over. "You ever jump-started a car before?"

Luke shrugged. "Mary, I've lived on this island my whole life. Of course, I can jumpstart a car." He couldn't, of course. He had seen his boss do it countless times as he stood nearby, watching, but not learning. He had seen others do it as well in person and at least a dozen films. But he had never actually jump-started someone else's car, and so today had become a red-letter day for him.

Mary took a sip of her coffee. "Ok, just don't fuck my car up. It's all I got." Luke popped the hood of her car and rested the cables on the bumper. *How hard can it be?* he thought. He'd seen these hicks do it all his life, and if they could, he certainly could. He went to college, after all. "Ok," he said, making sure he was loud enough for Mary to hear. "Let's see what we have here."

As Luke began to play *Operation* on the car, he could hear footsteps approaching in the snow from a distance. Here on Sandy Stone, whenever there were two people, there was always at least one more bound to join. It was their way.

"Morning, Mark!" Luke heard Mary say, and he could feel the strength of his headache growing.

"Hey, Mary," Mark said. "You got somebody trying to break into your car through the hood. Look!"

Luke sighed again and stepped away. As he did, he saw Mark in his Hawaiian shirt, shorts, and ushanka hat. "Morning, Mark. Reverse psychology?"

"What?" Mark looked down at his attire. "Nah, all my shit's in the wash. Don't I look sexy today, though?"

Mary giggled and Luke shook his head. "You know, I never did get my space heater back. It's been two months."

Mark smiled. "Space heater? Nah, I gave that to the Mayor."

Luke put his hands on his hips. "He said he gave it to you."

Mark scratched his chin. "Space heater? Hmm. Nope. Gave it to the Mayor last month. He still has it."

Luke shook his head. "Every time I tell myself I'm not going to lend anything out to you all and then break my oath and do it, I never see it back. It never fails."

Mark laughed. "If you're cold in that trailer of yours, I'll gladly come over tonight and keep you warm." He started making kissing sounds at Luke, who went back under the hood of Mary's car.

Mary crossed her arms and laughed. "Luke says he almost hit a white fox on the way here."

Mark shook his head. "No white foxes here. It may be cold here, but it ain't the Arctic, kid."

"I know." Luke sighed and threw his arms up in resignation.

Mary looked at the package Mark had in his hand. "Is that for me?"

"Nah, this is for Sarah. A little peace treaty for my behavior last night."

"I'm sure she's not still angry with you."

"Well, this will help if she is."

As they spoke, Luke took his cables and opened the hood of his car. When he knew their attention was diverted, he took out his phone and pulled up a YouTube video on jumpstarting cars. The moment Luke hit 'play' on the video, Mark snuck up behind him.

"Hey, Luke!" he yelled. "Whatcha doing?"

"You don't have to yell," Luke sighed. "I'm right here, helping Mary start her car."

"You need a phone for that?"

"Nope."

"Ever done this before?"

"Sure."

"I'm on my way over to Sarah's. Anything I can pass along for you?" Mark began making kissing sounds again, and Luke could hear Mary giggle.

"You can tell her I said 'hi.'"

"I could do that, *or* I could tell her that Luke sends lots of hugs and kisses her way."

Luke sighed. "You know, Mark, I'm really busy right now. Why don't you run along and go bother someone else?"

"Ok, just trying to be friendly. I'll let Sarah know I ran into you." He looked over at Mary and waved. "Have a good day, Madame."

Mark walked away, and Luke got into his car as Mary watched him nervously. He forced a smile and waved, then muttered to himself, "I hope this works." He started the car and let the engine rev, and as he did so, he saw smoke and sparks rising from the other car. "Shit," he said.

Mary screamed and ran inside, then ran back out with a pitcher of water and dumped it over her engine. She looked up at Luke through the dirty windshield, flustered and angry.

"Damnit, Luke!" she laughed. "You fucked my car up!"

CHAPTER FIVE

the waves were larger now and sounded like thunder
● ● ● *every time they crashed up against the rocks. The sky*
was black, and the clouds were moving fast, faster than she'd
ever seen. She could just catch brief glimpses of the island,
which seemed so far away now. The whole world went dark
and screamed all around them, and the lake opened its great
mouth, ready to swallow them whole...

The moment Sarah awoke, she knew something was wrong. The room was dark, though it was late in the morning. The radiator hissed in the corner, but the spot on the wall where the morning sun usually shone its light was dark. Sarah slipped her hand underneath the pillow to pull out her phone. Gone. As she looked around the room, everything seemed out of place, as if each object had been displaced just enough that only her naked eye would notice. The room was quiet, but inside she felt panic. Then she thought about the herd of deer, their shadows disappearing over the white horizon, then gone, the frozen lake, and the dream.

She had dreamt something terrible, something that had awakened her in the night. She remembered now, or at least thought she did, and in the quiet gloom of the room, she sat on the edge of the bed and recalled herself awakening, trembling, stumbling out of bed, and pouring herself a glass of water. The window was open, but she had closed it as the shades beat against it. Now she remembered. Her phone had been vibrating, and she had tossed it into the drawer. She rolled and opened the drawer, pulling out her phone. 10 missed calls, all from Alice's number. Her heart beat fast again. Sarah called her sister back and paced the gloomy room. She noticed that the old clock on the wall read 3:00. *But my phone says 9 am*, she thought. And then she remembered the clock at the bar the other night, stopping at the very same time.

Alice was still on Pacific Time in LA, undoubtedly fast asleep. The call went to voicemail. "Hey, it's me. Is everything ok? I guess we just keep missing each other." *If it had been important, she would have left a message, wouldn't she?* Sarah leaned against the window and felt the frigid draft creeping in. Outside, a hazy sun shone through darkening clouds. The street was still empty and would be until May, when the ice would finally break and give way to the long, glorious months of summer. *If it had been important, she would have left a message.* She repeated this thought to herself as she made her way down the steps to the kitchen, where she began brewing an especially strong pot of coffee. She felt drained, and fresh air would be the best thing for her, but today she didn't want to trek down her usual path along the perimeters of the island into the forest. Just the thought of it made her shudder, and she wanted to forget all of it. This was her island, her home. She wouldn't let something like that poison her. She only had so many places she could go, and this place would not become her prison.

Sarah sat on the piano bench and played Chopin's Nocturne No. 2 as the first few flakes of snow began to fall. It was an older piano and a little out of tune, while some of the keys stuck. But it was by the window looking out over the lake, and Sarah could play and watch the storms come and go. She had played more this winter and found it a better way to pass the time than rolling joints she had bought from Mark and binge-watching videos. On top of the piano sat a picture of her father, Alice, and herself. They would have been about nine and ten, respectively.

She recalled how their father always had a piano teacher come during the summer months. Alice was, of course, a natural musician but never developed the fondness for it that Sarah did. So, as she practiced more and more, Sarah became the superior player, but she never gloated about it. When she played, her father would lean in the doorway and watch her, and she would pretend not to know he was there. She had done that often as a child, and now that he was gone, she wished that she hadn't. When she played now, she liked to think of him still behind her, still watching and smiling. But she played for no one at that moment, and as she began to play the notes a little softly, another noise rose above the sound of her playing.

When the sound started, it seemed far away, as if emanating from the most distant reaches of the island. Sarah stepped outside but could not locate the source or place exactly what it was. As she stepped out into the cold, the sound began to build. The rest of the world around her remained still. There was no wind, and the crows that were there earlier had flown off to some hidden haven in the forest. But the sound continued to rise, and as she walked down the street, it grew. At first, it sounded almost like static, simple white noise, as if a giant TV had been left on after the program had ended. But as she walked down Main Street, it began to build, and as it grew louder, the sound grew clearer. From within the static came what sounded like whispers. Soft and indistinguishable and slow, then more of them layered upon each other.

A chill ran down her spine, and though it was just past noon, she felt a great sense of unease. The sky had darkened with snow clouds, and the air smelled foully of dead fish and toxic chemicals. She could see the light on in Amy and Dan's pizzeria, but it gave her no comfort as the Closed sign was still up, just as it was on most of the doors and windows of the adjacent stores. The whispers grew, and Sarah's light jacket did not shield her from the bitter cold front that had begun to make its way south from Canada: brutal, arctic air cold enough to burst pipes and drain car batteries. It was always cold on the island in the winter, but arctic deep freezes like this were even more unwelcome.

Whisper upon whisper, frantic and fast. She neared the loudspeaker at the top of the street, and she could hear it growing louder. She looked around and would have felt better if anyone else had stepped outside to listen. But she was alone. The loudspeakers. Mark was the only one who had access to them in the winter. One of his many "part-time duties" during the off-season, and though Sarah adored his company, she often wondered why anyone would entrust him with any semblance of responsibility on the island. But they had, and in all fairness, Mark had never burned the island down.

To stomp out her loneliness, Sarah decided to make her way toward the control tower, where she hoped that Mark—or someone—would be. She had planned a day of playing the piano and finishing Shakespeare's The Tempest, but after her dream last night, alone was the last thing she wanted to be. As the whispers grew louder, she began to whistle an old tune in the hope of blocking it out.

Living on the other side of the island from the others, the sounds from the speakers had always comforted her during the long gray days of winter. Here she would leave behind the flat, frozen beaches of one coast for the rocky, steep cliffs of the other. There was a steady incline that led to the end, to the section where many of the islanders lived, far away from the tourist nonsense during the warmest months. There were three paths to get there: Either of the two sidewalks that outlined the perimeter of the island and would take a few hours to trek, or the central path through the tundra of the island, where there were no roads.

She trekked through the vacant amusement park: the carousel horses all covered in snow and ice, macabre, unnatural smiles frozen on all the multicolored beasts. Long, jagged icicles dangled from their frozen bodies like dragons' teeth. The swing sets that danced gently in the cold wind, the Ferris wheel that spun all year round like a restless windmill. Not far past, she walked alongside the ruins of an old church, dilapidated and unused since the 90s, when a portion of it had burnt down. She had heard more than a few whispers that some off-island buyers wanted to transform it into a brewery. *People will turn anything into a goddamn brewery*, Mark had said. At least someone would use it. Behind the church was the graveyard, which was surprisingly maintained much better, with some of the oldest tombstones going back to the late 1800s. They did not frighten Sarah but rather comforted her. She liked the idea of so many people passing through here, coming and going. She felt lucky that she had met so many of them.

Mary's was the first cottage she passed, and she knew she was nearing the far side. Her calves were sore from the uphill walk, and the deep snow had made her journey more laborious. Hank was still sitting in his chair, dressed in New Year's celebration attire replete with a party hat and sunglasses. Sarah smiled. Even when the weather was at its worst, she never forgot to dress her skeleton. There were no lights on inside, and no doubt, Mary was taking care of her mother. Sarah stopped in her tracks and looked into the blackness of the windows, wondering and hoping to catch a glimpse of movement. But the house remained still, and she knew how important it was to sometimes be left alone.

Sarah realized she was just standing there, staring at the house. Mary was either not home or busy with something else. She would come back tomorrow. Maybe, she thought, she would have her palms read again. *Alice would laugh if she knew I still did that,* she thought. Alice, with her BMW stuck in 4 hours of LA traffic every day. Alice with a new model boyfriend every month. Alice, who never stopped talking about how many projects she was taking on, her yoga, and her many trips. They were all meant to goad Sarah, of course. But Sarah never took the bait, and behind every tall tale, she sensed traces of unhappiness and anger in her sister's voice.

Chapter Six

From behind the curtain, Mary watched as Sarah stood there momentarily gazing at her house. She had turned off the lights and stood still, appreciating the thrill of seeing someone unable to see her back. Though she had not had anything to drink the night before, she had not slept well, and her mother upstairs had awoken her early in the morning, screaming. She had woken up, disoriented with a throbbing headache, feeling both panicked and annoyed. She did not want visitors right now. She wanted to be alone.

Upstairs, her mother lay bedridden with dementia, her memory slowly eroding each day, just like the cliffs at the farthest end of the island. Wave upon wave slowly ate away at rock and earth, slowly shrinking the island, the world consuming itself. This is how she felt about the island, which, like her mother, had not aged with grace. She was tired of researching nursing homes back on the mainland, all the assisted living spaces that seemed to care only about payday and little else. She wouldn't let her mother rot in one of those. As she watched Sarah continue to make her way up to the northern part of the island—no doubt seeking out Mark about the infernal noise coming from the loudspeakers—her mother cried out again upstairs.

"Mary! Mary!" she called. Mary turned up the music, an oldies station on her antiquated radio that would often soothe her mother. Now, she simply used it to drown out the cries upstairs, and the higher she turned up the volume, the louder her mother seemed to scream. She looked at the clock and saw that it was half past one.

"Fuck it," she muttered. She poured herself a glass of wine. She knew that by around 5, when the last of the daylight had gone, she'd be drunk. It was her Saturday routine, after all. But no one else had to know that. Mother upstairs wouldn't recognize the smell on her breath anyway. It was one of the few things that made her happy during the wintertime. But today, the first drink didn't help. She felt exhausted and restless. She wouldn't have gone out last night had she not been ready to throw a chair through the window, stuck inside all week. And the dreams. The dreams had been worse this week. She remembered each one and wrote them down when she woke. They had been about the little girl again, and each time she had awoken, she couldn't seem to get warm for the rest of the day. Everything seemed cold here. Cold and empty and dark. In the darkest hours before sleep had taken her, she had worried that she was bound for the same fate as her mother, bedridden and helpless, remembering everything and nothing all at once, slowly losing her entire library of memories and, eventually, self. Seeing things, hearing things beyond any sane person's perception of time and space. She had told her mother about the dreams each time she had them, and her mother just lay there, eyes open but not registering anything.

As she drifted into thought, she heard a loud crash upstairs, followed by more screaming. It could only be one thing, and Mary could feel her headache grow stronger and feel the last bit of patience she had leave her. Gone. She set down her glass and stormed up the old wooden stairs.

"Mother? Mother!"

As Mary slammed open the door, her mother was crying, and on the floor were the spilled contents from her soiled bedpan. The room smelled like piss and shit. A rage flew into her, and before she could figure out if it were the wine, the sleepless nights, or any lingering resentment toward her mother that she had buried away all these years, she grabbed her mother's hand and bit three of her fingers. She clenched down hard, and her mother screamed again and began to wail in pain. Just as soon as she had finished, her face went red with shame. She bent over her mother and held her.

"I'm sorry, Mom. I'm so sorry." She kissed her mother's warm forehead as she continued to whimper, then hurried over to the dresser where she kept some spare towels for just such an accident. As she wiped her mother's mess over the floor and watched it sink deep into the wood, she felt ugly inside and out. *If the others could see me*, she thought. *If only Mark could see me right now.* As she smeared the shit over the floor, she told herself that she would stop the drinking and that she would go to church first thing tomorrow. But just as quickly, she remembered that the old church had been in disuse for the better part of a decade, and her freshly poured glass of wine was waiting for her on the counter, right where she had left it.

Her head pounded, and with about half the mess cleaned up, she walked over to her mother's old record player. She grabbed one of the older albums on the table, placed the needle on it, and turned the volume up as the music played.

"I'll come back later to clean the rest, ma. Get some rest. I'm sorry."

She was well aware of the stench in the air, but she felt weaker and weaker, and, despite her sweater, still felt cold. Downstairs, as she drank from her glass, she felt glad that

none of the others could see her, and then she pulled the
drapes closed even tighter.

He had transported his murals to the radio room so that he could paint and work at the same time. Though his paintings never sold well during the summer art walks, he loved being a painter and had always loved the act of creating. While many of the others on the island loathed the wintery months, he loved the solitude and peace it brought him, the time to work without interruption. He had photographed the southern shore of the island afar from his boat during the golden hours of sunset, and painting with the yellow and orange hues brought back all the forgotten glory of warmer months to come.

He heard a quick knock at the door and smiled. Although he was deep in thought with his work, he still appreciated company, especially Sarah's. "Get your ass in here."

Sarah entered and was overwhelmed by both the heat and fumes from Mark's painting oils. "Jesus, it feels like Africa in here."

He put down his paintbrush and poured himself a cup of coffee, then added a generous portion of whiskey. "But which country in Africa? I've been to many of them."

Sarah walked over to a window and pulled it wide open. "Mark, you've been everywhere."

"Actually, the hottest place I've ever been was Bangkok during their summer season. Between the concrete and the

CHAPTER SEVEN

Inside the "control room" in the old town hall building with the clock tower, Mark watched Sarah plod through the deep snow toward him. He, too, had been startled by the sounds of strange static making their way across the island and figured it was only a matter of time before someone else came looking for him. He had shut off the console and found no evidence of anyone else tampering with it (anonymous residents had, in the past, pulled the plug on some of his more eccentric musical choices). He had brought a bottle of Johnnie Walker Red with him—he would save the good stuff for later—and slipped in a Beach Boys cassette. As he pressed play, the first notes of *"Don't Worry Baby"* began to blast over the loudspeakers. As he closed his eyes, he imagined the roads and sidewalks full of people. But when he opened them, the streets were still just as desolate and empty. Sarah had disappeared beyond his line of sight, and only her footprints remained.

heat, you'd swear you were in hell. Great place, though. Great women."

Sarah walked over to his painting, now just a shell of the island, lined with little dots that might or might not be people. Much of it portrayed a serene day on the water, with little dots swimming and others on the beach. "I like when you do ones of the island."

Mark took a sip of his coffee and slurped it loudly. "Yeah, but everyone does those. I think I'm just doing this one to pass the time."

"You should put one in this summer's show."

"If I even get the invite. I didn't sell a single piece last summer."

Sarah walked over to Mark's cocktail bar. "May I?" She poured herself a small glass of red label, and the two toasted each other in silence. "Yeah, but we had fun, didn't we?"

"If I recall, we all got rip-roaring drunk."

"Yeah, but we always get rip-roaring drunk."

He took a generous sip of his glass and looked at Sarah. "I'm sorry about the other night."

Sarah smiled. "No harm done. You were just being you and got carried away."

Mark reached over for a cigar and lit it. "All the same, I don't want there to be any bad blood between us. Your dad would never forgive me for it."

"Dad would have said, 'You're a jackass,' then moved on. 'Cause that's what Dad did."

Mark winced as he accidentally inhaled the smoke from his cigar.

"I miss him," Sarah said.

"Me too. Frank was a good guy." He cleared his throat. "A good friend, too." As Sarah's eyes scanned the room, she caught something moving from the corner of her eye. Crawling out of a hole behind the kitchen sink were a few small cockroaches, scurrying about in the hopes of hiding under the fridge before they were spotted. "Jesus, Mark, you have roaches again."

"What?" Mark spun around so quickly that he almost fell over. "Goddamnit!" He took his shoe off, threw it hard across the room, then took off the other, ran over, and began pounding away even after the pests were safely out of his reach. "Dirty little fucking bastards. Little mooching fuckers, crawling under every nook and cranny on this goddamn island."

Sarah stood there, quiet and uncomfortable. "They're just bugs, Mark. It's no big deal."

He sighed. "What are you still doing here, Sarah?

"What are you talking about? I just got here."

Mark walked back to his canvas and continued to paint, working on the tiny, indistinguishable dots that would become people. He did not turn around to face her as he continued to speak. "I mean, what are you still doing here, on this island?"

"I like it here. This is my home." Sarah drank more from her glass. She knew Mark was tipsy. She forced a smile. "Why are *you* still here, Mark?"

"Lady, I've been all over. Nearly broke myself after years of logging, then spent more time than I care to remember jumping from one country to another. I'm too old for any of that now. My mom used to take me here during the summertime. We'd come all the way from Chicago. She loved it here, mostly because they had a pretty religious thing going on. But that's all gone now. I told her that I wanted to live here one day. And now here I am. But you're what... 32?"

"32 this fall."

"And you haven't been off the island since you were a kid? A teenager."

Sarah swallowed hard. "Nineteen. I was nineteen. And I didn't make it very far off the island. You know why I can't leave."

"All I'm saying is, you're still so young. You're smart, people like being around you—except me—and you're the youngest one on the island right now."

"That'll change come summer."

"But don't you want to see some other places? There's more to the world than Sandy Stone. Look, I know I'm the last one to be giving you advice on anything, but I think when you get to be my age, you'll regret the hell out of it if you didn't at least try to get out of here. You don't want to be a bartender here for the rest of your life, do you?"

"And turn out like my sister, right?" She tried to smile, but it was short and forced.

"Alice does what she wants," Mark said. "Even your dad admitted as much. How is she these days, anyway?"

Sarah thought of the missed calls and texts. "I think she's ok? We've been having trouble getting a hold of each other."

"Why, because she's partying in LA and you're stuck on an island in the middle of winter?" He chuckled.

"I don't know if there's even a word for the kind of hours she keeps. I'm sure I'll catch her soon."

"Is she still sour about the funeral thing?"

Sarah took a long swig of whiskey and winced at the bitterness of it. "I think she's sour about a lot of things. But yes, I'm sure she is."

"She'll get over it."

"Dad's been gone for five years. If she hasn't gotten over it by now, then she never will. Besides, I didn't even tell her about the big news."

"Big news?"

"Miss Paskert's going to sell me the bed and breakfast."

Mark stopped painting and turned around. "She told you that?"

"She told me she was getting tired of coming back here and managing the place. She's got her properties in Cleveland, and some over on the West Coast as well."

"Did she actually say that she was going to sell it to you?"

Sarah lit one of Mark's cigars. "Basically, yeah. She did. Why?"

"Well," Mark turned around and continued to paint. "Hannah Paskert says a lot of things."

"What do you mean?"

"I mean, I just don't want you waiting around while someone else dangles a carrot in front of you."

Sarah finished her glass and poured another. "May I?"

"Help yourself," he said, without turning around.

"I don't think Hannah would do that to me. I don't think she would lead me on like that. She knows I take good care of that place. She knows I know this island better than most. She's practically taken me on as an apprentice."

"She's an odd person. She's said a lot of things."

Sarah laughed and nearly spilled her drink. "She's odd? You're the Dalai Lama of odd on this island, Mark."

Mark chuckled as he examined his tiny figures, each one coming to life before him. He wriggled his tiny stub where his ring finger should have been. "We're all strange on this island, sweetheart. Stay here too long, and you'll end up just like us." He took a long drink from his glass. "And I don't want you to end up like us."

Sarah clenched her knuckles. She had come to Mark to forget all these things, but here they came anyway, spilling into the room. "Of course I don't want to be on this island, Mark! You have no idea how goddamn lonely I am. Don't you think I see them? See all the normal people coming here every summer, talking about the world, and then getting to leave to go back to it? Do you think I don't see the young couples come and go here? I see the men come and then leave my life because I'm stuck here. Because I'm fucking crazy!" Tears streamed down her cheeks.

"You're not crazy, Sarah." Mark looked down, like a child being scolded by their parents.

"If I'm not crazy, then why can't I leave this island?!" Sarah screamed. It felt good to her to scream it. She had wanted to for so very long. "Don't you think about how I can't go there for anything? I couldn't even go to my own father's funeral back on the mainland, and now my sister won't talk to me because of it. Don't you think about how fucked up it is that I'm stuck on the island where my father killed himself?!"

He had wanted to talk to her about that. He had never discussed that with her, and she rarely brought it up, but it was always present in the room with them, with her. He felt that she had become a daughter to him after Frank had died, and every time, he felt he let her down. Mark's father had told him that he would make an awful father many years ago. That he was unfit for marriage and the ability to be a "working man." He had laughed at his son as he had laughed at his son's paintings. *And right he was*, Mark thought. And then his self-pity drove him to say, "It wasn't your fault, Sarah. None of it was. It wasn't your father's either. What happened on the lake..." He smiled dumbly and scratched the back of his head. "I'm sorry. I'm always saying or doing the wrong thing."

As she stared at him with red, tired eyes, the sound of static broke out from Mark's walkie-talkie on the table: "Mark... Mark, are you there? Over." It was Jack.

Mark set his paintbrush down. "Never a moment's peace in this place." He made a clumsy attempt at a smile and stumbled over to the table, picking up the walkie-talkie. "This had better be good."

"Town meeting tonight at 7 at the hall. I'd appreciate it if you could pass on the good word to Sarah."

"I just saw all your ugly fucking faces the other night."

"No one wants to see your face either. Big storm's coming. Gotta go over protocol."

"How big?"

"Big. Big and nasty. Over and out."

CHAPTER EIGHT

Not far from the farthest reaches of the coast, where the pine trees sit petrified and cast in ice along the shore, Adam Lang watched his dog race out onto the ice, sending huge flocks of seagulls to scatter into the gray sky. Four months from now, all the ice and snow would be a distant memory, and waves would once again come crashing over the treacherous rocks that jutted out through most of the coastline. It was why he loved living on this part of the island, the farthest reaches where neither tourists nor locals visited. All through the year, he could sit and watch the seasons change from his back deck. If he ever grew restless, he had his yacht and his dock out back, and he'd make his way up to Canada to visit his favorite places along the shore. That was his idea of getting away. From here on the island, he could navigate his real estate kingdom and live on the cheap. No traffic jams, no cabs, no disturbances. Just the others on the island and him. He stood near the edge of the cliff, dressed in clothes 20 years too young for him and 10 years too tight, a fake gold chain dangling from his neck. He was always well dressed, even in the winter. *You never know who might be watching,* he thought. *People like me.* He smiled.

As his Great Dane, Gabriel, ran across the ice, Adam lifted his binoculars again, watching as Sarah and Mark left the tower. It was easy for him to watch others, and he enjoyed living on the highest point of the island and looking down on the rest of them. Beyond them, he could see the rows of old cottages and stores. He curled his lips. *Eyesores,* he thought. *Embarrassing.* It had taken him years to build the condos on the outskirts of Missoula. Miles and miles of mountains and trees and hicks. No one supported him or believed in him. But then the Californians came, and he never stopped building. *Build,* his father had told him, *until there's nothing left. If you don't, then someone else will.* And he would do the same with this island.

During the warmest months of the summer, he would watch the tourists spilling out from the ferries onto the island, all with money to spend. All he had to do was wait for the warmer weather to come, and the lake would bring them to him. But those days were distant, and this time of year, Gabriel was the only thing that brought him outdoors. Indoors, he had his gym, his private movie theater, and groceries delivered for a generous fee from the market by snowmobile or flown in from the mainland. He had stockpiled supplies for this winter, as he did every year. If he grew restless, he could take his private plane up to Toronto, where he could pay for the companionship he sorely missed during the cold winter months. Or, he could call Susan. She would come to him. She always did. He took his phone out to text her, then thought better of it. *She's probably with Jack and that dumb kid now, anyway,* he thought. Susan was a large part of why Adam chose to spend his winters on the island tundra and not some tropical paradise. 'Free sex will always be better than the kind you have to pay for,' he had told his friends on their last yacht booze cruise before the weather turned sour for the season. He laughed out loud at his own joke again.

As he followed Gabriel at a distance, he shifted his binoculars away from the two figures to the miles and miles of frozen landscape, pure ice and white as far as the eye could see. He scanned along the ice until he came across a peculiar dark stretch. He focused on it. It looked almost as if someone had spilled black ink over a small patch of ice. It wasn't very far from the coast, just a stone's throw away from the Thunder Cliffs, where the waters were especially rough. They called it something else years ago, before the accident. The accident. *How long has it been?* he thought.

It couldn't have been very far from that spot. His eyes focused intently on the spot, half wanting to go out there. His memory drifted far back to that stormy day. He had not forgotten it. He never would.

Adam could still hear the thunder from the crashing waves and the way the wind roared, carrying those sounds through the rocky cliffs. The sentinel lighthouse had watched over these cliffs for over a hundred years. It sat silent and nestled upon the highest point facing north, watching the ships and the storms coming from the north, watching the waves break and shatter against impervious rock, the two always clashing. It was here where he felt both the strangeness and the magic of the island, where its beauty was matched only by the fury of the summer thunderstorms, the unending winters, and clippers from far across the lake. Many a ship had crashed into the rocks near the cliffs, swallowed by the dark waves. People had even jumped to their deaths.

Carved into the rocks closer to shore were the names of young lovers, well-travelled captains, and children daring enough to brave the treacherous riptides. Here, the history of the island was recorded, and many of the unwritten stories had been lost, their wreckage scattered on the ragged floors in the deepest depths. As he watched Gabriel make his way back with the ball, the dark patch seemed to spread, appearing to move the way heat does in a mirage. He knew this was where the others wouldn't go, not only because he owned most of these parts, but because of what was lost there so many years ago. As Gabriel dropped the ball into his hand, Adam calculated the distance, then tossed the ball directly at the spot. Gabriel chased after it—faster this time—but as the ball met ice and bounced toward the spot, he stopped in his tracks and watched as if it had crossed some invisible barrier. Gabriel paced around the spot from a safe distance, quietly whimpering, desperately wanting the ball but even more afraid of what was beneath, some ancient instinct warning him of a danger that even he could not understand. He walked closer to it but not too close, then barked in anger. Or fear.

Careful, you dumb creature, he thought. *If you fall in, I'm not going in there after you.*

Adam whistled for him to return, and Gabriel left the ball behind to disappear into that inky blackness that was neither ice nor water. *Buried is buried*, he thought. *Best to leave it that way.* Gabriel walked alongside him, occasionally looking back at the lake and whimpering. Adam began whistling, and Gabriel forgot about his ball, and the two of them walked back to their house by the cliffs.

CHAPTER NINE

Luke and the Mayor waited in the truck near the airfield as they watched the plane land. A cloud of angry seagulls ascended from its path into the dark gray sky, almost invisible against it. It was an ugly day. The sharp, biting wind that came in from the shore brought with it the stench of dead fish and something fouler, something rotting. The cargo shipments rarely held scheduled drop-offs or pickups during the winter, and when they did, gossip would spread like wildfire. Everyone knew it was a mere 20-minute ferry ride to the mainland, but during the winter, transportation to and from the island was at times sparse and at times impossible. But that was the gamble they had all wagered, the small price to pay for their island paradise.

The Mayor wore a 1920s tweed three-piece suit and a white skimmer hat. He spread his coat open like a peacock to Luke, who always seemed to wear clothes two sizes too large. He looked like a child who had gone through his father's wardrobe and was pretending to play grown-up.

"Well, what do you think?"

Luke sighed. "Let me guess, Joseph and the Technicolor Dreamcoat?"

The Mayor threw his coat shut in protest. "Oh, you're not even trying!"

Luke shook his head as he began to make out the small dot of the cargo plane in the sky. "Whatever it is, I'm guessing you swiped it from the museum."

"*MY* museum."

"I'm willing to bet some of the Museum Board might take issue with the fact you're prancing around in the clothes they are paying top dollar to preserve for the island."

The Mayor waved him away with both hands. "Top dollar!? Those cheapskates give just enough so that they can see their stupid little names on the museum pamphlets. Who takes care of all their little precious items when they're back at their day jobs on the mainland, hmmm? And why are you extra testy today? Mommy not send a care package this winter?"

Luke frowned. "Mark said you have my space heater. He said he gave it to you." He watched the plane get closer and closer until it touched down on the landing strip. The sound of tires on the ground always felt comforting to him.

The Mayor shrugged. "What the hell do I need a space heater for, anyway?"

"Look, I don't care which one of you has it; I just want it back. My trailer is freezing, and I don't have a spare."

The Mayor watched the plane come to a complete stop on the small airstrip. "If I had it—which I don't—I'd give it back. I'm not a thief."

"Why would Mark tell me you had it?"

"He's probably so drunk he forgot where he put it."

Luke clicked his tongue. "The same could very easily be said of you, too."

Joshua, the pilot, opened the hatch and waved them over.

The Mayor waved. "Good day to you, sir!" He said as he took off his hat.

Joshua stared at him for a moment, then looked at Luke. "The hell's wrong with him?"

Luke shrugged. "Stroke."

"What, really?"

Luke sighed. "No, he's just playing house with the museum clothes. And he's been drinking."

"Jesus," Joshua said, as he began unloading the crates. "Is that all you guys do here all winter?"

Luke shrugged. "Yeah, but I imagine it's pretty much the same everywhere in this country during winters like this. Why, what do the people in your neck of the woods do when the weather sucks?"

"Meth." Joshua walked over to the hatch and pulled it back. He looked back over the Mayor's outfit. "Lookin' snazzy there, Mayor. World War 2 era?"

The Mayor smiled at Joshua. "20s, actually. But good guess." He peeked into the crates. "Just three?"

"A lot of the crap you guys asked for was on back order. Probably won't get it in until next week."

Luke placed his hands on his hips and sighed. "Let's get this over with. Inventory check."

Joshua pulled out his pad and went through the piles, crate by crate. "Twenty pounds of coffee, thirty frozen chickens—that's including the thighs—forty pounds of flour. TWENTY bottles of red label. Check or money order?"

Luke handed him the money order, and Joshua went back over to the plane.

The Mayor slipped one of the bottles into his coat pocket. "Not staying for happy hour?"

"Nah, just fifteen minutes on this island makes me edgy. Besides, I'm headed back to the mainland before that storm hits. You all enjoy."

"What storm?" Luke asked, his tone changing.

Joshua flipped up the cockpit door. "You folks really do live in your own little world out here, don't you?"

"Joshua, seriously, what storm? If something was coming our way, we would have heard about it."

"Well, I reckon, come tomorrow night, you all won't be able to miss it. Hey, Mayor, have one for me, would ya, pal?"

He slid the cover over the cockpit, and just as fast, he started the motors running.

"Goddamn prick," the Mayor said, hugging himself in the cold. "What is it with goddamn pilots, anyway?"

As the two of them stood watching the plane take off from the small landing strip, static erupted from Luke's walkie-talkie.

"Luke, are you there? Over?"

The Mayor looked at Luke. "That sounds like Jack."

Luke sighed again. "I just spoke with him this morning. Probably wants to know if we got the shipment. I'll tell him the good news." He spoke into the walkie-talkie. "Luke here, over."

"Meeting tonight at 7 at the Hall."

"Didn't we just have a meeting?"

"Not like this. Storm's coming in from the north. Bad one. We'll detail you when you get here. Over and out."

Luke looked at the Mayor. "We might need that Red Label after all, Mayor."

"He say anything about the generators?"

Luke shrugged. "The generator will be fine. We'll be fine."

As they both watched the plane taking off into the sky, Luke tried to ignore the chill that went down his spine, and suddenly the air became much colder than before. Then everything was still and silent, and even the trees stood motionless. All was quiet and cold, and for the first time in years, Luke felt a million worlds away from the mainland. *Sarah,* he thought. *I have to warn Sarah.*

Chapter Ten

Sarah held on behind Mark on the snowmobile as it sped through the pines. She covered her face with her free hand to shield it from the brutal wind. Mark, all smiles and full speed, wore his goggles and aviator hat as they swerved between the trees.

"If you go too fast, you'll smash into a tree, and I won't be able to carry your old ass back to town."

"Relax, I could do this route in my sleep."

"You've been drinking all day."

"That just makes me sharper."

"Why are we going this way?"

"I'm going to cut through the amusement park. It's a faster route to town."

"Billy's going to be pissed if he finds out you've been in there."

"Yeah, well, Billy would be pissed if he found out about most of the shit we did in there."

It was true. Many a dull night they had broken into the park, turned on some of the rides, and gotten high. Only last week had Mark, Sarah, and Amy rolled a few joints, rode out to the park, and turned on the merry-go-round at 1 am. Sarah had been feeling depressed that day, tired of the cold gray days and wishing for warmer ones, like everyone else on the island. It was cold and dark and late, and even though they were all stoned, it brought Sarah back to warmer places and times. Her father used to take her and Alice here just before the summer season started, before the tourists began spilling in and congesting nearly every inch of the island. The place smelled of popcorn and sweets, and sometimes she could smell the fumes of metal and rubber from the inner workings of the rides. But she had loved it all for years, and that night she felt young again and wanted nothing more than to stay in that place forever.

She remembered when Alice saw the tiny rollercoaster, the little dipper, and when their father gave them a few dollars for a frozen lemon ice, she had spotted the short line for the ride. She even remembered the teenage, pimple-faced operator, bored and looking for young, pretty faces in a sea of people.

'Dad will kill us,' she said.

'*You're so boring,*' Alice said. '*Look how short the line is. Dad will never know.*'

'*We said we'd be right back.*'

'*And we will be.*'

She grabbed Sarah's hand—she was always bigger and stronger than Sarah, and as they grew older, she became cleverer as well—and Sarah found herself being dragged up the steps. There was a height measuring stick, but the attendant, indifferent to the clientele who would dare to ride such a small rollercoaster, barely even glanced at the two of them.

"You two been on a coaster before?" he asked, taking their ride tickets and yawning.

"Of course." Alice rolled her eyes. She was great at selling lies. It was a skill that had followed her throughout her life. They sat down on the hard plastic seats, and the attendant pulled down the bar, checked that it was tight, and then went back to the control panel.

Sarah could still remember how she felt at that moment, how hot it was on that July day, the smell of grease coming from the tracks, and how hot the metal felt. She remembered the feeling of her heart racing as the coaster started, first slowly, then faster as it approached the hill, the slow churning sound like metal gnashing teeth.

Chapter Eleven

A s they approached the park's boundaries, Mark came to a stop and ran off to the gate. From his bundle of dungeon master keys, he selected a large silver one and unlocked the front gate.

Sarah laughed. "Does anyone know you have that?"

"No, Jack made me a copy years ago and then forgot about it."

"What the hell was he thinking, giving you the keys to the castle?"

"Got drunk one day, gave me the keys to check on the place. Never asked for it back."

As Mark walked back to the snowmobile, a small slit in the sky opened and a fiery orange beam of sunlight broke through, causing all the metal in the park to glow. The wind stopped, and both Mark and Sarah looked up. For a moment, it looked as though the deep grayness was breaking, and the blue skies would return. And then they heard them. First, it was distant, a faint sound of birds cawing from far away. But then it grew so loud the ground almost seemed to shake.

"What the hell is that?"

"Fucked if I know."

"Is it the loudspeaker again?"

"I don't think so."

As the sound grew, they both placed their hands over their ears. The air grew colder, and Sarah could smell something foul. The wind began to pick up again, and old remnants from summers past scraped and clawed across the concrete all around them. Above them, the sky went dark and then black. Eclipsing the streak of sunlight were hundreds, if not thousands, of seagulls, flying above in a black cloud of a flock, heading south toward the mainland. The entire sky was filled with them, all cawing and screaming. It seemed as if it would never end. And then, just as quickly as they had appeared, they were gone, along with the orange sliver of light in the sky. The day seemed darker now, colder.

Mark stepped off the snowmobile. "I've never seen anything like that."

"Something must have startled them off," Sarah said.

"What the hell startles off an entire island worth of seagulls?"

"Jack said something about a storm coming. Maybe it's that."

Mark walked back over to the snowmobile. "Maybe. That must be some goddamn storm to chase that many gulls away."

Sarah looked back up at the sky, then at the clock tower near the roller coaster, which was stopped at 3:00. "Mark, what time is it?"

"Nearly 3."

"It looks like dusk already."

All around them, tiny little flakes began to fall, and Sarah once again wished she had dressed more warmly for the elements. She always felt closer to home than she was.

"Let's get going," said Mark, starting up the engine. "Or else it'll be dark before we get there."

Sarah's gloves did not prevent her hands from going numb in the cold, and all she could think about was warming them over the fire in the hall (if Jack had remembered to light it). Even though she had just seen everyone a few nights ago, she felt grateful to once again surround herself with the others, even if only for a few hours. The island suddenly felt very empty, as large as it was. As Sarah continued to brace herself through the winds on the snowmobile behind Mark, she did not feel her phone vibrating with Alice's calls.

Chapter Twelve

I nside, many of them had brought food, which was placed on the back table. The place smelled of smoke and every dish imaginable: kielbasa mac and cheese, corn chowder, fried white perch, and Mary's famous bourbon chicken. Most of the residents had shown up, save for Adam, who never appeared at such meetings. Mark and Sarah found themselves by the fire, both with hot cups of coffee. The Mayor was pouring some of the red label into his own brew while Mary sat in the back, dressed for the deepest of arctic expeditions.

At the front of the room, Jack had positioned himself behind the old podium that he had pushed away from the wall. He looked tired—he always did—and he waited patiently for the incomers to grab their refreshments and return to the seats he had set up for them. The residents had always turned such gatherings into potlucks or drink-a-thons, and he spared them the urgency that normally would have been called for such a meeting. The night felt strange, and it had come early. A few in the room muttered about how everything had gone dark at 4 and how there was no dusk. Luke, seated in the back, was doing what he did best: complaining about complaints, mostly about the residents' pets—screaming, barking at nothing, clawing at things that weren't there. Luke, who had always felt people should be licensed and trained to own the pets they tried to train, had assured them it was merely cabin fever, which both humans and animals were prone to. Of course, he knew this to be bullshit, but it was enough to stop the calls from coming in or, God forbid, an in-person visit. From the corner of his eye, he watched Sarah talking to Mark. Though he looked sullen about the unscheduled meeting, he was secretly glad it had been called. He knew she would be here.

Jack cleared his throat and brought his voice to a polite level. "Hi, everyone, if I could just have your attention..."

Mark stared at him and grinned. It was his favorite thing to do: make people uncomfortable and feel even more uncomfortable in his presence. Jack scanned the crowd—scanned past Mark's wild grin—and found that very few were listening. What gossip on this godforsaken island could they not have caught up on a few nights ago, he thought. Mark cupped his hands to his mouth.

"Everybody sit the fuck down! Let Jack talk so we can all go home!"

Jack sighed, "Thanks, Mark."

The others quickly grabbed their meals from the back table and took their seats. In the back, there was a strange glitch in the large TV screen on the wall. Jack's eyes were drawn to it only a few times: Strange flickers on what should have been a blank screen. But the room, the hall, hell, the entire island had been glitchy for years, ever since his parents brought him here. What was coming wasn't here yet. Panic could wait.

Jack cleared his throat again. He forced a smile, which was greeted by blank, impatient faces. "I appreciate all of you coming here on such short notice. I'm sure all of you had big plans for the evening." He was cut off by groans, his weak attempt at humor missing by a large margin.

The Mayor stood up and saluted him. "Skip to the good shit, captain."

For reasons he could not explain, Jack's heart began to beat faster. He had not planned on delivering the message this way. He had it mapped out in his head for hours, but it all faded before them, before his crowd. "There's a storm coming in from the north."

His declaration was met with a collective shrug.

"It's another polar vortex, and there's a blizzard coming along with it."

This drew Luke's attention. "How bad?"

"Well, NOAA says the temps are dropping down to negative teens."

There was silence in the room now. They were all ears, all eyes on him. He was happy to finally have their attention, and felt free to layer it with more bad news. "We're also looking at about fifteen to eighteen inches of snow. Wind is coming in around 60 mph. It's already hit the northern peninsula in Michigan, and they haven't been online since the stormfall. The way it's moving, it may be a multi-day event. Now we could get lucky and just get the southern tip of it, which would be about half as bad. But this storm...this one's big, and it's headed right for us."

Mark cleared his throat. "So, when is stormfall expected?"

"We're guestimating sometime in the evening tomorrow, around 6. Then we can pretty much expect to be shut down for at least a few days. Now I've called the mainland and they're on standby. But they said if we lose power, or if some kind of emergency happens here, they may not be able to come over until after the storm passes."

Mark leaned into Sarah and whispered into her ear, "Why are you Ohioans so obsessed with the weather?"

Sarah smiled. "It's our special thing. Let us have it."

There were a handful of chuckles in the room, and Jack shrugged at the suggestion as well. Dan, his feet up on the empty chair in front of him, stopped laughing. "Jack, we've been on this island now through how many storms? Remember that blizzard back in '78, the one that they said would shut down the island for months? We all lived through that. Our houses and stores did too. This island was made to withstand the elements."

Luke stood up, arms still crossed. "Jack's right. Let's not make light of this. It's an old island with old houses, and yeah, they've seen some shit but all it would take would be one big storm—just one—to shut this place down."

Everyone in the room began to roll their eyes and "BOO," and as Luke's face turned dark crimson, Jack tried hard to hide his laugh. How the higher-ups had left him in charge of the law for the better part of the winter was beyond Jack. *Thank God nothing ever happens here*, he thought.

Mark clicked his tongue. "No storm is a good one without some drama, huh, guys?"

Luke didn't smile. "All the same, I'd still like for us to make sure we all have good batteries for our walkie-talkies. Take inventory of what we have; let's not all rush to Amy's shop at once. Let's make sure those of us with snowmobiles have enough gas to make it to the mainland just in case. And we also ask that everyone stay inside during the storm. If something happens to you, the Coast Guard won't be able to get you out until the storm passes. And I know I don't have to remind you all that our tower signal may very well go out, so there's a good chance we won't be able to use our phones to call for help. So just be safe."

Mark had both arms raised across the seats on either side of him. "Luke, if you're the first one to leave, then we're raiding the shit out of your place when you're gone."

As Sarah chuckled, the phone in her pocket vibrated again. She felt a mad throbbing in her chest, and the room suddenly felt warmer than it was. The smell of the food from the back was no longer appetizing. It made her sick. The phone vibrated again.

"You gonna' answer that vibrator in your pocket, or do you want me to?" Mark grinned, and Sarah realized just how unpleasant it could be sometimes. She could see a few gaps from the missing teeth he had never bothered to replace.

She forced a smile. "I'll be right back."

"If it's one of your boy toys, tell him he can come to the island and get stranded here in time for the storm."

She didn't smile this time. She motioned to Luke that she had to take the call, and he did not bother to hide his irritation. They never all stayed for his meetings, and if they did, they rarely listened.

"Look, I'm not asking anyone here to jump ship, just to understand the gravity of the situation."

Dan stirred in his chair. "How much longer are we gonna play this duck-duck-goose shit? This whole island has enough booze to last all through three winters, let alone three days. I say we all shack up in the old Sandy Stone hotel."

Luke stared at him in disbelief. "Have you been drunk all day? Starnes isn't even on the island, and even if he were, he wouldn't let all you assclowns in there. And even if he did, we don't have the key."

Mark smiled and held up his dungeon master key chain. Even Mary giggled. "Jesus, Mark, do you have a key for everyone's place here?"

Mark turned around fast, his wide, semi-toothless grin ear-to-ear. "That's right, and every night when you fall asleep, I come and WATCH YOU." Mary stopped giggling and rolled her eyes. "I see everything you do, Mary."

Luke sighed heavily. "Guys, can we please get back to baseline here? I promise when we're done, you'll go back to shoving food in your faces 'til you get sick."

Jack walked over to Chris, who was busy helping himself to the food in the back.

"We still on for tomorrow night?" Chris said, his mouth full of carrots and dip.

Jack nodded. "Bill's coming too. I think he'll have fun."

"He ever been out on the ice before?"

Jack shook his head. "Not like this. Not ice-fishing at night."

"The wife okay with it?"

Jack scoffed. "I'm okay with it."

They both laughed and watched as Luke continued to speak while others spoke over him. As they talked amongst themselves, Luke approached Jack.

"Would you mind showing me how to get the generator running one more time?"

Jack coughed. "What? I've already shown you a dozen times. I'll show you tomorrow before the storm hits. Maybe you should film it on your goddamn phone next time."

"What if something happens tonight? What if we lose power?"

"Relax, Luke, if something happens tonight, no one will have to depend upon you to fix it." He said this last part very loudly, and a few eavesdroppers sitting close by let out big, boisterous laughter. Luke could feel his body cooking underneath his snow gear.

None of them saw Sarah sneak out the back exit.

Chapter Thirteen

Outside, a few stray snowflakes fell, and Sarah could see the faint, lonely flicker of the moon behind the thick layer of clouds. The air already seemed ten degrees colder, and even with Mark's jacket over her shoulders, she shivered. Three missed calls, all from Alice. Sarah dialed her, and once again the signal died.

"Goddammit!" Sarah knew most of the best spots for cell signals on the island, and this was not one of them. Her inn was on the other side of the island, and the only other spot was the lighthouse. She had resolved not to miss another call from her sister. And with the news of the impending storm, she knew the window for clear communication was closing fast. The keys were still in the ignition of Mark's snowmobile, and she could see the others still bickering inside, silent smart-ass exchanges she had all heard before.

As she arrived at the base of the lighthouse, everything was still, just like the rest of the island. The wind swept over the frozen surface of the lake, and Sarah held her arm over her face to shield herself. The ancient sentinel stood tall and defiant against the wind. It had weathered thousands of storms, and if properly cared for, it would last another 100 years. It was the quiet friend on the island that strangely comforted Sarah, and although it stood on the most touristy part of the island, it was beloved by both islanders and visitors alike. Its storied history made it the most important landmark on the island and perhaps all of Lake Erie. Over 70 feet tall, its glow could be seen from the shores of the mainland, a silent beacon that guided all safely through the darkest of nights. When the lighthouse was built in the early 1820s, a young ex-soldier was hired for the post and shipped out to the island, leaving his wife and infant behind until he had set up a home for them. One night, a strong storm blew in and sent waves crashing over the barricades that lined the streets. Meanwhile, out on the lake, his wife and son were on a small cargo boat crossing the deadly passage. Somewhere between the two bodies of land, the lake had swallowed them up, and in days to come, it surrendered only pieces of wood from the ship, their bodies never to be found. As legend had it, the soldier kept watch every night from the tower, looking out over the sea, waiting for them to come back to him.

The island's history was full of stories like that, as Sarah well knew. The Mayor, who was the island's historian as well as her father, had told her many of them. They kept the myth of the island alive, these old stories that gave it a history. It wasn't just a vacation getaway forgotten by the rest of the world. It was a home to her.

She climbed the old staircase that spiraled around the perimeter of the tower all the way to the top, where the automated system kept things whirring day in and day out. The wind was harshest up here, but she knew the door would be unlocked. Once inside, she could hear the wind breaking on the metal and glass, hear it moaning through the tiny slits between the windows. But it was quiet enough, and as she took out her phone, she felt relief when the signal was strong enough for a phone call. She dialed her sister's number and looked out into the darkness over the lake. She was still shaking from the cold. Her heart pounded, and she worried that, again, Alice would not answer. But she did.

"Sarah?" Her voice trembled, its clarity muffled between bursts of static.

"Alice, what is it? What's wrong?" The wind picked up outside, and Sarah placed her hand over her other ear.

"What the hell have you been doing? Why haven't you returned any of my messages?"

"Alice, calm down. Don't you remember how fucking hard it is to get a signal here? What's wrong? What's going on?"

Her voice began breaking up, and Sarah felt her patience running out. Between bursts of static, she could hear Alice sobbing. "Alice, please, please calm down! I can't understand anything you're—

"Sarah, you have to get off that island."

"What? Get off the island? Alice, are you drunk?"

"No, Sarah, you have to get off that island tonight!"

Sarah found herself shouting. "I'm not going anywhere tonight, Alice! Look, what happened? What's wrong?"

More static, and the bits of Alice's voice were indecipherable. Sarah paced around the tower, trying to find a space that would give her a clearer signal.

"...then I'm coming there to get you!" The line dropped. Sarah tried to redial again, and again but to no avail. "Fuck!" She screamed, and it echoed down the inside staircase. *Coming here to get me,* she thought. *But she was in LA! She was supposed to be in LA, anyway.* The call had left her feeling shaken, and part of her wished it had not gone through at all. At that moment, everything felt silent and still, and for the first time in ages, she felt truly, horribly alone. Out on the blackness of the ice, there were no boats or ferries headed to their island. Nor was the familiar light of the sister lighthouse flickering on the mainland. The moon was not visible in the sky to illuminate the whiteness of the ice. *Last one left, turn out the lights,* she thought. But out over the frozen lake, something caught her eye.

Out across the ice, she saw a strange red glow, and from the distanc,e she could not tell if it was above or beneath the ice. In the darkness, the glow grew brighter, then died down again, like some phantasmagoric firefly out on the lake. The night was still, and all Sarah could do was focus on the red glow. Her memories ran as deep as the waters that struggled with the fury of a trapped current under the ice, and she remembered:

Sarah couldn't hear the others from the boat screaming their names. Thousands of spiderwebbed flashes of light and heat. Alice held her tightly as the boat was tossed by indifferent waves.

"Everything is going to be okay, I promise!" Who had screamed that? Did it matter?

Dad. Where was Dad? He'll be here soon. I promise. I promise.

And then he came, she thought. Just like he always did. But when they sped away back to the island on mountainous waves, the young girl on the other boat watched as they left them behind, watched with hateful eyes and her fists clenched tight, fingernails drawing blood.

Sarah snapped suddenly from her vision to find that the red glow had disappeared, and all was black once again. Whether it was from exhaustion, loneliness or the awful memory returning, she knelt and cried.

Part Two

The Three Boats

BAYNAM BOOKS PRESS

Chapter Fourteen

20 Years Earlier

As she watched the cotton floating like snow across the island, Sarah felt this was by far the most beautiful day she had seen all summer. The weeks leading up to this day had been scorching hot, and she had stayed inside watching the sun slowly drift and cast long shadows across the backyard. The streets should have been filled with children—herself included—but were lava-hot asphalt. She felt as if she were being robbed of her summer vacation and did not wish to spend it cooped up inside watching the days pass her by. That was what winters were for. But there was a cooler breeze today, and everything felt fresh and new. Their father missed the ice cream trucks back home and always had a cooler full of frozen treats here. Sarah sat on the steps as the clock struck noon, wondering where the day would take her. The amusement park would no doubt be crowded, as would the beaches and the dock. Everyone had emerged from their cottages and hotels to finally get their first taste of summer.

Alice walked out through the screen door, letting it slam behind her as she always did. Everything she did was loud: she talked loudly, ate loudly, and stomped loudly around the hardwood floor of their cottage. Even the way she ate her ice cream as she walked down the steps and sat down a stair above Sarah was loud. It was easy to find Alice; her father joked that even if you were on the opposite side of the island, you could hear her.

"What are we doing today?" Sarah asked, taking her time with her chocolate-dipped cone.

"You mean, what am *I* doing today?" Alice crunched down on her cone.

"Dad said you have to bring me." She hated being left behind, feeling left out. Her quiet demeanor meant that outgoing Alice always made more new friends on the island. Even from a young age, Sarah felt like a shadow in her sister's footsteps, one she could never seem to step away from. Alice was the firstborn, and their father gave her more freedom. Alice was quick to learn all the rules and, almost as fast, how to break them. She had bewitched their father with her gregariousness, so her willfulness was often overlooked.

But then Sarah had come along, little Sarah, who seemed small for her age. Unlike her sister, she was more pensive, almost withdrawn. If Alice was the life of the party, then Sarah was the guest who always came late and left early, the one no one really noticed. This feeling would follow Sarah all her life, and the more she tried to be like her sister, the more she reverted to her quiet self. Later in her life, she would understand that part of her nature, but until then, she would never be at peace with it. She was aware of being someone who was always on the outside looking in, watching others have fun, but not aware enough to understand why.

Although different in so many ways, the two of them often spent their summer days together—Sarah accepting her role as sidekick and Alice appreciating someone who followed along. They made a world of their summer island, and there were always new adventures to be explored. Though Sarah dreamed one day of having her own group of friends, for now, these adventures were her life.

Today, their father had planned a day of cards and cold adult beverages with friends and had given Alice $100, a fortune in the hands of any child. Enough for dinner for the two of them, perhaps at Sam's hot dog Shack, or there was the Crab Grill, where they never actually served crabs but made delicious burgers and milkshakes in every flavor imaginable. There was a putt-putt course near midtown, which, despite the puddles, was open for all. And, of course, there was the movie theater, which played movies that were two or three years old for two dollars. Sarah had suggested all of these options, but Alice had other things on her mind that day.

They walked alongside each other as the hot sun beat down, melting the ice cream cone in Sarah's hand. "We could go to the theater."

Alice tied her long hair back into a ponytail. "You've seen all those movies already this summer. Don't you want to do something outside?"

Sarah shrugged. Outside or in, both were fine. "Do you want to go to the beach?"

Alice groaned. "Everyone is going to be at the beach."

"So? You love crowds."

"I'm not in a beach mood."

"Want to go to the putt-putt course?"

"I'm sick of that place. Besides, I always win. You know I always win."

"Well, what do you want to do?" Sarah never had a say in things, and if she did, she would have to do it alone. She could only hope that her sister's choice would not involve being around a lot of people, especially ones she didn't know.

The two of them walked to the end of the street, where the chain-link fence separated them from the rocks along the shore and, beyond that, the lake. They both rested their arms and chins on the fence, facing south. They could see in a hazy distance, the mainland, which now seemed far away and a place to be avoided, as once they did return, they would have to return to school, marking the end of their summer.

Alice watched a sailboat drifting across the smooth waters, hardly a break in its trek. Onboard, she could make out the silhouettes of two people who were unaware of them watching. Alice smiled. "I want to go out on one of those."

Sarah finished the last of her cone and stared at the boat as well. "We don't know how to sail. Dad hasn't taught us yet."

Alice rolled her eyes. "Not a sailboat, dummy. We can go on a sea canoe."

Sarah could feel the hot fence against her skin. "A what?"

Alice pointed to another spot out on the lake, a small object that drifted slowly in the water.

"That, dummy."

"Dad says we're not allowed to be on those on our own."

Alice clicked her tongue, a habit she had learned from their father. "Dad is having drinks with our stupid neighbors. They won't know or care which side of the island we're on today."

"But what if they find out? What if they see us?"

"All you do is worry. Try to start having a little fun sometimes. Dad says you'll live longer if you do."

"Dad doesn't say that. *You* say that."

"Well, whatever, don't be boring. Come on, you know it's gonna' be fun. Once we're out there on the lake, we can go wherever we want."

"But what if we get lost? What if we drift out to somewhere where no one can find us?"

"Don't be such a child. Where would we get lost? It's a lake, not an ocean. Look out there on the lake. Look at all those people out there. The weather's fine, there's not a cloud in the sky, and we have the whole afternoon to ourselves. We'll be back before dark, and Dad won't even know what we've done."

"And if they ask what we did?"

"Then we went to play putt-putt, went to the beach, and went to the movies. They won't care."

"But we don't have a boat."

"We don't have a boat *yet*, kid."

As they paddled upon a trail of shimmering water, Sarah watched the rocky shore growing farther and farther away. She would not lie to herself and pretend she was not thrilled to be out here, with no adults and only the two of them to set course on their adventures. It was every child's dream. Though the sun was lower in the sky than it had been when they set off on their small boat, and the shadows from a passing sailboat grew longer, it was still hours away from dark. The water was cool and calm, and for a short whil,e Sarah felt as if she were drifting along in one of her dreams, all the familiar shapes and terrains slowly fading beyond her line of sight.

Alice smiled as she clasped what was left of their father's money—not much to dine on, but she cared little. This was what she wanted so badly: to be away from control, out on the water, just like in films. Their cupboards back home would be filled with snacks anyway, and surely there would be leftovers once the adults were done drinking their sobriety away. That would be their dinner. They had convinced the teenage worker at the rental desk that they had been out on a canoe many times. The teen—whose teeth were so crooked even his braces would never fully straighten them into a proper smile—caved against his better judgement and rented them a boat for the day. Sarah had done what she always did: said little and let Alice run the show. But Sarah worried about more practical things as their funds quickly dwindled.

"What are we going to do for dinner, then?"

Alice looked past her as she paddled. The paddles were becoming heavier, and during brief moments she simply let the boat drift, letting the calm lake waters dip them up and down while she regained the strength to carry on. "We have some money left. We can pick up some snacks on the way back home. If Dad asks what we ate, we'll tell him we stopped at Sam's hot dogs." She gave her sister an assertive look, implying that her commands trumped any rules their father had set for them.

Sarah simply nodded as her sister did most of the paddling. This being their first time out on the lake, they had forgotten the things their father would have reminded them of: suntan lotion and water. Sarah could feel the low sun growing warmer, and though there was a breeze over the lake, she felt her discomfort growing. She slumped over the side of the boat and watched as water bugs skimmed across the surface of the water with alien-like agility. Playing over the loudspeakers, they could hear the garbled, slightly off-key notes of "Ebb Tide" by the Righteous Brothers. Though the lyrics were muffled, they knew that song—like every other song that came from the speakers—by heart. The songs were played in a continuous week-long loop, and people often found themselves singing or whistling along without even realizing it.

Not far from them was another canoe, which, like theirs, had ventured farther from the coast to escape the summer crowds. From a distance, Sarah could make out the silhouette of a man and a young girl, probably around her age. The man navigated the boat while the young girl sat back and watched the lake around her. Spotting their boat, the little girl in the back of the boat waved, and Sarah waved back.

"Who are you waving at?" Alice asked, still paddling on.

"There's some people over there on that boat. One of them waved at me."

Alice glanced for a moment at the boat, then continued on. The girls felt lost in the moment, and as they looked ahead toward the horizon where sky met ocean, they did not realize the sky was beginning to darken. They were too far from the island to notice the tree branches ripping wildly in the wind or see the weather vanes madly spinning. As the wind began to pick up, so too did the waves, and Alice found it much more difficult to navigate through the choppy waters.

"Hey Sarah, help me," she ordered.

Sarah grabbed the extra oars and began to row. As she looked back, she could just barely see the island. The sky above was growing darker by the minute until it was black. The sunlight had suddenly been swallowed by the approaching storm. Then they heard it: The sound of storm sirens from the island, blasting loud and clear over the loudspeakers. Up in the sky, they began to see quick flashes of light.

Sarah could feel her heart beating faster. Already, the temperature had dropped, and she felt both hot and cold simultaneously. "Alice, we need to go back."

"I'm trying."

"Alice, I can't see the island."

Alice was paddling harder now, but the boat did not seem to move an inch in the choppy waves. Her arms felt tired. "If you want to get back, you have to row faster."

"Alice, I'm scared."

The sirens grew louder now, as if the island was screaming for them both to come back. "We'll be okay. I promise."

Sarah tried to row harder, but the oar was too heavy for her, and she knew Alice was doing most of the work. Their boat rocked up and down, and Sarah nearly lost her oar several times. As the sky blackened above them, Sarah could picture their father wondering where they were, getting worried or angry about them not coming home when the sirens blared their warning. He'd be anxious, just as she was, looking out at the dark sky. She felt the awful despair of one who lies: her father did not know where they were. He would not know where to look for them. At that moment, she was angry with Alice for taking her out here, taking her far away from the safety of the island where they could have taken shelter. But now the storm was nearly upon them, and they were miles from the shore.

Sarah looked out across the lake to see how the other boat was faring. They seemed closer now, and Sarah could see the man rowing frantically as the little girl cried. The man was saying something to her, perhaps consoling her, but the girl did not seem to respond. At that moment, she wanted to hold the little girl's hand and tell her exactly what Alice had said: That everything would be okay. But land and shelter seemed so far away now, and as thunder began to boom in the distance, for the first time in her life, Sarah entertained the thought of death in her mind.

Back at home, their father had jumped in his car and driven to all the places he thought they might be. He had already called the sheriff, and on his walkie-talkie, he heard other reports of missing persons. The storm had not been in the forecast and had popped up unexpectedly, moving fast. The afternoon looked like dusk, and the once-crowded streets were empty as everyone took shelter. As the first raindrops began to fall, he knew the storm had already reached the island. It would hit soon, and it would hit hard. He had not felt such a panic in years. He prayed long-forgotten prayers, hoping he had said them right.

Years later, he could still recall exactly when he got the message on his walkie-talkie. But he remembered that it was Jack on the other end, along with Mark and a few others. The owner of the boat shop had been concerned when the storm moved in and called Jack, who was the sheriff at the time. The girls had last been spotted drifting south on the lake. After that, they had lost sight of them.

Out on the lake, Sarah and Alice held hands and prayed. The rain had grown harder now, and the waves grew angrier, tossing them about. Sarah looked out across the crashing waves and could still see the other boat, struggling as they were against the storm. She saw the muddied image of what must have been the girl's father, trying to both maintain control of the boat and comfort his daughter. Sarah wished her father were in the boat with them. He would know what to do and would have guided them over the treacherous waves, carrying them both safely back to shore.

The sky filled with relentless spiderwebbed lightning. Above the island, they could see quick flashes of white light striking down, followed immediately by deafening thunder. A streak of lightning struck the short distance between them and the other boat, and Alice covered Sarah's body with her own as she cried.

"Don't touch the water!" Alice screamed.

Sarah nodded tearfully, even though she already knew. She held onto her sister tightly. They both felt a million miles away from land, and the thought of dying out here, their bodies lost to the waters, far from everything they knew and loved, was too great to bear.

When their father finally arrived, Mark and Jack were already at the dock, bracing themselves against the wind. Jack explained that most of the boats had been rented, but there was one speedboat meant for emergencies. They had called the coast guard, but to their dismay, they already had multiple units out rescuing other boaters trapped in the sudden storm. Jack had warned them of the potential danger, but their father heard none of it. They had to find the two children. The sky was black as night, and only through quick flashes could they see the waters before them. Off in the distance, the sirens still sounded, though their warning had diminished in the force of the storm.

Mark and Jack were dressed in ponchos, but their father had only his summer clothes on and was soaked to his skin. The expanse of the lake appeared infinite in the storm, as if the whole world consisted of raging waves, thunder, and lightning. Their father waited to catch sight of them, but as the wind grew stronger and the lightning more frequent, his heart sank like a boulder tossed into the deepest depths of the lake.

At first, they could not hear the woman's voice over the walkie-talkie. Gabriella had called their names several times, and it was only by chance that Jack checked to see if any transmissions were coming through.

"They're on the north side of the lake, the two girls, and there's another boat near them. They're hanging on, but just barely."

Jack spoke into the device: "Who is this?"

"Gabriella. I'm at the north shore, by the lighthouse. I can see them, but you have to hurry."

The men were on the eastern side of the island, and though their speed was fast, the waves were fierce and would impede what should have been a quick trek to the northern rim of the island.

As Sarah held Alice's hand tightly, their boat began to fill with water. As they tried to bail it out with their hands, the boat slowly took on more and more water as the waves grew higher. Sarah had lost her paddles to the tides, and Alice had abandoned hers, now floating at the bottom of the boat. Across the water, they could see the light from the lighthouse, a beacon of hope that somehow managed to tear through the darkness and reach out to them, reminding them that land and home were not too far off. Alice shook her sister and pointed.

"Look, it's the lighthouse!"

Sarah looked out over the waters and saw it. "It doesn't look that far." She looked desperately at Alice as she clutched her hand. "Do you think we can make it?"

Alice nodded frantically back. "We can make our way in that direction. The closer we get, maybe someone on the island might see us!"

"Do you think Dad is looking for us?"

"I know Dad is looking for us. He'll find us! Just hang in there, okay?"

Sarah fought back her tears, and Alice picked up the paddles. But the more she tried to fight against the waves, the more they seemed to push back, keeping them in a kind of strange whirlpool. Alice almost wished she had not seen the lighthouse; the hope she had felt for a brief moment had risen and crashed like the waves around them.

Sarah looked out and saw the other boat struggling, and through the fury of the storm, she could see the child looking back in her direction. Sarah pointed to the lighthouse, but the child just watched the two of them trying to make their way toward the island.

Adam watched as all this unfolded through his binoculars. He could hear the force of the wind against the windows, and from sheltered safety, he watched both boats struggling against the storm. His yacht was being tossed about in the wind and waves. Such matters were out of his hands, he felt, because there was always somebody else to take care of these kinds of things. He had not phoned the police because he assumed someone else already had, and he didn't consider taking his yacht out because more skilled men were no doubt on their way. *If I sink and die, then what good will I do anyone?* he thought. *Tourists. Always tourists who don't listen and don't understand the ebbs and flows of the lake or its unpredictable weather.*

Out on the rocks, he could see a woman standing, and then he felt his blood run cold. She stood out where the steepest cliff overlooked the raging waters, her hair and clothing flapping in the wind, watching the boats just as he was. Within minutes, he recognized her. It was Gabriella. The island "witch," or so she sold herself to the bumpkins who stumbled onto his island every summer and disturbed his peace. Out on the lake, he saw a speedboat approach, and though he couldn't see those on board, he was confident one of them must have been the police. *See, there's always someone to take care of nasty business here.*

The ice in his drink had melted and diluted his top-shelf whiskey, and when he drank from it, he winced. As he watched the scene before him unfold, he wondered how many lives the lake had claimed during such storms. How many had survived? If the lake wished to spare their lives, then it would. If not, then there was no point in adding another life to that list. Inside his boathouse, the yacht waited, no doubt heavy enough to withstand these waves.

Perhaps. He didn't like the little voice inside him, the implications.

You know you could reach them both. And you know you could make it back alive.

I'm worth more to this island alive than dead.

But think how much everyone would love you, instead of just kissing your ass every time you write a check.

The people here respect me...

But you could be more than just this. You could do something bigger than yourself, instead of watching your life unfold here alone for the rest of your-

Enough. He had turned it off, just as one turns off a light switch. And then it was gone. He chuckled to himself. *How wonderful to be able to turn that off.* And as he watched the boat drift further away from view, he thought, *I wonder if everyone feels that way?*

Gabriella feared the wind would sweep her off the side of the cliff. Never had she felt so close to touching death. Though she worried about her daughter, she knew she was old enough to care for herself if something should happen to her. She had seen this happening years ago, back when she was a teenager. It was a vision so powerful it nearly blinded her: she knew she would die on this island, and it would not be a quiet, peaceful death. She could not see how or when, but she felt the certainty of it and did not question it. She had never told anyone this, not even her daughter. She had merely written it in her journal, which would most likely be tossed or buried with her when her time came. If that time were today, then she would be ready.

Here at the thunder cliffs, the roaring winds seemed to call her name. As she watched both boats struggle against the waves, she saw Jack's speedboat approaching, bouncing perilously against the waves. It was like watching a memory that she'd seen a thousand times. She knew this event had many possible paths, and not all of them ended well.

As Alice and Sarah continued their futile attempts to bail water from the bottom of their boat, they heard the faint noise of a horn of some kind. It stood apart from the sporadic, angry booming of the thunder and the constant humming of the island sirens. This was something else, something that was coming closer, headed in their direction. Alice looked up and saw the outline of a speedboat tearing through the unstable waters, tossing about as it cut wave after wave. On board, she could barely make out three shapes. She clutched Sarah's face in her hands.

"Help is coming soon! Look!" She pointed out over the rough waters, and as a large wave lifted them, Sarah could see the speedboat headed in their direction.

"Is it Dad?!" she cried out.

"I don't know who it is, but they're coming for us!

Sarah turned her head and looked back over the waters behind them. The other boat was still there, the two figures still aboard. From a distance, she could see that they, too, had spotted the boat; the taller one, most likely the father, had seen it. Then a large wave struck their boat, blindsiding them, and the man was swept off his feet into the bottom of the boat. The child disappeared as well. As she went to tell her sister, Alice interrupted her:

"It's Dad!"

Those words were more powerful than anything the storm could conjure, more powerful than the waves that rocked them or the raging winds. Their father had arrived to rescue them, just as they had prayed for. But as the boat grew closer, they could see it was small, barely big enough to carry the weight of its three passengers. Their father had thrown a life preserver out into the water. Sarah and Alice could hear him shouting, but could not decipher his words through the storm. He gestured wildly for them to jump. But brave as she was and confident as a swimmer, Alice did not want to jump into those waters, nor did she want Sarah to. With the water level now up to their knees in the boat, Alice held her sister closer and cried.

Their father, realizing that time was running out and seeing that the girls were in shock, dove into the waters himself. He grabbed onto the life preserver, and as the waves began to engulf him, he cried out their names. It was Sarah, not Alice, who grabbed her sister's hand and told her to jump. Alice shook her head no, but Sarah urged her:

"We'll jump together!"

Alice finally nodded yes, just as a large wave rocked their boat and sent Sarah into the raging waters. She sank underwater, and the world seemed to disappear forever. With the few precious moments of breath she had left in her lungs, she prayed she would see home again and feel the warm sun on her face one more time before it was taken away from her forever.

Sarah couldn't remember the moment when her father grabbed her tiny arm and pulled her from the violent currents. Years later, that moment would still visit her in her dreams. She would recall the muted sound of thunder under the water, quick flashes of light through the darkness, the sound of rushing water filling her ears, and then the brightest light she had ever known. She felt whole and unafraid both at once, and by the time her father grabbed hold of her arm, she was caught between two worlds—and pulled away from a wholeness that she would never feel again.

Their father encircled both children in his large right arm, and in his other hand, he held tightly to the rope Jack and Mark pulled him in with. Alice held onto Sarah as she drifted between two worlds, and the boat they were pulled toward seemed miles away. Every time they seemed to be getting closer, a large wave would push them back like a giant hand, farther into the dark waters. But Mark and Jack did not give up, and the girls felt their father's strength as he held them tight.

The two men aboard the boat struggled to keep their footing in the churning waters, but they had enough strength to pull the three closer until their father grabbed onto the edge of the boat.

"Hold the line!" Jack yelled as he pulled the children up first. Once they were safely aboard, he pulled their father up as well. There was no time for celebration or tears. They were all exhausted, and the storm had grown even more powerful.

Their father looked up at Jack and Mark, whose attention was now focused on the other boat, both passengers desperately watching their potential rescuers. Sarah heard the man arguing, but she could not make out their words over the sounds of the storm. Mark was adamantly pointing toward the other boat, while Jack was shaking his head no. They both looked up at their father. He still held them tightly, as another large wave nearly capsized their boat.

"There's too many of us on this thing!" Jack screamed.

"There's only two of them on that boat! How much farther can they be, for Christ's sake?"

"Listen to me! This boat can't take much more of a beating from these waves. We're already heavier than we should be! We take on any more weight, and we won't—none of us make it back to shore, I fucking guarantee it!"

"Can't you get through on the radio?"

"Nobody's getting through in this storm! We'll have to call in when we get back!" The world continued to rock and fall apart around them, indifferent to their arguments. Then they turned and looked at their father, making him their tiebreaker.

Sarah felt him squeeze her tighter at that moment, and though the storm was only now reaching its zenith, she felt safe and knew her father would not let any harm come to them. He had come this far to bring them back, and she knew they would make it back to the island alive. Their father looked over at the two men. Almost out of breath, he could only shout, "Let's go back! Call for help when we get there!"

It was settled. Jack fired up the engine, and they began their way across the waves. Alice held her arm tightly around her father's neck.

Sarah looked behind them as the other boat grew smaller and smaller. She could see the man shouting and waving his fist. Standing behind him was the girl, just staring at them.

Sarah looked at her father. "What about them, Daddy?!" she screamed.

"We can't help them now! We'll have to call for help when we get back!"

"But they might die!" she pleaded tearfully.

Sarah watched as the girl watched her back, staring without expression, no hate, no fear, just staring blankly. And then the other boat was just a tiny dot, a fragile toy lost amongst the gargantuan waves, illuminated briefly by lightning. And then it was gone. Guilt-stricken in a way that she never had been before, she turned to her father: "Please, let's go back for them!"

"We can't! We're too heavy, and now we're too far!" He looked back where the boat had been, now gone. "We'll go back for them, I promise!" He held her tight as the boat rocked in every direction, speeding defiantly against the tempest winds.

Once they had returned safely to shore, they were finally able to reach out to other boats, and eventually, the coast guard made it through the storm to the island. Nearly a dozen boats braved the storm and searched the area where they had last seen the boat. The worst of the storm had passed, and while the waves were still strong, the rain and lightning had subsided. The blackness that had seemed to swallow the island whole had begun moving south toward the mainland, where eventually it would die out.

Come evening, a strange blood-red sun had broken through the clouds just in time for a mournful dusk. As the boats circled the crimson waters, they found no signs of the boat or its passengers. The air had grown cooler, and the frenzy of the storm had been replaced by a more ominous stillness. They had searched deep into the night, and from the shore, people could see stray rays of light circling back and forth, then disappearing into the inky blackness of the summer night.

Three days later, they had called off the search. The bed and breakfast where the two had stayed reported them missing. The father and daughter were tourists, both from an Ohio town nearly forgotten on modern maps. No family had come to claim them or spoken with the police. They had disappeared from the island as anonymously as they had arrived there. Both the Mayor and the island's newsletter had done their best with damage control, noting that, although the loss was tragic, the island was still as safe as ever, and the only people prone to danger were those who didn't follow the rules of safety. This was enough to satisfy the tourists, and by the end of the summer, the incident had nearly been forgotten. The islanders prepared for the epilogue of summer, in which vacation ends and school and work resume, and for nine long months, everyone longs for the moment when it can all begin again.

But for Sarah and Alice, the memory lingered on, tainting them no matter where they went or what they did. The last of the summer sun only darkened the shadows on the island, and to Sarah, the mainland seemed farther away, as if this island were the last remnant of human civilization. The air no longer smelled of cotton candy or suntan lotion; it smelled of dead fish and rotting wood. Both children refused their friends' offers to venture out for the remainder of the summer, instead choosing to watch the days pass by from the back of their house, which was all glass and looked out over the waters of the lake. They half expected that other boat to appear in the distance, both occupants smiling and waving, all things forgiven. But it never did, and so the darkness lingered.

As for the two people on the boat, a brief memorial ceremony was held for them before their belongings were shipped back home. Only a few of the locals attended. Gabriella and her daughter Mary were there, as was Jack, along with Sarah, Alice, and their father. Mark had not attended, nor had the Mayor, who wanted the matter to be over and done with. Few words were spoken.

Sarah would not grow to realize her fear of leaving the island until years later. Up until college, she had left the island for school trips or on weekend getaways. But during her first semester away at college, Sarah began experiencing the attacks. They came on slowly at first, minor meltdowns in class or alone in her room. She often felt dizzy, and although the campus was large, she found its remote location disorienting. She had called home several times, and her father assured her it was normal to feel homesick. But the attacks grew worse, and her sleepless nights caused her to miss nearly all of her classes.

The winter following her first semester, Sarah returned home to the island. The day she stepped back onto the island for good was cold and gray. Her father embraced her as she stepped off the last ferry of the season, and she felt whole again. She was home. Knowing she could never again leave the island, she acted fast to find work. She soon found herself bartending at the local tourist hotspots, with the dream of one day owning one of them, or all of them. It was the only dream she could have.

One morning, Sarah woke up to an empty house, silence instead of music, and the smell of coffee she was accustomed to in her father's house. When the police arrived, they told her that sometime during the night, their father had walked to the edge of the Thunder Cliffs and jumped. Some fishermen had discovered his body lying on the rocks at dawn. They had asked Sarah if he had left behind a note or if he had said anything to her that might hint at his condition. But like Sarah, her father had never been the same after the incident, though he never talked about it. It was always just a silent understanding between them. Alice had moved on to college by then, and now he was gone, too.

As the seasons passed and she said goodbye to the last of her twenties, Sarah never forgot about what happened out there on the water. When the summer storms rolled in, she could almost see them out there, waving their arms and pleading for help, watching Sarah and the others slowly drift away from them, the little girl with the unblinking eyes that would never forget...

Part Three

Stormfall

Chapter Fifteen

From her window on the plane, Alice looked out over the bleak grayness of it all. She was only six hours removed from the sunny West Coast weather. Here, the land matched the sky in its milky whiteness. Far off on the horizon where land met sky, there was no distinguishing between the two, and Alice felt as if she was floating in a gray abyss, never to land. She had packed very little and was annoyed with herself for not grabbing something to eat on the way. She had hoped to sleep on the flight, but found that she could not. The valium she had taken did little to help her relax on the small aircraft.

The flight was empty, save the pilot. He seemed highly entertained by every little thing, and a few times he caught her glancing at him. *Both of us are thinking the same thing,* she thought. *What the fuck are you going to this island for in the middle of winter?* She smiled to herself, realizing she was leaving behind one group of weirdos for another. She had not been to the island in years. She couldn't stand its touristy fabrication: the same people, the same things to do, and the same events all summer round. Alice had always wondered how Sarah could stay there without going insane. True, the city she was leaving behind was also fake—as were the people—but the culture and the energy felt real to her. The island she was headed to had none of that. And she was coming at a time when most of the island would be deserted. *Winter on a deserted island,* Alice thought. *Oh, Sarah.*

But she had grown tired of trying to coax Sarah from the island years ago. Even after they lost their father, and Sarah had refused to attend her father's burial on the mainland—which Alice had never forgiven her for. She had resigned herself to letting her sister live out her life on that prison isle. The two of them were so different, and she had also stopped trying to understand why her sister did the things she did. Alice's own life in LA was exciting and fast-paced. The blue skies and proximity to the ocean, the beautiful fake freaks, the high-end cars that most people couldn't afford but drove anyway—it was all absurd, but it still felt real, and she loved every minute of it. But Sarah, working at bars with the oversexed boys and cheap liquor and old men with their potbellies and Hawaiian shirts—it was all so...tacky. Why anyone would willingly choose to live there any time of year was beyond her. But she was tired of trying to figure out everyone else. She had spent most of her life trying to find the things that made her happy, and now she was.

The pilot glanced behind him at Alice and smiled at her. He was a bit unshaven and looked uncomfortable in his own skin. She could see holes worn in his sneakers. "I take it you're not headed to Sandy Stone for the beaches." He smiled, and it seemed fake to her, like all the other tourists on the island.

The flight was only two hours from Detroit, but it already felt more than twice that. She looked away, out over the gray ugliness outside. "Good guess."

"You a local? On the island, I mean." He turned sideways in his seat. This wasn't going to be a short conversation, she realized.

She sighed, then turned toward him slowly. "Do I look like one of the locals there?"

"Well, I've never stayed there during the winter. I'm a weird guy, but not weird enough to live on that island during this season. You couldn't pay me enough."

"That makes both of us."

The small plane shook violently in the fingertips of the stormfront moving in, now just a line of black clouds on the distant horizon. Alice heard strange sounds, possibly wing flaps or an old engine. It looked like an old plane. Very old. She had been on hundreds of flights, most of them first class. But she had never been in a plane so small, and the sounds it emitted made her worry that it might not get them to the island. *Thanks again, little sister*, she thought bitterly.

"I'm Blake Reese, by the way. All the locals know me there. I love Sandy Stone."

Alice, arms folded, sat back in her seat.

Blake cleared his throat. "I love places like that. Little communities you'd never know about."

"...or care about," Alice said, under her breath. She took out a flask with her initials etched on it and poured from it into a little plastic cup.

"I'm sorry?"

"I said that's interesting. So, Blake Reese, how did you ever come about choosing to be a pilot way the hell up here? Have you ever been anywhere else?"

"Well, I grew up spending the summers going to islands like this with my folks. I'm guessing you did too?"

She nodded without blinking, enjoying his discomfort.

"My parents used to take me to some of the islands in the summertime. I guess I always wondered what it would be like to be there in the wintertime. And when I found out there were people who lived there all year round, I really wanted to know what they were like."

Alice drank slowly from her cup until it was finished. "Well, Blake Reese, you've come all this way; let me tell you about the kind of people who live on islands during the winter. Let me tell you exactly the kind of person who would willingly live on an isolated, frozen piece of rock away from the rest of civilization." She leaned forward. "They're trash, Blake Reese. They're the worst kind of trash. They're people whose families have lived there for generations, waiting all winter long, drinking and waiting and waiting and drinking until the summer comes, and all the little tourist families come from all over, to their little, tiny island. And you know what, Blake Reese? The people on that island think they're the center of the fucking universe. But they're not. Far from it. No, Blake Reese, I hate the people on that island because the people on that island think they are so goddamn special for living on an island. And if that's the kind of people you'd like to meet, well then, cheers to you."

Blake stared at her for some time as she continued looking out the window, any semblance of politeness gone. "Well, Miss, then why the fuck are you going there?"

Alice looked over at him and smiled. "Just visiting family."

Chapter Sixteen

Jack threw an armful of Bill's clothes onto an already impressive pile of equipment, food, and other items while Susan leaned up against the wall, staring at him in disbelief.

"And this is your idea of a good time, how?" she asked, staring in awe at the pile of junk her husband had created in such a short time.

Jack did not look up from his inventory list. "That polar vortex is headed through this afternoon. Gonna make that ice on the lake nice and hard. From the sounds of it, this storm's gonna be sticking around for at least a few days." He began wrapping sandwiches and placing them in a large green cooler.

She crossed her arms. "Don't you think Bill would rather do anything other than spend the night out on the ice?"

"Jesus, it's not like he has any other kids his age to play with on this goddamn island."

"Keep your voice down," Susan shot back in an elevated whisper. "You think he needs to hear us remind him that all the other kids have left for the winter? He's lonely enough as it is."

Jack clicked his tongue. "You know he can't hear us. Look, my dad took me out on the ice a million times when I was a kid. His dad did the same. It's a family tradition."

"Not mine. Wouldn't you two rather stay inside by the fireplace, watch movies and drink hot chocolate like most normal human beings do during a fucking blizzard?"

"Sweetheart, we've got all winter long to sit on our asses in front of the fireplace. You'll thank me when I come home with a cooler full of perch."

"That you're going to clean and gut yourself."

"That I'm going to clean and gut myself, yes. And we're not spending the night out there."

"Will you be home before midnight?"

"Not exactly."

"Then you'll be out all night. You're going to freeze out there."

"Sweetheart, I've been out on that ice a million times, and I'm fine. Do you really think I'd bring Bill if I thought for one minute that he'd be in harm's way?"

She folded her arms. "You men do the dumbest things."

"Just satisfying my primal urges to kill and hunt, and also getting out of the house for an evening. Look, I'm sure you're getting just as stir crazy as I am in this house. Tonight, you can crack open a bottle of wine, watch some *Sex and the City*, and talk to your sister all night."

"Thank you for your permission. I'd be doing those things anyway. And at what point should I call the Coast Guard to start looking for you?" Alice took her cellphone out of her pocket. *Good*, she thought. *Let him think I don't want him to go. He's too thick-headed and stupid to let me stop him anyway. I could sneak out of here to see Adam, or he could come here to see me.* She smiled. It meant another night with Adam. She texted him:

I'm alone tonight.

Tigger came in and began barking at them, hungry for his lunch, which he had not yet received. "And why don't you take Tigger with you? If you're so concerned about us being cramped up in here, he needs more exercise than any of us."

Jack turned around and smiled. "But if we're all out on the ice, who's going to protect you?"

"Oh, please. Tigger can't even protect himself. And look how restless he's been these past few days. He's woken me up three nights in a row, just barking at nothing."

"Probably just more deer in the backyard."

"No, Jack, I got up last night when you refused to, remember? There was nothing outside. He's been acting strange all day. When he's not barking at nothing, he's hiding under the bed. He never does that."

"Look, it's just the storm coming. Animals always get riled up before a storm. It's that sixth sense bullshit they're always talking about. Remember that TV special we saw about that Thailand tsunami, and how all those animals were heading to high ground before the people even knew what hit them?"

"Well, if that's the case, then shouldn't we be worried? I mean, if this storm is so big that it spooks Tigger, shouldn't you be taking it a little more seriously?"

"I am taking it seriously."

"How? By walking onto a frozen lake in the middle of a blizzard? How is that taking it seriously, Jack?"

Jack had his mining flashlight on top of his head, and it flashed into Susan's eyes. She flinched.

"Look, we'll be back before the rough stuff hits, I promise. I haven't gotten my fishing on all goddamn winter 'cause the ice hasn't been strong enough, and now it is. I promise you we'll be safe."

"Will you please stop shining that damn thing in my face? You're wasting the battery. That thing will die out while you're on the lake, and you'll be lost out there in the dark." *Maybe he will die out there in the dark, too,* she thought. *No, I don't mean that.* She winced. *Where did that thought come from?*

Bill was playing video games, oblivious to his parents' conversation. When he turned around and saw them fighting, he already knew what they were fighting about. *We'll just follow the north star, Mom,* he signed.

There won't be a north star in the storm, Bill, she signed back.

Bill was lost in his digital world. *Then we'll just follow the light from the lighthouse.*

Susan threw her arms up in resignation. "Fine. Great. And why don't you take Tigger with you? At least he knows his way back without a flashlight..."

Jack was stuffing more items into his bag than the bag could hold. "He'll scare away the fish. Besides, he'll keep you company."

Tigger, oblivious to the three of them, kept watch at the far back of the house, looking out the glass sliding doors, past the snow-covered leafless trees that swayed in the strengthening winds. He was restless and scratched at the cold glass as he whimpered. Then he began to growl, then bark at the wintry evening outside. The others did not see the dark, snow-filled clouds approaching from the north, daylight disappearing, and tree branches swaying faster as the Arctic front crawled its way slowly toward their island.

Outside, there were no birds perched on the bare tree limbs, nor any fresh hoof prints in the snow that had fallen during the night. On the south side of the island, no one saw the mainland quietly dissolving to white and the horizon slowly dissipating into oblivion. As the first flakes of the storm began to fall, no one noticed the lights from the mainland slowly began to disappear, leaving them encased in their own little frozen world. The barometer had begun to drop, and no one heard the slow, painful moan of the shifting of the ice as the tundra molded its own arcane shapes: violent, twisted sculptures of ice that slowly rose from the lake and inched toward land.

The sky grew dark at midday. Already, the storm had brought its false night upon the greater part of the lake, and soon, the island as well.

Chapter Seventeen

Sarah awoke on the living room sofa, with no recollection of how she had gotten home or even when she had left the lighthouse. All of her clothes—save her shoes—were still on, and the curtains were wide open. She sat up quickly. Looking over at the door, she saw that she had locked it, whenever it was she had come home last night. Her hands were cold, and she went to the radiator to warm them up.

She heard the familiar vibrating of her phone nearby, and approaching the table where it lay, she saw Alice's name appear on the screen. She swiped the phone up and answered it.

"Alice?"

"Sarah? Where the hell have you been all morning?"

"I'm sorry, I was still sleeping."

"Didn't you get any of my messages?"

"Alice, we talked about this last night."

"Talked about what? Are you still drunk? Look, I'm at the airfield now and freezing my ass off. Would you please come pick me up?"

Sarah paused a moment. "Wait, what do you mean you're at the airfield?"

"I'm on the goddamn island, Sarah. Now, please come pick me up before one of the other island fuck-jobs does." She hung up.

Sarah stood in awed silence for a moment. She had talked to Alice last night; she remembered that much. The reception was poor, but she knew that she had. Sarah walked slowly over to the hissing radiator by the window. Despite its warmth, she could still feel the cool blast of winter snaking its way around the edges of the old window. She placed a finger on the radiator and felt the quick, sharp sting of heat on her index finger. It throbbed for a moment. "Ok," she thought, "I'm not dreaming."

Chapter Eighteen

Mary could feel it in the air, but not like the warm, sunny days of summer when the energy was constant, and the warmth and light seemed everlasting. This was different. No matter how many lights she turned on, everything still felt dark. She had lit all the candles she could find and thought it strange that the wicks seemed to flicker violently, without even the slightest draft in the room. She had been preparing oatmeal for her mother, and when her eyes lingered on the drawer with the little dark bottle, she stopped the thought before it could take root. Just at that moment, the room—and the entire house—had grown cold and dark, and she had felt suddenly, unexplainably sick.

From upstairs, she could hear her mother's old records playing on the antique Edison. Mary muttered along with them and sometimes even sang, but those old crackling songs did not bring her any peace today. She continued making her mother's oatmeal, and, feeling guilty about the previous day's events, she added some extra cinnamon and chopped apple slices to the bowl. The house began to moan and creak, and for a moment, Mary felt as if she were in the hull of a ship.

Mary turned on her own music—The Platters—but still couldn't shake the negative energy that permeated her house. The more bright and cheerier she tried to make things, the more everything seemed to darken. She felt a heavy weight upon her heart that seemed to slow her every move. It seemed to creep in with the wind. It felt tangible. She walked to the old wooden cabinet, splintered and scratched with time, opened the bottom drawer, and began removing all her candles and crystals. She unwrapped four white candles and broke each one at the center. She remembered her mother yelling at her as a child when Mary had lit one, not yet understanding its true purpose. Her mother yelled at her a lot, but the lessons instilled in her had not been lost after all these years. She had never really felt she had the gift—not like her mother—and whatever she did possess, she had "whored" out to the tourists that swamped their island every summer.

Her mother spoke less and less now, for which Mary was somewhat grateful. But her fits had grown worse, and once the season changed and winter gripped the island, she had slipped beyond Mary's grasp. It made her feel lonely and a million miles away from help, even with all the others on the island. Come spring, when the ice melted and the ferries ran regular routes, she would take her mother back to the mainland for tests. But part of her already knew what they would tell her: that her mother would need constant, professional care, the kind Mary could not afford, and that meant she would have to leave the island. Their shop had been enough to keep them afloat during the winter months, but that was about it. She placed the candles at each of the four corners of the house, and in the center of the room, a white rock. She had already placed one such rock under her mother's bed, out of her reach, so it would not be shattered during one of her fits.

Upstairs, the record began to skip. Mary turned down The Platters. The first floor was quiet again, and the house had stopped creaking. She tilted her head in puzzlement, realizing that the clock on her wall had died. *It's later than two thirty*, she thought. *And I just changed those batteries.* Upstairs, the record continued to skip. *It would have to wait.* Mary began to climb the stairs. She could hear the skipping record, stuck on a word she couldn't understand, on one of her mother's older albums. As she reached the landing, she saw that her mother's door was slightly ajar. Though she could see the trees outside bending from the force of the wind, everything inside had suddenly gone still.

"Mother?" No reply but the skipping record, caught in a never-ending loop. She knocked on the door, and still there was no sound from within.

Mary pushed the door open and found her mother standing naked in the middle of the room, with the windows wide open. She stood there in a strange trance, arms outstretched, snowflakes and wind coming in. The curtains fluttered madly as she stood there, arms open, looking out into white nothingness. She appeared almost unreal at that moment, standing upright like she had so many years ago, no expression on her face.

"Mother!" She shouted out. The room seemed deafening between the roaring of the wind and the skipping record.

Her mother turned toward her, her eyes rolling back into her skull.

"She says she's coming soon now," she whispered. Then she screamed so loud that Mary had to hold her hands over her ears to shut it out. She ran to the bed and grabbed a blanket to wrap around her mother, who was still screaming. She collapsed to the floor as Mary shut and locked the windows.

"What were you thinking?" She began to shake her mother, first gently, then harder as she felt a strange anger grow over her. Her mother continued to wail.

"Stop screaming and tell me what happened!" Mary felt the room spinning. Then, it was as if someone else's hand rose slowly up into the air and landed hard across her mother's face. Her palm stung, and as her mother continued, so did the slaps, each one landing with more force and fury. As hard as she slapped, her mother's screams only grew louder and more horrible. Mary finally sat back and cried, her arm tired, her palm on fire. As she watched her mother scream and cry, she looked toward the open windows and thought about jumping. She thought about the bottle of antifreeze out in the garage. She could just put some in both their drinks at dinner, watch her mother eat, help her finish her final cocktail, then have one herself and be rid of all this.

Her mother had stopped screaming now and looked blankly up at the ceiling, her eyes focused on nothing at all.

"I'm a monster," Mary whispered. "Are you proud to see what your daughter has become?" She got up to close the windows and locked them tight. She helped her mother to her feet. "Did you make me like this, Mom, or was I always going to be like this?"

She tucked her mother in under the blanket. "You probably wish that I had never been born, if you could wish for anything right now." Next to the nightstand lay her mother's old journals. She had been ferocious about documenting everything—and everyone—on the island, and Mary would read it to her in the hopes of bringing back better memories she had of growing up on the island. Her mother closed her eyes slowly, then lost herself in sleep.

"In the morning, you won't remember any of this," Mary said, wiping her tears away. "But I hope you do. I hope you remember how horrible your daughter is."

Mary grabbed one of the journals and found a peaceful excerpt dated about fifteen years ago. Better years. She began:

"...the storm had come in quickly over the lake. It hadn't been in the weather forecast. The day had started out so clear, and I was out for a walk with Helen and a few friends who had come over on the ferry for a few days. We had put a little "something special" in our lemonade, and we'd lost track of time—who kept track of time on the weekends anyway? That's why we were here. It seemed like everyone was outside that day: grilling out, riding their bikes, or simply sitting on a bench. We noticed the air getting

cooler, and the weathervanes were going crazy up on the rooftops. Helen was talking about her daughter going to college and how happy she was about being an empty nester when suddenly the music on the loudspeakers stopped, and the storm sirens came on, and at first we all stopped and wondered if it was just a drill. Then everything went dark. The blue sky was gone, and it looked like evening. And then I just got an awful feeling...

I don't know what possessed me to go to the north shore that day. Normally, I would have gone home and finished my cocktails and watched the storm pass over the lake as I always did. But there was a dark energy, and the foul smell of dead fish grew strong in the air. Almost in a daze, I took one of the golf carts and drove to the north shore, where the storm front had come from. I remember how hard the wind was coming in, and huge branches came down on either side of me. People watching through their curtains must have thought me mad—of course, they had already thought that for years. 'There she goes, that nutty psychic lady. Taking her joyride through the middle of a storm. Maybe this one will finally sweep her away.' By the time I got to the shore, most of the pier was already submerged in water. Huge waves, like the ones in a hurricane. As I looked out over the lake, I saw their small boat bobbing helplessly and being tossed around like a toy on the giant waves. From my distance, I couldn't see their faces. How terrified they must have been. But why on earth had they come up this far north of the island, with no place to dock and no lifeguards to help them? Perhaps they had drifted in the storm? I never got a clear answer, but Alice is a real hell-child, and I wouldn't be shocked if she had been behind the idea. I took my walkie-talkie out and called Jack and Mark, both of whom were already on the lake looking for the children. I told them to hurry their asses up, that the two girls were stuck out there. I told them to phone their parents.

As I waited, I looked out and saw another boat beyond them rocking just as violently on the waves. In the darkness, I could only make out the silhouettes of two people, just as helpless and hopeless as the two girls. I thought, My God. I hope they have enough rescue boats."

Mary's eyelids grew heavy, and as the journal slipped from her hands, a few newspaper clippings came loose and fluttered slowly to the floor. Mary joined her mother in sleep, and the two rested quietly as the storm grew outside and the bare tree limbs clawed at the windows. They could not see beyond the white wall outside the window, as the mouth of the storm began to open, making its way toward the island. Beneath the ice, something else began to awaken and made its way slowly to the surface, where it would join the front of the storm and reach landfall on the island before the witching hour struck.

CHAPTER NINETEEN

Mark poured himself another half glass of Red Label, relit the end of his Java cigar, and went back to working on his shoreline portrait. He had not noticed the sky darkening outside, nor would he have cared if he had. The canvas before him was still unfinished—a scene of the lake that he had been working on for the better part of winter. As he examined the small figures on the painting, he quietly lamented how slowly this piece had come along. Sarah had been right about him not selling any work the summer before. The quality pieces sat untouched and unsold in storage back at his cottage. But these paintings, whether or not they sold in the summer shows, were what helped him get through the long winters.

He had considered traveling again this winter, spending these long months someplace nicer, someplace brighter. But he had started this piece in the fall and was determined to have it done by Spring. Come summer, he would sneak it in with the other paintings he had for sale. He always mixed his art in with the others that he sold, but they still never seemed to sell. He stood back and looked upon it; it was the beachfront on the southern point of the island, lined with sunbathers, picnic-goers, and swimmers submerged in the water. He had allowed himself to indulge a bit in the anatomy of his female characters, many of whom he created with large breasts and revealing backsides. Those were the moments he missed the most, when all the vacationing beauties came to the island, and the air smelled of suntan lotion and barbeques. He had even incorporated several of the locals on the island, including Sarah, her outline barely recognizable, reading a book on a large rock overlooking the lake. He had spotted her there many times during the summers and had enjoyed making her part of his permanent creations. He had done so many times before, only some of which he had shown her.

Out on his greenish lake, he had created a small number of sailboats and speedboats, but not so many as to crowd the picture. Just enough to give the lake light and motion. As he set his brush to the board to add another sunbather, he noticed a smaller boat that he did not remember painting before. The boat appeared to be lost amongst the waves, and now he noticed that he had painted these waves in the far corner much larger and more violent than the rest. He hadn't done so intentionally. In the far-left corner, he had also made the sky darker, perhaps the line where dusk meets night. As he stood back to look at it all as a whole, he hadn't remembered painting that corner. To be fair, on many a restless night, he had woken up, poured himself a generous glass of whiskey, and worked until the dawn broke outside his windows. He'd make breakfast, then head back to bed around noon. In retirement, he loved dictating his schedule the way he had in his early college days, especially when the island was barren during the winter months.

But as he stood and watched his painting seem to unfold before him, the scene had evolved unbeknownst to him. What was meant to be a beautiful, peaceful evening on the beach had become something more. Though he did not remember painting it, he recognized the scene. There on the water were not one but two small boats, both lost amongst the large waves, and in each boat were two figures. Their faces were small, dark, and almost indistinct, yet they had looked exactly the same so many years ago.

The room felt very cold and quiet now—even with the radio on—and he felt as if the whole island was motionless. He had survived storms all over the world: typhoons in the Philippines, blizzards in Russia, forest fires in Montana, and tornadoes throughout the states. But this felt different.

He went to the control panel, flipped through a few CDs, and found a classics collection that he quickly slipped into the player. Any song would do. The sky grew darker now, and Mark felt the music might prevent the island from being swallowed up by it. The others would appreciate it, he thought. Santo and Johnny's "Sleepwalk" began to play, and its warm sadness relaxed him. From the window, he watched two snowmobiles drive past his control tower. He saw Jack and his mute son. On the other was Chris, with his bushy beard and pirate-like eyepatch. Mark knocked on the window, forgetting for a moment that they could not hear him. They were headed toward the lake, for what reason he could not fathom.

He poured another drink and suddenly wished that he had not painted that scene. He wished that summer truly was here, that when he walked outside, he would feel the humid warmth, smell the lake, and see the many faces out for a walk before the sun set and the moon rose over the island. But as the music faded, so did his daydream, and he was left alone with his painting, whiskey in hand.

Chapter Twenty

In his jeep, Luke could feel the force of the wind fighting against him as he drove down the main road. Traces of snowflakes fell, and it seemed the storm was waiting for something at the farthest reaches of the island. Next to him sat the Mayor, happily swigging from his flask, his luggage and other personal effects loaded into the backseat.

"Just so you know," Luke said, "I think this is a really dumb idea."

The Mayor finished his drink. "Just so you know, I think it's a dumb idea for all of us to be on our own through this."

"You just want an excuse to drink and throw parties."

"I don't need an excuse to do that."

"If anyone finds out that you guys broke in there, I had nothing to do with it."

"You're missing out on a good time."

The road was slick, and Luke could feel his jeep slide through a few turns. "I'll do just fine on my own, thank you very much."

"We got groceries, games, and enough bottles of booze to bring Oliver Reed back from the dead."

"I don't get that reference, but I wish you well on your blizzard bender anyway." The jeep slid again. "So, if your phones go dead—and they will—you've got the walkie-talkies, right?"

"Yes, Dad."

"Christ, you're 20 years older than me. You guys all make me feel like I'm the only adult on the island."

"You'll grow old fast thinking like that."

"I grow old fast when you and your buddies go fucking around the island like teenagers and I have to clean up the mess."

The Mayor laughed and finished what was left in his flask. Drops of whiskey dribbled down his chin. "Word of advice: if you ever wanna' get into someone like Sarah's pants, you're gonna have to lighten up that attitude of yours a little bit."

Luke gripped the wheel more tightly. He was silent for a moment. "You talk as if you have experience with this matter?"

The Mayor laughed. "Sarah can do better than both of us. I just mean, maybe you'd find more women swooning over you if you weren't the island's Uncle Scrooge."

"I really don't see how protecting the well-being of the island and keeping all of you safe makes me Uncle Scrooge. And Sarah and I are just friends."

The Mayor laughed again. "Luke, I love you to death, but you're an awful liar."

"I'm not lying."

"You asked her out."

"I asked her out five years ago, she politely declined, and I politely accepted her decision. That hardly makes me a liar. And when does my business suddenly become everyone else's business, anyway?"

"On an island this small, your business becomes everyone's business, whether you like it or not."

"I feel like I can't even take a leak around here without someone knowing about it."

"You can't. We'd all talk about that too." He laughed again.

Luke took his eyes off the road and glanced at the Mayor. "First of all, I am entitled to some privacy, even if your gossip helps you get through the—

"Look out!" The Mayor seamlessly snapped back into sobriety. Luke slammed on his brakes, and the two of them slid across the street. As calmly as he could, he pulled the steering wheel into the spin—not against it—and tapped the brakes as gently as he could. Yet the jeep was still beyond his control, and as an oak tree grew larger and larger ahead of them, he threw an arm out to protect the Mayor.

"Brace yourself!"

The jeep met the tree with a dull thud, not the loud crashing sound Luke had anticipated. Then everything was still. Both of them breathed heavily, staring at the large oak in front of them. Luke could see the hood was bent upwards a bit, smoke was rising, and there was a small crack in the windshield.

"You ok?"

The Mayor felt his extremities. "Probably be a little sore tomorrow, but yeah, I'm okay."

Luke looked over at the Mayor, who still seemed distracted. "Let's take a look at the good news."

Luke attempted to open the door and found he had to force it partially open. Probably a bent frame, he thought. Among other things. His heart was still racing, and the unreality of it all distracted him from the gust of wind that hit him as he stepped out into the cold winter air. Beneath the jeep, he could see that oil was leaking.

"Shit," Luke muttered. "I hope you brought some warm clothes with you, Mayor. We're gonna have to walk on foot from here." The Mayor did not respond. "Mayor?"

Luke turned around and saw the Mayor standing in the street, looking ahead. Having seen enough damage to know they were as good as stranded, Luke walked over to the Mayor. As he approached the Mayor, he could see the focus of his attention.

On the road ahead was a circle of human-shaped ice sculptures, standing in a circle in the center of the road—all holding hands, and all headless. The two of them stood there for a few minutes, just watching them, as if waiting to see if they would come to life.

"What the hell?" The Mayor stood with his hands on his hips. "Who do you suppose put those there?"

"No idea." Luke took out a cigarette and lit it. "A better question would be *why*?"

The Mayor slowly walked over to them and reached a hand out to touch one of them. "All ice, all of them. But where are the goddamn heads?"

"I intend to ask him when I find him."

The Mayor turned around. "Ask who?"

"Mark."

"Why do you think it was him?"

Luke exhaled smoke and walked over to the Mayor. "Because a) Mark is the only artist on the island right now, and b) he's the only one who would do something this weird and asshole-ish."

The Mayor looked at them. "Kind of a strange thing to do."

"I won't say you're wrong about that."

As they stood there gazing upon the ice sculptures, the flakes began to fall faster until there was a steady stream of snow.

Luke looked down the road. "We should get going."

"What about these damn things?"

"First, we're gonna' get you to the hotel. Then I intend to have Mark come out here, move this shit and pay for the damage to my jeep, which isn't even really my jeep."

"What about my stuff in the car?"

"We'll take what we can carry."

The two of them grabbed a few bags from the backseat and began to make their way.

As the snowfall grew in intensity, the Mayor looked over at Luke and smiled. "I guess the storm's finally arrived, huh?"

Luke grimaced in the cold wind. "I guess so."

"Don't feel bad about the jeep, Luke. You can always borrow my jalopy."

"Thanks, Mayor, but I don't want a goddamn jalopy; I want the jeep fixed before my boss comes back."

Once the ice statues were out of sight behind them, Luke finally breathed a sigh of relief.

CHAPTER TWENTY-ONE

As Sarah pulled up in her car, she saw Alice standing in the falling snow, arms crossed, bags at her feet, and completely underdressed. She would have laughed at the sight had it not come under the pretense of something urgent. Alice had been trying to call her for days, and now she was actually here, standing in the snow, looking impatient and angry as always. She had not driven a car all winter, and the sedan did not handle the snowy roads well, even as slowly as she went. She was not prepared for any of this.

Alice looked almost comical, standing there under the pathetic wooden shack that operated as a waiting area for the airfield. Three luggage bags sat at her feet. As Sarah pulled up and got out of the car, Alice snapped:

"Please tell me the heat works in that thing."

Sarah smiled. "Blasting at full force, sis."

They hugged each other in the falling snow. Sarah had forgotten how long it had been since she last held her sister. It all seemed unreal, and for a moment, she was not concerned with why or how, just glad that Alice was here.

As Sarah drove, Alice looked out the window at all of the vacant cottages and shops. A wintry ghost town, still ages away from rebirth. She shook her head, but was already tired of expressing how she felt about it.

"I'm surprised you were able to get a flight in with this storm coming, I mean."

Alice was only half-listening, applying lip balm to her chapped lips. "What storm?"

Sarah sighed heavily. "The storm that's gonna' keep your ass stranded here for at least the next few days."

"Wonderful." Alice tried to check her wi-fi signal. "Don't tell me you guys don't get wi-fi here."

"It should be on when we get back to the bed and breakfast."

"How the hell do you guys communicate here in the winter?"

'You know, when Dad grew up here, he didn't have wi-fi, and he did just fine."

The car swerved a bit on the snowy road, and as she hit a bend in the road, the tail end fishtailed.

"You don't drive here much, do you?"

"Don't need to usually."

After a short pause, "Well, are you gonna' tell me now or tell me when we get back to your place?"

Sarah gripped the steering wheel tightly. She hadn't driven on snow in years and felt it best if Alice did not know that. "Tell you what?"

Alice looked over at her, arms folded. "Tell me about whatever trouble you're in. That's why you called and told me to come here as soon as possible, right?"

Sarah was darting glances between Alice and the road. "What are you talking about? You called me. You called me the other night!"

"Yeah, I called you back after you called me. Once I booked my flight, I called to let you know I was coming. Don't tell me you were on one of your benders when you called."

"No, Alice, I didn't call you at all. I'm serious. You can check my call history. I only reached out to you after you tried to call me so many times!"

The car was sliding even more now. Sarah's foot pressed down on the gas, and as the flurries fell harder, she found it becoming more difficult to steer. She was swerving left of center, weaving back and forth over the dividing line now made invisible by the drifting snow.

Alice stared at Sarah in disbelief. "Sarah, you called me! Saturday, remember? You were in tears! You said something awful had happened, and you needed me to come right away."

Sarah shook her head. "I was at a party here last Saturday, with everyone else. I never tried to call you. Not once! The only time I checked my phone was to try and call you back after I saw all your missed calls."

"Sarah, I only called you because after you spoke with me, you hung up. Or got cut off."

"Look, I don't know who you spoke with, but it wasn't me."

"Ok, if it wasn't you, then who the hell called me from your phone, Sarah? One of the other freaks here on this island?"

Sarah could feel the anger building on top of her anxiety, which was already near the boiling point. "Alice, did you come all this way just to insult me, or are you going to calm down and tell me what the hell is going on?"

The car was no longer driving—it was sliding, and Sarah felt caught between her fight with her sister and her growing loss of control behind the wheel. This was the stretch of main road that ran alongside the icy wasteland, a beautiful bumper-to-bumper drive in the summertime, now made treacherous by ice. Large snowdrifts slithered their way onto the road, creating virtual dunes of thick, blinding snow. The winds coming in off the lake were spilling snow in every direction, causing momentary whiteouts. Sarah knew that if any cars were coming the other way, she wouldn't be able to swerve.

Alice was now starting to realize the severity of the situation. "Hey Sarah, these roads are pretty bad. Maybe you should ease up a bit?"

"Trust me, I've driven these roads more than you have. This is the only way to get home."

Alice pulled out her cellphone. "Look, I even have the voicemail message you left me."

"I didn't leave you any voicemails."

She pulled up her voicemail and pressed play. "Just listen."

But as the message began to play, it became clear that the voice was not Sarah's at all. It was that of a little girl's voice and sounded almost as if it was coming from underwater. The words were gargled and strained, as if water were coming into her lungs as she spoke:

"Alice, I'm in trouble. I need you to come here, Alice. I need you to save me. Please come soon. I'm so sorry about everything."

Strange humming sounds and static followed, not unlike the static Sarah had heard before on the island's loudspeakers. Then the message abruptly ended.

Sarah had stopped focusing on the road now and eased her foot off the gas pedal. "That's not me!" she protested in confusion.

Alice looked again at her phone. "No, that's not you. But it was. I swear it was—

This time, Sarah could not swerve fast enough to avoid a snowdrift, and the balding tires slid and spun them hard against the weak fence railing that separated the road from the frozen lake. The car spun out of control, and the front end crashed into the fence, tearing through it easily. They plummeted over the edge and onto the frozen lake below, both screaming as they fell.

As if in a nightmare, Sarah was powerless to do anything but helplessly watch as the car carried them over the edge and down onto the ice. The boundary, invisible to most, was nearly blinding to her, and she had not stepped one foot off the island in over a decade. Now she became hysterical, placing her hands over her face and screaming, hoping it would all soon come to a merciful end. Alice tried to grab the wheel several times, but her efforts were futile.

As the car struck the frozen lake, it did not roll over and over as they always did in the movies, Sarah thought strangely. She found herself removed from her body, watching them spin and careen off the cliff. She could see the car bouncing around on the ice like some absurd pinball game. Sarah felt herself floating higher, above the wreckage, until she could see the entire island through the thickness of the growing storm. Here, all was quiet and peaceful, and she could float as freely as she wished. She thought this must be how astronauts feel in zero gravity, where objects float gracefully without all the sounds of madness, crashing, and screaming back on Earth. But then, in a quick flash, she saw it all: the island, the lake, the world, consumed by a blackness she had never before seen in her life. Darker than the farthest reaches of space, this whirlpool of nothingness lacked any form. Yet she could sense it approaching, ready to consume her along with everything she loved. All around her, the muted silence had been replaced by a horrible shrieking sound. Sarah could not tell where it came from, or if it was simply the earth being torn to pieces by this unseen force. It lurked as if it had malicious intent and would not stop until all light and hope had faded from the world forever.

As Sarah was jolted from these abstract thoughts, she could once again hear Alice's screams. As she looked around, she realized that neither of them had died, but their car had rolled far from the shore. She screamed so loudly that Alice had to cover her mouth.

"It's okay, we're okay!" Alice kept saying. But she didn't understand.

Sarah ripped Alice's hand away and screamed back, "We're not fucking okay! We have to get back to shore!"

Chapter Twenty-Two

As Alice held Sarah and cried, she could already begin to hear the slow cracking of the ice beneath them. The lake was frozen, but just how solid Alice could not be sure. She wiped the blood from the cut on Sarah's forehead and cursed the island again when neither of their cellphones had a signal.

"Why do you fucking live here?" she said aloud, angry with her sister's stubbornness and the sheer remoteness of their situation. She had come from a warmer climate where there were people shoulder to shoulder everywhere. She had vowed never to return to this island once she was old enough to leave, and yet here she was.

The car shifted. Alice heard a loud crack. Outside the shattered car window, the distance back to shore seemed mere steps away. But Sarah was still unconscious, and Alice could already tell the surface could break through at any moment. She took Sarah's face into her hands.

"Sarah, please wake up! Sarah, we have to get out of here!"

Sarah stirred from her injured slumber, and as her eyelids flickered, Alice quickly removed her seat belt. Sarah's head hung limp on her shoulder, and as the car shifted again with their movement, Alice knew she could no longer wait. She would have to remove Sarah from the car, conscious or not. The interior of the car was freezing, and the snow obscured her vision through the cracked windshield. But she could not hear the sound of any other car or person nearby. The world seemed dead, and they were all alone.

Alice felt her fingers—along with the rest of her body—going numb from the cold, and she could not tell which parts were numb and which were hurt. She tried not to think about this as she unbuckled her sister from the seatbelt. The metal stuck in the socket and would not free her. Desperate and feeling almost ridiculous, she tugged on the device with all her might and screamed until finally it unlatched, and Sarah's body fell limply out.

"Alright," she said. The car's frame had been bent, and Sarah's door would not open. Alice lay her back upon the seat and with both feet kicked at the passenger door. Like the seatbelt, the door refused to budge. Upon the third try, she heard the ice beneath them cracking again, and this time the car moved. It shifted and sank, not much, but enough for Alice to realize that her borrowed time was running out. And then with one final thrust of her feet, the door opened halfway, just enough for them to get out.

Alice crawled over Sarah and pushed the door further open, squeezed herself out, and took both of her sister's arms and pulled. She had not truly felt the cold until now, and though it stung her like a thousand angry bees, she did not care. Sarah was light—she always had been—but as Alice pulled, she had little of the strength she thought she might have now. The weight of everything had become suddenly real at that moment—the long flight, the bitter cold, Sarah's strange phone call, and now this. Though she hoped to feel a pulse as she grabbed her sister by the wrists, she felt nothing.

As she pulled Sarah's torso, then legs and feet, out of the vehicle, Alice could see the spiderwebbed cracks all around them, encircling the car. As the ice began to slowly break apart and consume the car, she dragged her sister across as fast as she could, crying, freezing, and alone. This all somehow felt familiar to her, but at that moment, she could not place it. The ice beneath her feet was slick, even under the snow, and several times she lost her footing and slipped. The shore was just out of reach. Then Sarah's eyes fluttered open, and for a quick moment their gaze met.

Then Sarah remembered where she was. She saw where the island was and realized that she was not on it. And then she screamed. Alice was not sure if it was from shock; she had never really believed her sister's phobia of leaving the island. As the car behind them slowly began to sink into the icy waters, she could hear the ice begin to crack all around them.

"Sarah, listen to me!" Alice was now beyond pleading and angry, her words sharp. "You have to shut up and listen!"

But Sarah couldn't. She had no control, and her hysteria seemed to crack the unsettled ice even further. Her unwillingness to help drew Alice's ire, and she slapped his sister's face.

"Snap out of it! If you don't stop, we'll both die out here!"

She had regained enough of her strength to pull Sarah the rest of the way across the ice, and finally they both fell onto land. Sarah continued to sob, and Alice held her as they watched their car sink slowly underneath the ice.

"I hope that wasn't the only car you had on this island."

Sarah wept, covering her eyes, trying to pull herself together. She hid her face in shame, not wanting her sister to see her like this. She had wanted her to see a woman finally in control of her life, confident, and ready to do things the way she wanted, without any outside interference. Someone who didn't need to be rescued anymore. But instead, she felt herself go limp and helpless as her sister dragged her to safety. *Was it always going to be this way?* She stopped feeling sorry for herself, uncovered her eyes, and watched as the last of the car sank under the ice.

"That's *my* last car on the island." Sarah's tears were freezing on her face as the temperature continued to drop. "But it's not *the* last car on the island."

Alice nodded. "Come on, let's get you home. We'll warm up there and figure things out, okay, sis?"

Sarah said nothing, only nodded. As they climbed up the rocky slope, the world seemed to darken all around them.

Chapter Twenty-Three

As Luke and the Mayor approached the Sandy Stone Hotel, Amy and Dan emerged outside, both without winter jackets and holding drinks in their hands. Luke already felt his irritation building as neither offered to help with the huge crates they carried.

Amy took a giant swig from her steaming thermos, undoubtedly filled with alcohol. "What the hell took you guys so long?"

"We had an accident." Luke's feet were freezing and numb. Just as well. It had made the long walk more bearable.

Dan looked past them. "Where'd you park the car?"

"In the trees," Luke muttered. "Would you guys mind giving us a hand? We just walked a mile in this shit."

The two stared at them, not moving. "Why'd you park in the trees?"

"I fucking crashed the car, Dan. I crashed the car and we just walked a mile in this shit to deliver you survival booze."

Amy and Dan continued staring, then began mock-clapping slowly.

To no one in particular, Luke said, "I honestly don't know why I still live on this fucking island."

The Mayor grinned, happy to have the accident—and long walk—behind him. The remnants of his buzz were fading, and he was ready for a refresher. "We brought our survival kits. What did you guys get your hands on?"

Dan lit a cigarette. "I brought some boxes from the store. Amy brought a bunch of games. We've got enough crap here to get us through three storms."

Amy brightened as if suddenly remembering. "And we have a special guest! Some journalist guy came in on the last plane. We ran into him looking for a place to crash. It'll be nice to have a fresh face around for a change."

Luke placed his box of bottles on the ground. He was tired and even more tired of surprises. "Now I've done my good deed for the day, I'm gonna get back to the station and keep an eye on all the other children on this island. Dan, I'm gonna' need to borrow your snowmobile."

Dan took a key from his pocket, then overthrew it. It landed in the snow behind Luke, who sighed again, removed his glove, and dug into the snow to retrieve it.

"Sorry, man."

Luke shook his head. "You all have working walkie-talkies?"

Amy laughed. "Yes, Dad. Here's an idea: Why don't you just stay here with us instead of going back to the station by yourself? You'll enjoy this storm a lot more if you make the most of it."

"Amy, I would love nothing more than to spend the next few days drinking myself stupid as a giant blizzard blows through. But unfortunately, some of us have to keep an eye on things while the rest of you have fun. Now, if you don't need anything else, I have a long ride back. And when I call to check in on you, I expect you guys to answer." He looked over at the Mayor. "You're in charge, chief. God help us all."

Luke boarded the snowmobile, fired it up, and sped away without even a goodbye.

Amy frowned, crossing her arms. "You know he's just going back to check on his girlfriend."

Dan laughed. "You mean the one who doesn't acknowledge his existence?"

Chapter Twenty-Four

Mary sat in her sunroom while her mother slept upstairs. She had been reading her mother's diary for hours, searching for patterns, remembering things she had half-forgotten. After the accident with the girls on the lake, she could clearly see that her mother's writing—and memory—had slowly started to fade. She had always wondered when it began. As the snow continued to fall, obscuring her view outside, Mary found little comfort in her hot chocolate, the glowing fireplace, or soft jazz that played in the background. Her mother's writing removed her from all that as she continued to read:

... 10 years have passed, and I still can't forget that day. I can see that girl's face in my dreams as if I had seen her clearly out on the lake. I've taken walks out to the Thunder Cliffs, trying to relive that moment and remember how it all unfolded. From where I stood, I saw the girls, saw the other boat, and watched the rescue, and then I saw the other

boat disappear into the waves. There's a dark spot in that water now, but nobody wants to talk about it. It's like black oil, so thick and so dark you can't look into it. Everyone just pretends that spot doesn't exist, like nothing bad ever happened there. But I wonder if they think about it too, if they dream about it the way I do? I've seen the look on their faces, the quiet shame. I wish I'd had the courage to speak out. Everyone else had a right to know. I still see that girl's face, her blue eyes that never blink. I can see them when I close my eyes, and I can't help but wonder if there's something we haven't yet paid for, something that isn't finished with us yet...

Mary closed the diary. She hadn't been there to see it as her mother had, but she still remembered that day. And like her mother, she remembered how everyone had just stopped talking about it, as if it had never even happened. Her mother had been different after that, even before her mind slowly started to leave her. But her mother had never told her about it. And now she, too, was afraid to close her eyes and see that face that lay frozen beneath the ice.

She put the diary down, then looked at the two newspaper clippings that had fallen out of the diary. They were both identically dated July 10th, 1994, but there was one difference between the two. One mentioned the deaths of the two tourists, while the other did not. *Why would they publish two different articles*, she thought? She looked outside and saw that the whole world had gone white.

Chapter Twenty-Five

Back at the bed and breakfast, Sarah was wrapped in a blanket and drinking hot tea. Alice was examining the pictures displayed on the wall, recognizing some. In these photographs, she became aware of a strange split in time that made her sad, and for a moment, she almost understood her sister. There were so many pictures of the two of them when they were young, always together. Then, after their early 20s, it was suddenly just Sarah in the pictures. When she had left the island, Alice never had any intentions of returning. She had fire and adventure in her heart from a very young age—she had her father to thank for that—and the very thought of staying on the island—on any island—was unthinkable. But here she was once again, back on that sliver of rock she had sworn never to return to.

Sarah set her tea down on the table. Her hands were still shaking a bit, but whether it was from the cold or the wreck, she was not sure. She couldn't get warm. Outside, she could hear the storm growing stronger, the wind howling and creeping its way through the slits in the wood. The radiators hissed in defiance, but the two of them could still feel the cold. The last of the dull winter light began to fade as the skies darkened to a jagged sliver of dull yellow light, barely visible through the heavy snow. Then it too was gone.

"I'm sorry about what happened," was all Sarah could manage to say. Her head still throbbed, and most of the incident was now buried in the deepest remnants of her subconscious.

"I'm just relieved that you're ok." Alice looked through the wine cabinet, finding most of the bottles were from local wineries. She selected a Cabernet, took out the bottle, and examined it.

"Ms. Paskert won't mind if I help myself to a glass of this, will she?"

"When I explain why we needed it, I think she'll understand."

Alice found two wine glasses on a nearby shelf and poured generous amounts of the dry red into both. She placed a glass in front of Sarah.

"How's your head?"

Sarah rubbed her forehead. "Not too bad right now. Tomorrow's gonna be a different story."

"Is there a doctor of any kind on this rock, or do you all have to go to the mainland?"

"Luke's a medic."

Alice laughed. "Luke's still here? Oh, good old Luke. Man, that boy loved you."

"I think he still does."

"Probably why he's still on the island. Lucky you, if you ever want to get married before 40, you'll have someone waiting in the wings."

"I'm never getting married."

Alice took a long sip of wine. "Never getting married, never going to grow up, right, Sarah?" She chuckled.

"Just because I don't want to get married doesn't make me less of an adult. You're not married."

"Divorced. I tried it once. Once was enough."

"Well, what makes you think I have any interest in that?"

"Sarah, I love you to death, but let's be honest: You've been Peter Pan-ing it here since you left college. Working in a bar, one-night stands with guys you'll never see again, staying up all night drinking with the tourists...it's the same thing you've been doing since your teens. Is that really what makes you happy?"

There was a long moment of silence between them as Sarah finished her tea. "I am happy here, Alice. I have to be happy here. I have to be happy here because I can't go anywhere else."

"That's ridiculous."

"It's not." Her tone was getting more agitated now. "You know goddamn well why I don't leave this island. Why is this something you refuse to comprehend?"

"I'm sorry, but I'm just not buying it. A grown woman in her 30s, phobic about leaving an island? I've never heard of that. Has any doctor or therapist ever diagnosed you?"

"Look, I tried to leave the island, and I couldn't do it. I don't know why you're giving me such a hard time. I'm living, I'm working; I mean, Christ, I'm not the happiest person in the world, but there are people far more miserable than I am. I make it work because I have to."

Alice shook her head. "How did you ever end up this way?"

"We were both on that boat, Alice. I just wasn't as lucky as you to be able to walk away from it perfectly fine."

Alice stared at her. "You think I walked away from that day perfectly fine? Like I just flipped a switch and forgot the whole fucking thing? There's rarely a night that goes by when I don't have a nightmare about what happened, and most of the time it doesn't end so well. It doesn't end the way it did in real life. And then even when I wake up, I have to worry about my kid sister still stuck on that horrible island." Alice stepped closer to her. "And after all that, you left me with cleaning up the mess. I had to arrange for Dad's burial. And where were you? Here. I had to explain to everyone why my own sister wasn't there for our father's funeral. It was bad enough that Dad died the way he did."

Sarah turned around, making no effort to hide her tears. "Don't you think that I want to jump off the northern shore of this island like Dad did? I run by there every day and think about it. Because every day, I'm constantly reminded that I'm stuck on the same small island where Dad killed himself. Sometimes that pain in my chest hurts so bad, I swear I feel the same emptiness Dad must have felt. I see that cliff where he jumped and goddamnit, I think about it too. But I don't. Unlike you, I can't just run away from my problems. I have to face them. Every day."

Alice looked at her, shocked. "If you hate me so much, then why did you call me?"

Sarah looked out the window. She could see the heavy snow falling in the dull halos from the lamp posts lining her street. "I didn't call you! I didn't tell you to come here! How do you explain that?! Why do you think I would want the one person in the world who constantly berates me to come back to the place I can't get away from?!"

Sarah got up, stormed upstairs, and slammed the bathroom door.

"Shit," Alice said. From her black leather purse, she pulled out a pack of Camels and stepped outside without bothering to put on her jacket.

Chapter Twenty-Six

D arkness fell upon the island. As the winds roared, even the strongest trees bent against their will. Out on the ice, no one would see the snow devils forming, twisting in their cold fury, dancing upon the jagged tips and crevices of the lake, then dissipating back into formlessness. Every house and building on the island creaked and moaned in the wind, and the few remaining inhabitants turned on all their lights, a beacon to the rest of the world.

Up in the control tower, Mark stood alone. His record had faded out and spun soundlessly on the loudspeakers. He finished the last of his drink, took the record off, and replaced it with Adam Khachaturian's Adagio from Spartacus to calm him as the storm gained strength. He'd leave for the hotel soon, but before that, he'd stop and check on Sarah. And his painting...his painting he'd touch up later. He would get rid of that boat, once again erasing it from existence.

Tigger barked as he and Susan watched Jack and Bill leave for their ice-fishing trip, their snowmobiles loaded up with their gear. She felt a calm silence settle around her, as any time spent alone was rare. She kept checking her phone for a reply from Adam. Nothing. Tigger ran to the window, whined a little, then got up on his hind legs and began barking out into the night. Though she was annoyed that they had left in such conditions, having the house to herself for the night was too good to pass up. She texted him again:

I have the whole house to myself tonight.

As the snowmobile's taillights faded into the darkness, her smile faded when Tigger continued his frenzied barking.

"Shut up!" she yelled. "There's nothing out there."

Tigger began to scratch at the window, and the sound of his nails clawing at the glass sent a shiver down her spine. She opened the sliding door and let Tigger out.

"See? This is what happens when you don't shut up."

As she dragged him through the snow, she could hear him whimpering.

"Too bad. You had your chance to calm down. I'll let you back in when you decide to behave."

She latched his collar onto the leash tied to the oak in the backyard, now coated in snow and ice. She cursed under her breath as her hands began to go numb.

"See? See what you make me do when you drag me out here in this shit? You think I want to be out here?"

Finally, the collar latched onto the leash, and as Tigger tried to follow her back, his slack ran out, and all he could do was bark. Susan closed the sliding door behind her. "Stupid fucking dog," she muttered to herself.

Far out on the frozen lake, Jack, Bill, and Chris set up their camp and began to drill into the ice. They could not see the island, and no one on the island could see them. A whirlwind of white snow eclipsed them, cutting them off from the rest of the world.

Alice had heard Sarah's crying through the door, and when she knocked, she found no reply and a locked door.

She took her cellphone out of her purse. The screen had cracked, and she could not get it turned on. Now she felt truly stranded, back on the island she had never wanted to return to, at the mercy of a storm she had no idea how long it would last. She had been there for less than four hours and had already alienated the one person on the island she wanted to see. Was this how Sarah felt all the time? she thought. Alone in this shack, miles away from any real civilization. She couldn't decide whether she should feel sorry for her sister for being trapped here or if Sarah was simply a frightened child who was too scared to leave what had become safe and familiar to her.

Tired, she sat down on the piano bench, occasionally checking to see if her phone would, by some miracle, turn back on. She turned toward the keys and ran her fingers across them. They sounded in tune, and she surmised that Sarah must have played it often during the long, dark winter nights here.

She began to play. She had learned dozens of songs from her piano lessons as a child, but now remembered only a few. As she played Beethoven's Moonlight Sonata, her fingers faltered over the notes. It did not sound overly pleasant to her, but she was momentarily pleased that she remembered most of it. Slow and sad, the kind of music Sarah used to play. Now the room was filled with sad music, and Alice felt its calming effect on her. There was nothing else to pass the time. As she played, she did not hear Sarah open her door and come down the carpeted stairs.

Sarah leaned against the wall behind Alice and watched her play. For a moment, she felt as if she was back at their old house on the other side of the island. Alice played well, as she had, but Sarah could tell she hadn't practiced in some time. With the howling of the wind snaking its way through the cracks in the house, she felt the scene only needed a Christmas tree and a lit fireplace to make it complete. For the first time in the past few days, she felt at ease.

"You haven't forgotten the classics," Sarah remarked.

Alice turned briefly, then went back to playing again. "Haven't forgotten what I never really learned well before. You were always the pro."

"I was only better because I didn't have your social skills, so this was what I did instead."

Sarah sat down on the bench beside Alice and began to play along with her.

"I haven't played this piece in a while, either," she said.

"I don't believe that for a second. You always played the sad ones."

"I've learned some much sadder ones since then."

"Maybe you'd feel happier if you played something happier. What did our piano teacher used to want us to play? Wasn't it Elton John?"

Sarah laughed. "Elton John and Billy Joel. To this day, I can't stomach either one of them on the radio. Their music is forbidden at my bar."

Alice laughed without missing a key. "Even 'Piano Man'?"

"Especially 'Piano Man'."

Alice saw a photo of the three of them: Sarah, their father, and herself. Her smile faded. "I miss Dad."

"Me too. I like to think of him when I play."

"That's a nice picture. I'd forgotten about it."

The two played quietly side by side for some time as the storm continued. Outside, it was now completely dark, and they could hear the winds continue to howl and batter against the walls of the house.

As the trees bent and swayed against the wind, the lampposts and streetlights began to flicker, and the music playing from the loudspeakers began to slow down and eventually stopped altogether.

Part Four

The Tempest

BAYNAM BOOKS PRESS

Chapter Twenty-Seven

The floodlights from the camp shook in the wind, and long shadows danced back and forth as Jack and Chris drilled their augers into the ice. The snow was coming down harder now, and the two men dressed in winter gear repeatedly cleared it from their digging site as Bill watched, cold hands in pockets, no comfort to be found for miles in every direction.

"How thick is the ice?" Jack asked, most of his face concealed by a ski mask and goggles. He hugged himself, not comfortable using the new tools they had brought, and would instead wait his turn to lower the line in once all seven holes were completed. He wore an aviator hat to match his black aviator leather jacket and looked fifty years out of place, even on the barren ice. Despite his attire, he could not fly a plane, nor could he drill fishing holes in the ice, and he felt useless and emasculated as he stood with Bill, watching.

"About four to five inches thick," Chris yelled out over the sound of his own drilling. His mouth too was covered, but instead of goggles, an eye patch covered one eye and left the other naked and unprotected against the frigid gales. He seemed not to notice or care. "It's not as thick the farther from the mainland you get, but it's strong enough to hold up our fat asses out of the water until we're done."

Jack nodded and looked back at their shanty village of tents and cots, now struggling against the growing wind. "You really think that storm is gonna hit? We'll be sitting ducks out here in the open." The thought of sitting next to the fireplace back home with a cup of coffee and a few healthy shots of Jameson mixed in sounded better and better. Although they had started their expedition well before the sun rose that morning, their catch thus far had been far from bountiful, and to return now would mean precious time lost. Chris had made this pilgrimage every year for the past ten years, making his way out onto the lake when it was solid enough and setting up a base camp where they could lose all their troubles in fishing and beer until they had had their fill, then return home.

Jack always felt like he was one of the few to truly look forward to the winters along the lake. Last year had been unseasonably warm for much of the winter, and they had been unable to make their way out onto the ice. But this winter over the island—over all of Lake Erie—had been merciless, and fortune was in their favor with ice thick enough for basecamp and the snowmobiles they brought. The threat of breaking ice was a distant one; they now only had to worry about the strength of the winds. Bill stomped impatiently in place. This was his first time staying overnight on the ice. Bill had been looking forward to it until the moment the sun went down, and they were surrounded by cold and darkness. But no matter what he did, he could not get warm.

Chris walked back over to the camp and hammered more stakes into the ice to give more support for their tents. He knew even if the tents did not blow away, they would never sleep with all the noise. And it was now almost deafening: the wailing of the winds, the scratching of snow on the ice, and even their own drilling. He liked coming out here during this time because of the peace and quiet, but now it seemed as if they were all operating within some sort of arctic factory, and all comfort dissipated with each gust of wind that seemed determined to ruin their camp. Chris wasn't married; he was always on the ice because he could be. But Jack knew this was his only time away from home. Almost every aspect of his life had become family-oriented, and although he hadn't come to resent it just yet, he had become familiar with the restlessness that arose this time of season, and an ice fishing trip was his only ticket out of the house and spousal duties.

They had chosen this week after all the forecasts had been nearly unanimous about the agreeable weather: Clear but cold, and cold enough to keep the ice strong for their trip. But they had not predicted this storm, much to the delight of Chris. One by one, they drilled holes in the ice, their fingers and toes cold but not yet freezing, and the thrill of a good catch was always enough to warm their blood until the alcohol came after (Jack had already poured some rum into his cocoa). Once the holes had been drilled and the water could be reached, they baited their lines and submerged them. They found it hard to stay upright against the wind, and Chris found himself knocked back several times. With no particular role to play, Bill was handed a flashlight from his father and stood there as a silent sentinel as the others continued their frantic drilling.

"If we head back now, we can still grab dinner at my house."

Underneath his Eskimo hood, Chris shook his head. "You can head back if you want. I'm not leaving this place 'til we get what we came for."

"The storm is picking up." Jack found it hard to see any of them. If the floodlights went out, it would be darkness for miles and miles in every direction, with only their flashlights and headlamps to guide them. "Are you sure this is safe?"

"I'm not taking these fucking snowmobiles *all* the way back to shore only to come back again tomorrow morning and set up camp all over again. We're here, we're set up, and this storm will pass, just like all the others."

The ice here was uneven, and they tripped several times while fighting the wind and holding the fishing line steady. The temperature was dropping. They could feel the cold wetness of it, through their many layers of clothing, deep into their bones. Jack had had hypothermia twice—once as a child—and he had not forgotten how long it had taken him to get warm again, how cold he had felt for days.

Bill stood there holding a flashlight, but he shone it on neither of the men. Instead, the young boy of age twelve shone his light into a random patch of darkness just beyond the group, the ray unable to penetrate the infinite darkness that surrounded the perimeters of their encampment, until the very blackness itself swallowed it, as if it were something tangible. The boy stared into it, and the darkness stared back.

Chris glanced over as he continued to drill. "Hey kid, shine that thing over here, would ya?"

Bill stood there, motionless, his back still turned to Chris. Chris hoisted himself up, heard his knees crack, and then stumbled over to the boy, both his legs having nearly fallen asleep. He gave Bill a quick shove from behind and startled the kid so much that he spun around and shined the light right into Chris' one good eye.

"Get that shit out of my eyes, boy. Didn't you hear me calling you back there?"

Bill looked at him but said nothing.

"I said, didn't you hear me?"

Jack came up from behind him and knelt beside his son. "No, he didn't hear you. He can't hear you. He can't hear a goddamn thing."

Chris looked down a bit in shame. "I thought he just couldn't talk."

"He can't talk, and he can't hear. Christ, he's been on the island as long as you have. It's no secret. What did you want from him, anyway?"

Chris shrugged. "Just needed some more light where I'm digging, that's all."

"I'll tell him. Get back to it."

Jack turned toward his son and signed to him. *I'm sorry; he didn't know.*

Everybody else here knows.

He's a bit thick and a bit drunk. Just forget about it. Are you warm enough out here?

Bill shrugged. *I saw something out on the ice.*

What do you mean?

I saw something. Moving around out there.

Something? Like someone?

Bill shrugged again. *I don't know.*

Jack looked off into the darkness and saw nothing outside the limits of their lights. *Well, if you see something again, let me know. Just keep your lights on us.*

As the snow picked up, they all became very aware of a sound far off in the distance. It started low, almost inaudible. The first few times, they simply shrugged it off and continued, but again, they heard it. Louder this time. And closer. Coming from not one direction but many.

"What the hell is that?" Jack asked, holding his line firm against the wind. "That's not the storm siren, is it?"

Chris continued his drilling, hearing the question but ignoring it. But despite his constant drilling, he had heard the sound too: the sound of ice shoals shifting, the way they tend to do when the temperature warms, during a fair dusk or dawn. But the temperature was dropping, and fast. Jack tapped Chris on the shoulder. He stopped but did not turn around. "What the hell is it now?"

"Just shut up and listen." Jack left his hand on Chris' shoulder. Over the shrieking of the wind, they both could hear the sound of the siren coming from the island. "It's the siren."

Chris shook his head. "Yeah, so?"

"There's no one at the operating tower to turn it on."

Chris looked at Jack, then went back to his drill. "Maybe Mark went back and turned it on. Because of the storm."

Jack turned around to face the darkness. "Yeah, maybe." He looked at his son, who stood there shaking with the flashlight in his hands. The beam of its light trembled as it shone on Chris, casting a long, distorted shadow of him that spread out over the ice like ink on paper. Jack turned back to Chris. "All the same, if someone did turn them on, maybe we should go back?"

Chris waved him away. "Go back if you want to. Don't expect any help from me."

Just then, something else began to drown out the wail from the sirens. All around them, they could hear what sounded like glass breaking and strange, almost whale-like moaning—painful and slow—coming from underneath the thick surface of the ice. Chris and Jack didn't know which direction to step away from. The thunderous sound of ice breaking was almost deafening now, and although the ice beneath them seemed stable, the wind had become strong enough to knock them over. Strange shadows cast from the lights danced across the ice, arcane figures streaking across frozen water and dancing and disappearing back into the darkness that seemed to spread out forever, a darkness with no end in every direction.

The winds ripped the lights from their stands and shattered them on the ice. They stood there, the three of them, trapped in wind, snow, and darkness. They could no longer see the lights from the shores of the mainland nor those of the island. It was as if they had been removed from their world, transported, the winds carrying them to dark places unknown. All they had was Bill's lone light, which trembled now as the cold grew to embrace him. Jack knelt next to him and could feel the cold of the ice burn its way through his jeans and his long johns underneath until it reached his flesh.

It's going to be ok, he signed to his son.

I'm scared. I think we should go back.

I think we should go back too.

Then all at once they were able to see each other and see their surroundings, and for a moment they believed their smashed lights had somehow come back on. But this light was different; it was a strange red glow, emanating from deep underneath the ice.

"What the hell is that?" Chris held tight onto one of the last standing poles. The whole surface of the lake had become luminescent, and as the red glow grew brighter, the sound of ice breaking grew louder. The ice began to shift underneath them, breaking apart and smashing in a fury of otherworldly noise.

"How far are we from the shore?" Jack yelled over the wind.

"Twenty minutes if we can find the shore!" Chris was almost crawling on all fours now against the force of the wind. Jack grabbed his arm and dragged him over to the second snowmobile. Already, he could feel his exposed skin go numb. Another twenty minutes of this and they both would succumb to frostbite and hypothermia. He had never been this cold in his life, and he found it difficult to move. His survivalist instinct was just barely enough to overtake his panic over what was going on all around them. Adrenaline gave him the last bit of warmth he could hope to grasp on to. It had to be enough to get them to the shores.

Jack looked down at his son, who was trying hard to fight back tears. He was in the presence of adults; surely, they would protect him. Then all around the ice broke in a giant circle, encompassing them, tearing them away from the main shelf of ice on the lake. Their ice island now began to break into smaller and smaller parts.

"We'll never make it out of here on that thing!" Chris was hugging himself for warmth now. The contacts in his eyes had frozen, and his whole world was just a white blur. Jack quickly scanned the ice, hoping to see some solid ground left for them to make their escape.

All around them, the ice was breaking apart and encroaching upon them quickly. The moaning beneath grew louder. Behind them, their camp was slowly being taken apart now by both wind and moving ice, and the last of their tents had crumpled to the ground and was drifting away.

"We'll have to jump to the main part of the ice or we'll die here!" Jack was doing everything he could to keep Chris moving.

Chris staggered over to the snowmobiles, still parked at the base camp. Without looking back at his comrades, he jumped on the machine, turned it on, and sped off. There was one left, for they had only brought the two.

"What the hell are you doing?" Jack yelled. Chris did not answer as he sped off and left the two alone.

Together they raced toward the stable ice shelf, which seemed to drift farther and farther away from them. The ice beneath them cracked like glass as they ran over it, and he knew this entire pocket was thin enough for both of them to fall through. One dip underwater and they would be gone. Jack fell to his knees and held his son close to him. He could barely move now, and Jack found himself struggling with the elements. Only he wasn't cold anymore, and he knew now that he did not have much time for them to make it back. With any luck, Chris would call for help once he made it to the shore—if he made it that far. He had left them behind, but Jack would deal with that later. He gripped Bill's shoulder and realized that his hand had gone completely numb, each digit an unfamiliar part of his body. Each piece of him was slowly drifting away, too.

Jack fell to his knees, his body no longer willing to comply with his mind. *Let it be quick, Lord. But please protect my son.* Jack held his son tight as life slowly pulled away from him. And then their small piece of ice began to submerge as well. Jack went feet first into the ice water beneath him, but as Bill reached out to grab his hand, neither had the strength left to pull him out. He did not want his weight to pull his son under along with him, so he let go. His body was too numb to feel the icy water consume it, and as he went under, the red glow grew brighter, and soon he found himself deep beneath the ice, sinking fast. Somewhere beneath the surface, Jack knew he was not alone. His name was called, something beckoned him, and instead of sinking into darkness, he sank into something much brighter and emptier than darkness...

Chris sped away, hoping to leave his guilt behind. The splitting of the ice seemed to match his speed, and all around him, he could still hear the thunderous cracking. He had driven some ways but could still not make out the lights from the mainland. Any direction was better than where he had just come from. His face was numb from the winds, raw now, his skin feeling ready to peel from his face. He wasn't a coward, he told himself. He would call for help as soon as he safely landed on the shores. The Coast Guard would ride out on a helicopter and find them, stuck on ice, pissed but alive, and they'd go back and warm up and have the Jameson in coffee by a nice fireplace.

Up ahead, he could barely make out the lonesome flicker from the lights on the mainland, shivering in the wind. He wasn't far now. Without looking behind him, he focused on the shimmering beacons as his face went numb, but the prospect of frostbite did not frighten him nearly as much as the thought of submerging beneath the ice. The other two would make it out alright. Tomorrow, they'd laugh it off. Then they'd return to their home, their families, who would receive their survival stories with keen interest. The warmth of his own house and the fireplace—that warmth was missed and greatly needed now. It seemed so far away, just like the mainland had moments ago. But now he was getting closer, and his spirits lifted as he thought he could make out the rocky shores covered in ice, and he laughed in relief. And then the lights and the shore disappeared in darkness. All traces of direction had been lost to him, and as his snowmobile hit full speed, he could hear the breaking of ice all around him, and then just as quickly as the lights had disappeared, so did he through the ice into the water.

It happened fast. His world went dark and unbearably cold, and though his eyes were closed, the sound of breaking ice was almost deafening under the water. It was a cold he had never known before, his body going numb, and the pain of his extremities losing all sensitivity faster than his brain could process. And he was sinking, fast. Although his legs had gone numb, he knew something was pulling him down—something gripping his ankle, weighing him down as if it were latched to an anchor. His eyes were closed, but even as he sank, he knew he was not alone. He could hear it. In his mind's eye, he could see the surface drifting further and further away as he was being pulled down into their world, and somehow, just like a dream, it all made sense. He was both sinking fast into the icy abyss and sitting at the fireplace, his Cleveland Browns coffee mug full of a generous portion of Jameson while watching the snowfall outside, and the cold then seemed very distant. And as he opened his eyes and saw her, he screamed and his lungs filled with putrid ice water, and within minutes his body was lost to the cavernous space beneath the ice, where dead men sank and something else would rise tonight...

Bill stood alone on the ice as all went quiet. The red light had gone, as had the thunderous sounds. The ice, too, had stopped cracking and breaking. Now there was only the wind. His father had disappeared into the dark fathoms below. Here, the boy imagined himself trapped forever on this sheet of ice, while his mother slept peacefully in her warm bed, not dreaming of this, not hearing him call her name in a world where he still had a voice.

Far off in the distance, he could hear tiny footsteps, little sounds of snow crunching, inching toward him somewhere in the darkness. He looked all around him, trying to find the source of the noise. He had dropped the flashlight, and all light had been lost to him as he stood there in the blinding, white fury of the storm. Perhaps it was Chris, he thought? But he could not call out his name. He could not call out anything. Maybe Chris had made it to the mainland after all and came back with help. Surely that man had not left them all alone to this cold fate.

Hello? He signed to empty air. *Is anyone there?*

There was no answer, just the continued footsteps, growing closer.

And then it appeared, the silhouette of some small figure walking toward him, hair and dress blowing in the wind. A girl. She was about his height. He looked to run but found himself all alone on a small slab of ice, just floating above the inky blackness of the frigid lake beneath him. His feet had gone numb, and he felt strangely warm. Warm like back at home.

And as the figure came closer, and he saw that smile that stretched from ear to ear—that horrible smile—he wanted to scream, but as he opened his mouth to do so, no sound came. And as he screamed in silence, she reached out with her hands and slowly clasped his, and his blood and limbs filled with ice until he could scream no more.

Chapter Twenty-Eight

S arah was back on the mainland and afraid, but not because she was off the island. Because back on the mainland, everyone was gone, all traces of people wiped clean from all major cities and highways, leaving her to wander alone, calling out the names of everyone she had ever loved or known. But no one answered back, and no matter how far she traveled, she found nothing, just the cold wind and echoes of her own voice. She somehow knows the cities have been deserted for years and will never be occupied again. All the food in the supermarkets will expire, and the meat will rot, and if she gets sick, there will be no one to care for her. She screams...

Sarah awoke at the front desk of the B&B, her head buried in bookkeeping paperwork. Both the radio and TV produced an unsettling static. The room was cold, but all the windows were closed, and radiators still hissed with steam. She put her Ohio State hoodie on and tiptoed up the stairs. *So quiet up here*, she thought. She had hoped that Alice would make this place come to life, as she had done so many times in the past. But now it seemed as if the inn was even emptier and farther away. She opened the door to Alice's room slightly, her heart pounding. There on the bed, she could see the blanketed form of her sister, still sleeping.

Sarah closed the door, knowing she would not sleep again tonight. 3:00 AM. Insomnia had rarely bothered her over the years, but tonight she was restless. As the storm approached, a strange feeling had come over her. She could hear the wind whistling through every crack and crevice in the old windows, blowing dead branches around outside, and rolling a metal trash can down the street. Normally, a storm like this would have lulled her to sleep, the winds whispering in her ear like a soothing midwinter lullaby. But not tonight. As she went back downstairs to prepare an unusual pot of morning coffee, she heard the static from the radio growing louder, filling every room with something tangible and menacing. The static began to form patterns until it became clearer; almost subliminal whispers began to echo from the radio. Sarah stood still and terrified, listening to the voices overlapping each other in desperate, hushed tones. She walked over to the radio and shut it off.

Over the screaming winds outside, she heard the familiar electrical crackle of the loudspeakers coming to life. But instead of Wagner or the Beach Boys, she could hear the same frantic whispering that had come from her radio. It was everywhere now, and unless she was losing her mind, she knew that everyone else who was awake could surely hear it as well. The idea that she might be the only person awake on the island right now made her blood run cold. Deep down inside, she felt a quiet dread that these whispers were somehow meant just for her. Outside, she could see nothing but the whiteness of snow and wind, and as the streetlights flickered on and off, so did the lights inside the B&B. In each period of darkness, Sarah held her breath and stood silent and still as the storm finally made landfall.

Gabriella sat awake in her bed, liquid debris still dribbling from her feeding tube. Ben Selvin's "*Love, Your Spell Is Everywhere*" played softly on the old record player. As Mary slept in the adjoining room, Gabriella looked out through the small, lone window into the whiteness beyond. Above the noise from the wind, she too could hear the whispers outside. They were growing louder, whisper layered upon whisper upon whisper, growing in intensity. As they fell upon Gabriella's ears, she understood them very well. She had heard them long ago in her childhood dreams, the dreams of a skeletal ferryman, reaching out his bony hand to grab onto hers, whisking her away on a ferry with a destination of no return. She had dreamt this many times as a child, and though she had lost most of her faculties, she had never forgotten those whispers. She lay in bed watching the storm unfold, unable to move or cry out for her daughter as the ferryman whispered her name.

Tigger fought madly against his leash. His owner had passed out on the sofa while watching late-night sitcom reruns. The dog barked, whimpered, and howled as the whispers made their way into his backyard, and the tree branches seemed to reach down and lunge for him. He made every last effort to break free from his leash, lunging repeatedly in fear and rage until one last thrust snapped his neck and his barking ceased, and nearby neighbors gratefully returned to their peaceful slumber.

Back at the hotel, cocktails were being passed around with great gusto. They were more booze than mix, and no one seemed to notice or care when the lights began to flicker. The Mayor had selected an old compilation of '60s hits on the jukebox. No one could see the snowdrifts outside piling up against the door, slowly burying the hotel in feet of unrelenting snow. Up on the vacant top floor, the lamps on the walls began to slowly dim. Outside the window at the end of the hallway, a wooden shutter banged again and again, as if some invisible hand was knocking at the door. Then suddenly the shutter shattered into pieces, and all was silent again.

All the lights around the island began to flicker on and off, the snowy halos disappearing and then reappearing again. As he walked back to his snowmobile, Mark flipped on his headlamp flashlight, undeterred by the storm or the loss of power. As he started up the engine, he too began to hear the whispers. It took him no more than a second to realize it was not the wind nor any part of the storm. It took even less time to realize it was coming from the loudspeakers on the island. The whispers of multiple voices, hushed but urgent, their words incomprehensible. Mark looked up at the control tower and saw that the lights were still on, just as he had left them. He would come back later, as now he was worried most about Sarah.

Chapter Twenty-Nine

Luke sped toward the main road under the cover of darkness. He had forgotten to borrow snow goggles and found it difficult navigating his shortcut through the woods. His eyes stung, and he could barely keep them open as he struggled to make out the path before him. The main road would undoubtedly be covered by snowdrifts. He felt relieved to leave the riffraff behind him, but worried about his name being mentioned if someone were to find out they had crashed the hotel. *Maybe they'd fire me, and I'd have to leave the island*, he thought, smiling as the wind stung his face. He could go someplace warm, with normal people. But then he thought of Sarah and knew he was not going anywhere.

He had not had a chance to talk with her at the town hall meeting, and it bothered him that she hadn't stayed around afterwards to seek him out. But no one ever did, even though he had cleaned up their messes or gotten them out of trouble. It seemed that the more he did for them, the less they respected him. Or maybe they were just assholes. Luke recalled a moment when he was a boy and his father had looked down at him and asked, What *would you like to be when you grow up, Luke?*"

He imagined a young Luke looking back up at his father, smiling and replying, *Become the island's fucking punching bag, sir.*"

Sarah rarely called him except when she needed something. He knew this and didn't care. Everybody needs something, he thought. The snow was coming down harder now, and he thought about her all alone in that ancient bed and breakfast, so far away from the rest of the island. In a way, he almost envied her, living a comfortable distance away from the others. He was excited about the possibility of being invited to stay in one of the vacant rooms, then waking up and sharing their morning coffee.

Chapter Thirty

Gabriel burst into Adam's room and jumped onto the bed, barking uncontrollably, whining, and howling. Adam had been lost in dreamland. "Quiet! What the hell is wrong with you?"

He looked over at the clock and saw that it read 3:00 am. Still hours away from daybreak. He reached for his cellphone, saw Susan's messages, and then disregarded them. *Not going anywhere tonight, darling.*

Gabriel was not easy to startle, and though the idea of someone attempting to break in seemed unlikely, he could think of no other explanation for his dog's behavior. The others on the island knew to keep their distance from his property. They could gaze upon it from a safe distance, but he was wary of guests—even during the empty months of winter—and longed for peace while he hibernated.

Then he heard it: the moaning and bending of metal pipes. He started to rise, then jumped back onto his bed and shrieked. The floor was freezing, as cold as ice.

Gabriel was on the bed now, whimpering as the moaning grew louder. If Adam had looked closer, he would have seen the frost on Gabriel's paws. But the dog would not abandon his master. Adam put his slippers on and walked to the door, which he had thought he locked. As he swung it open, a cold rush of air burst through.

"Jesus, Gabe." A broken window. That explained the cold floors. The blast of wind off the lake was now gusting into his bedroom from downstairs. The stench of dead fish and something fouler, more rotten. He tried for the lights again but found none of them working. No bars on his cellphone, either. Adam flipped the cellphone's light and began making his way down the hall towards the spiral staircase. He could hear the wind rushing up the stairs, and downstairs, he heard shards of glass blowing around. It sounded like a mess, and he knew he would have to find his walkie-talkie and contact Luke.

As he descended the stairs, Adam hugged himself, shivering. The temperature in the house seemed no warmer than outside, and even the cavernous hallways could not shield him from the winds. As he reached the bottom of the staircase, he could see his light reflecting off the shards of glass that covered the floor by the window. The curtains flapped madly in the wind as the storm made itself welcome in his house. From upstairs, he could hear

Gabriel's whimpers and barks but was unable to translate his pet's frantic plea for his master to return to safety.

"Gabriel, get your lazy ass down here!"

Gabriel made his way timidly down the hallway but would go no further than the top of the staircase, just beyond Adam's line of sight. Adam attempted to survey the scene as best he could in the darkness.

"What a mess," he muttered to himself.

Expecting to hear glass crunching beneath his feet, he heard only the sound of his footsteps on the wooden floor, along with the moaning of the pipes. The curtains were wide open, revealing his panoramic view of the icy lake that seemed to stretch on forever. He knew he had closed them before he went to bed. The curtains flailed wildly. Yet all the windows were closed. The door was still locked and closed as well. Yet his house felt violated. Upstairs, he could still hear Gabriel whimpering, letting out an occasional bark, begging his master to come back up to safety. But now something else had caught Adam's eye: a small glow out on the ice, distant but moving closer.

Someone out on the ice with a flashlight? Who could be crazy enough to be out there in this weather? He paused a moment to reflect on his island neighbors and realized that it was extremely possible. *If you're dumb enough to be out in this,* he thought, *don't expect any help from me.* The red glow seemed to be getting closer, and it was headed toward his house. The painful shrieking from the pipes grew louder still. From a closet, he pulled out his large telescope, which he primarily used during the summer to gaze upon young, tanned bodies out on their boats. He struggled in the darkness to focus on his subject, and the growing chill in the room made it difficult to steady his trembling hands.

As the lens came into focus, he saw that the object was much smaller than it had seemed from afar, a small red glow that seemed to move against the force of the wind. It never shifted from its course, which seemed to be directed straight toward him. As he twisted the lens and adjusted the image, Adam saw what appeared to be a small figure within the red glow, almost as if it were surrounded by torchlight. Yet he saw no fire or flashlight, just a luminous red light that defied the winds. And then he felt it on his ear. First one, then another, and another: icy, wet drips. *Something is leaking*, he thought. *Fucking wonderful.* As the drops became more frequent, he pulled away from the lens, took out his cellphone, and shone the light above him. Snowflakes were falling from the darkness above, without any window or door open. *What the hell is this?* Adam held out his hand and felt the flakes trickle onto it. He could feel the temperature dropping more and more.

He looked back out the window, and even without the aid of the telescope, he could see the figure, wrapped in a velvet red, walking toward him. He could make out her shape now and could see the long hair and the dress that went down to her knees. It looked like a little girl, walking calmly alone, undeterred.

Gabriel's barking suddenly stopped. "Gabe? Gabe, come here, boy!"

And as the shrieking pipes grew louder, they began to bend until they broke one by one, and then frigid water came pouring through the ceiling. The icy water quickly engulfed the floor, and within minutes, his feet were submerged. As he ran to the spiral staircase, he could see water gushing down in torrents above. Though he knew he was not dressed for the elements, he also knew he had to get out as quickly as possible. The town wasn't far, even on foot. As he went to grip the doorknob, he found that it would not give. He pushed his weight into it several times, throwing himself into the door.

"Fuck this," he said, and crossed the room to the large window overlooking the lake. He picked up a chair. *I'm not going to die like this in my own house.* He swung the chair with all his might, but to no avail. It bounced off the window, leaving not even a scratch on the glass.

"That's impossible," he muttered, then again, much louder, "That's fucking impossible!" The water had risen above his bare ankles, and he was so cold he could hardly move. He hoped he would awaken soon from this nightmare, and if it was not a nightmare, he hoped the end would come quickly. At that moment, he regretted living so far from the others, insisting his castle be as distant from them as possible. He knew it could be weeks before they found him, maybe even months. All the money in the world couldn't stop the deadly coldness that slowly filled the room. As his hands went numb, he dropped his phone into the water. He climbed up onto a table and clutched at himself in the cold.

Then he saw the red glow again. But this time, it wasn't a distant beacon out on the lake. It was climbing the side of the cliff, bright enough that it could be seen even through the swirling snow. It grew brighter until he could finally see a small figure emerging over the edge of the cliff. It was her again, hair blowing softly in the wind. She was moving toward him, her dress and hair, and body flowing almost as if they were submerged in water.

The water began to creep over the surface of his table, but now his extremities were too numb to feel its coldness. He could see nothing but the red image of the little girl slowly approaching his living room window. Soon enough, she was at the window. As he focused upon the red glow, he saw that face staring back at him, watching him watch her. Seeing him remember her. As his final thoughts drifted back to that summer day long ago when he watched those two tourists drown in the storm, he began to laugh, until finally his laughter grew louder than the rushing of the water. He laughed for some time, knowing the girl wasn't going to come take him; she would let the icy cold waters take him instead. He laughed until the water reached his face and filled his mouth, his throat, and his lungs.

The girl in red stood there for some time, watching Adam's body float like a phantasmagoric snow globe. His eyes were frozen wide open, as was his scream, frozen forever on his face. As the girl looked out upon the rest of the island, sirens began to howl. Leaving no footprints behind her, the girl in red moved past Adam's house, into the night, and down the main road that led into town.

Chapter Thirt-One

As Alice opened the door and saw Luke's frozen face staring back at her in surprise, all she did was burst into laughter. A hundred childhood memories flooded them both simultaneously, and Luke felt his crimson cheeks grow even redder as he stood there, dumbfounded.

"What the hell are you doing here?" he demanded in disbelief.

"Nice to see you too, Luke." Alice looked him up and down, smugly noting that little dorky Luke had grown up exactly the same as she had left him all those years ago.

"I thought you were in LA?"

"I was, Luke. And now I'm here."

Luke could see Sarah seated on the couch behind Alice, her swollen foot resting on the coffee table. She tried to hide her smile. "Thanks for coming, Luke."

He still held the wrapped flowers that Mark had left behind, unsure of what to do with them. Alice looked down and saw them, and her eyes gleamed with delight.

"Aww, Luke, did you bring flowers for Sarah?" She asked mockingly.

Luke looked down, feigning surprise. "Uh, yeah. These are for Sarah."

Alice snatched them away from him and looked at the card. "Oh Jesus, Luke, these are from Mark." She turned to Sarah. "They're from Mark."

Luke blushed. He felt too warm, even standing out in the cold. "Well, yeah, I meant to say that they were for Sarah, from Mark. I found them out here."

Sarah smiled. "It's okay, Luke."

Luke looked over at Sarah, whose foot was resting on the coffee table. "That's not elevated enough," was all he could say. It was late now, close to 2 am. "I have some bandages for it. Luckily, I had some in the med kit in Dan's ride. And I have some ibuprofen." He walked in and was struck by the hot temperature inside. His fingers and toes felt frozen, and he looked forward to holding them over the radiator in the corner of the room. He knelt next to Sarah. "Ouch."

"Yeah, I can't put much weight on it."

"I wouldn't try to. How'd it happen?"

Alice grabbed a chair from the dining room table, dragged it across the wooden floor, and sat down next to them. "We had a car accident."

"Jesus, you guys too? Nobody should be out in this mess anyway."

Sarah laughed. "I had to pick my sis up at the airport. What was your excuse?"

"I had to drop the mayor and some supplies off at the hotel."

"I bet you were thrilled."

Luke took some bandages from his bag. He removed the ice pack Alice had made for her and began to wrap her ankle slowly. "Well, as long as I know where everybody is and they're safe until this blows over, I can live with it. The more of them packed together in one place, the easier it is to get to them."

Something about that last comment sent a chill down Sarah's spine, though she could not say why. Luke's visit had distracted her from her earlier ominous thoughts. Though she noted the clumsiness of his bandage wrapping, she said nothing; Luke had many jobs on the island but was good at none of them. But he was loyal to his employer and to the island, and for that reason, he stayed. His hand trembled a bit as he held her foot to wrap her ankle. The bandage kept coming undone, and every time he sighed heavily, she struggled not to smile. His awkwardness around her hadn't changed since their teens.

Alice seemed to delight in staring at him with unblinking eyes, adding to his obvious discomfort.

"Sorry," Luke said. "I'm not great with these things."

"It's okay, Luke," Sarah said. "I'm glad you came by."

"Where's your car?" Luke asked, without looking up. He, too, had become aware of his shaking hands, and his heart beat fast as well. Perhaps, he thought, if he were to mention the treacherous conditions out there, she might invite him to stay.

"Probably at the bottom of the lake by now," Sarah said. "And I would be too if Alice hadn't pulled me out of the car."

"I'm sorry I wasn't there to help," Luke added quickly. "I was busy having an accident of my own."

Sarah smiled. "I hope that won't get you into too much trouble."

"Oh, I'm sure I'll catch shit for it, but Todd owes me one, and the mayor saw what happened too."

"What did happen?"

Luke had finished with the bandage and looked up at Sarah. "Good enough?" It wasn't. The dressing was loose in all the wrong places, and Sarah could tell she was going to have to redo it later. But she smiled anyway. "It's fine, thank you."

"Of course. Well, Mark's idea of a sick joke is to blame."

"Sick joke? I don't understand."

"We were driving—and the roads were already pretty bad at this point—and then he had the nerve to put these macabre snowmen in the middle of the goddamn road. I mean, he knows that people on this island still drive in the wintertime. I don't know who the fuck does that, who has the time to do that—"

If Sarah could have stood up, she would have. "Mark was with me earlier. He's been at the control tower all day. It must have been someone else."

"Well, unless our resident Howard Hughes has finally lost his mind, I can't imagine what sick fuck on this island would do that."

Alice came back into the room carrying two drinks. "Why were they macabre?" She placed one of the glasses in front of Sarah, then took a generous gulp of the other one in her hand. As Luke went to reach for it, Alice snapped, "That one's Sarah's."

Luke felt his face flush again. "There was a circle of snowmen in the middle of the road, with all their heads missing."

Alice looked at him for a moment. "That's pretty fucked up. Probably a kid."

Luke laughed. "The only kid on this island right now is Bill, and that kid never leaves his parents' sight. Look, I don't know who it was, but when I find out, I intend to have a nice long conversation with them."

Alice rolled her eyes again and finished her drink. Sarah took a sip from hers and winced. "Jesus, Alice. Is there even any mixer in here?"

"Just enough. Mixer ruins good liquor. You're a bartender; you should know that."

She stared blankly at Luke. "Oh, I'm sorry, Luke, did you want one?"

Luke flushed, shook his head, and sat back. "Nah, thanks. Somebody has to stay sober on this island with you, strange people."

Sarah shook her head. "Everyone seems a bit strange to you." She could still feel her ankle throbbing, despite the ibuprofen and liquor.

"Anyone who would want to stay on this island in the middle of winter, yes," Alice said as she made herself another cocktail.

Feeling his leg falling asleep beneath him, Luke stood up quickly to shake it awake. "Well, whoever it was is an asshole."

Outside, they could hear the wind banging the shutters against the windows. The lights flickered on and off. Though the radiators were still hissing, the room felt colder, and all three of them felt an invisible draft snaking its way through the crevices around the old windows.

Luke looked at Alice, then Sarah. "You know, this storm's not gonna let up for at least another day or so. I'd hate to leave you two here alone, especially since everyone else is on the other side of the island."

Sarah could feel her ankle throbbing, but the booze was beginning to dull the pain, and she was finally able to relax a bit. Knowing it had not been since their late teens that the three of them were in a room together, Sarah was filled with an overwhelming sense of lost days gone by. For a moment, she had almost forgotten about the accident and the storm outside. "You have a lot to do, Luke. You always do. I'm sure the others on the island all appreciate it."

Luke shrugged. "It's my job." His heart began to sink, and he dreaded the cold wind on his face during the long trek back.

Alice observed the two of them and found it difficult to hide her smile. "Or you could just stay here, Luke. We've got enough booze in this place to last a winter. We can stay up all night getting drunk and swapping old stories." She darted another look at her sister, but Sarah did not look amused. "How 'bout it, Luke?"

He could feel the room grow warm again and suddenly wanted to be back on the other side of the island. "Yeah,

I'd love to, but Sarah is right. I'll be on call until the storm passes." But the tension of the moment was interrupted by the flashing light coming through the window. Luke walked over and pulled the curtains back for all to see.

"Someone's headlights?" Sarah asked.

"No," Luke said. "I think it's lightning."

As the lightning followed the thunder outside, their lights again began to flicker, and they all looked up at the old chandelier that swayed above them, watching it flicker. In the sudden darkness, they could hear the thunder growing closer.

CHAPTER THIRTY-TWO

Mary had seen the lightning, too. She had fallen asleep on the couch watching a show she could not remember, and now the dark room lit up in quick, random flashes. The TV had gone to static, and Mary turned it off. Through the window, she could see the snow flailing madly in the wind. At least they hadn't lost power, she thought. Upstairs, everything was quiet, and Mary hoped the storm would not wake her mother. She slid her feet into a pair of slippers, threw on her robe, and walked to the bottom of the stairs. The house seemed larger in the dark, every creak and shadow amplified. The rooms felt unfamiliar and strange to her.

Outside came another flash of lightning, followed quickly by a rumble of thunder. *This storm is throwing everything at us,* she thought. The hands of the old grandfather clock rested at 3:00 am. Mary wondered how the others were faring in the storm. Everything suddenly felt small and closed off, the island just a flickering speck in the sea of blackness. She had awoken to strange thoughts for many years, lost in the halfway world between lucidness and dreaming. She had never mastered it the way her mother had, and the dream journals she found in the closet were filled with such strange and terrifying things she could hardly believe her mother wasn't terrified to fall asleep every night. Or maybe she was. Though she was tired, her senses were fully aware. She sat down and tried to close her eyes, but her mind wandered to strange places. The storm. The past. Her mother's journal. She wished she had read more of them. Now more than ever, she had so many questions, and she wondered if her mother was replaying these same memories right now, drifting through the same dream world.

Through half-remembered dreams, her mother spoke of places hidden under the deepest realms of the lake and things that lay waiting. She spoke of strange things, and frequently, Mary could hear her mother scream out things she did not understand. And these days, when darkness set in early, the island had been cast in the shadow of something just beyond her senses.

She tried to banish such thoughts, but in the darkness her mind seemed to swim in them. *Is this what it's like, getting old? Waking up confused and alone in the darkness? Will this happen to me?* She turned on the light, but when she reached for something to read, all she could find was her mother's journal she had brought downstairs earlier. She had written down so much that she didn't tell Mary, and it seemed almost as if she had lived another whole life on the island. In the dim light of the living room, Mary opened the journal with the hope that it would ease her back to sleep:

... We didn't tell the others, because they'd have thought we were crazy. They would have stopped us, too. Maybe they should have. When they finally came back with the girls, Frank held them tight, held them so close I thought he would suffocate them. But the storm wasn't over—it was still as strong as ever—and God, I remember those waves, the way they crashed over the break wall, and the deafening roar. I'd never seen waves so high. I saw them pull away from the storm, and I ran down the side of the cliff until I met them at the dock. Mark and Jack looked relieved to be back on solid land. Did they know I had been watching the whole time? Did they know I was crazy enough to stand out in the storm and watch them until they had made it back safely? I don't know why I did. There was nothing I could have done, and yet I stayed and watched anyway, as if I had some part to play. I've never spoken to Mary about this, and I never will. I ran up to them, already ankle deep in water. They

saw me and waved me over, as if they were almost expecting to see me there. Both girls were crying and clinging to their father. But I did not see the other girl and her father there with them. "Where are the other two?" I had to scream over the storm. Jack said nothing, only shook his head. Frank was still holding Sarah and Alice, and Mark just looked at me and then back out at the lake.

"You have to go back out there! They're still alive!" How did I know that? I couldn't say at the time. I still can't. But I knew they were.

"We barely made it back alive, woman!" Mark screamed at me. I could smell the alcohol on his breath. He was in my face, and Jack had to pull us apart. "Mark's right, we almost died out there," Jack pleaded with me. But I knew he was wrong. And for some reason, I knew something awful was going to happen if we didn't help them.

I yelled at them, calling them cowards. I told them the whole island would know that they let a little girl and her father die. I told them God was watching, and he wouldn't forgive them either. But that last part did no good—we were all God-fearing children once upon a time, but that was lost long ago. And now the three of us looked at each other, barely able to stand upright in the raging storm.

Frank came up from behind, his girls both still in his arms. "She's right. We have to go back."

I won't write about what we said to each other next. There was more arguing. But what Frank decided was always scripture, and then I took the girls in my arms as Frank looked back at me. 'I'll be back with both of them. Take care of my daughters.' And then they were gone. They went back out on the lake, and I wasn't sure if I would see any of them ever again. That part was beyond my vision.

Mary dropped the journal when she heard a knock at the sliding doors in the kitchen. It was a quick tap-tap, but deliberate and loud, and as she rose from her chair, the lone table lamp began to flicker. She stood there motionless for what seemed like some time, waiting for any sound to rise above the roaring of the wind. Upstairs, her mother was still silent. As her heart pounded and the blood rushed to her head, her senses heightened. She felt foolish, knowing full well there were others on the island. Maybe someone had lost power? Or worse yet, been in an accident? Surely she couldn't ignore a cry for help, even if it was the middle of the night. She would hope someone would do the same for her. Yet still she stood there, unable to make her way to the kitchen. The lights flickered again. And again, she heard the knock. Three knocks this time, quick but with purpose.

This time, Mary found the courage to move her feet slowly toward the door. She flipped on the light and tried to focus her eyes on the darkness beyond the windowpanes.

"Hello?" Not loud enough to wake her mother, and most likely not loud enough for her unknown visitor to hear either. There was no response. As she approached the door, she could feel the wind force its way through the cracks around the door, and she hugged herself for warmth. She had not left the backyard light on, but she could hear the storm's invisible fury in the darkness. Another two knocks, more insistent this time. Whoever it was must have seen her, standing there in the light? She knew everyone on the island and feared none of them. Mary called out again to the darkness, and again she received no reply. When she approached the door and flipped on the backyard light, she saw nothing on the other side of the door. Outside, the shadows of the tree limbs blow about madly in the storm like some tentacled creature, reaching out in a frenzy in every direction. She quickly caught a glimpse of something moving in the shadows, something small. It ran from shadow to shadow in the farthest reaches of her backyard, just out of sight. It was a child. It had to be. But the only child on the island she knew of was Jack's boy. She unlocked the door, bracing for the cold, and opened it.

The rush of cold wind nearly froze her where she stood. In an instant, she felt totally enveloped, and fearing the cold would creep its way up to her mother, she closed the door behind her.

"Hello?!" She yelled this time. "Who's out there?"

Again, there was no response, and once more she saw a small shape retreating further into her backyard. There was no point in going back inside now, she thought. She was wide awake, and it would take a good half bottle of wine to get her back to sleep. She was growing tired of this. The idea that this might be a prank—at this hour and in this weather—began to make her blood boil, warming her just enough to withstand the elements. The frigid cold made her forget her fear, and she marched out into the snow, still hugging herself, scanning every shadow, her eyes stinging from the unrelenting snow. She scanned the untouched snow, looking for footprints.

"If you're out here, say something!"

Mary was now beyond the reach of the backyard lights, and as she stumbled in the darkness, she felt the cold, snowy wood of the backyard fence. Nothing and no one. She stared straight into the darkness, and the darkness looked back at her. For a moment, she could almost see herself asleep on her couch, sleeping, her mother's journal resting on her lap, dreaming of this very moment. But the painful numbness of her toes and fingers told her otherwise, and she laughed as she imagined what she looked like, standing in her yard at 3:00 am in her nightgown in the middle of a storm. She was wide awake now and felt she had earned at least half a bottle of wine. Mother wouldn't be up for hours, and she was desperate for the few hours of peace she had to herself. As she turned around to head back toward the house, she saw that the back door was wide open.

I know I closed that, she thought to herself. *I know it.* She stepped out of the darkness, forgetting the numbness in her fingers and toes. As she approached the house and looked up, she saw the light was on in her mother's room, though she saw no movement. *Is she awake?* Mary thought. *Did the knocking wake her up, too?* She walked up the steps and back into the warmth of the kitchen, closed the door behind her, and locked it. She stood silently, waiting to hear the creak of floorboards. Nothing. Mary kicked off her slippers, which were soaked from the snow, and stepped onto the floor, leaving a trail of damp footprints behind her. As she stepped into the living room, she heard the faint sound of music coming from upstairs. She could hear the crackle of the record player but could not yet place the song. But there was no doubt it was her mother's record player.

"Mom?" she called up the stairs. The floorboards creaked under her weight as she ascended the stairs, and she no longer heard the hissing of the radiators. As the warmth of the house slowly thawed her, she became aware of a burning sensation in her extremities. She breathed deeply as she approached the top of the steps, now at the landing. The music was clearer now. The song playing was "Let the Sunshine In," an older, stranger version sung by children, which she had never heard before. She froze in her tracks.

"Mom?" She could hear the fear in her own voice. "Mom, are you awake?" There was no answer.

Mary turned down the hallway and saw that her mother's door was slightly ajar. Again, she could see the strange orange light glowing from her lamp, snaking its way across the floor, like a luminescent welcome mat. The music seemed much louder now; it must have been at full volume. Mary had never liked this song, even as a child, and couldn't even begin to guess why her mother had chosen it. She reached out and knocked on the door.

"Mom?"

She slowly pushed the door open and saw that her mother was fast asleep on the bed. But as she entered the room to turn the record player off, she saw another figure—a smaller one—standing in the corner of the room where the orange light did not reach.

She was a little girl again, playing on the beach in what must have been midsummer, still long enough from the start of school to enjoy. In the sky above her, swirling colors swam in the hot, humid air. A few people she did not recognize were stepping out of the water. She could feel the sand between her toes and smiled. Behind her stood a sandcastle larger than any she had ever seen, and in front of it was a picnic blanket set for two, yet she was all alone. *Where is Mother?* she thought. She had always been forbidden to wander the beach alone, especially when it was getting close to dark. Already, she could see stars forming at the black horizon line where sky met lake. As more and more people began emerging from the lake, Mary began to wade into it, the water cold even on the hottest of days. She could not see her mother in the water, and she began to feel scared.

"Mom!" she cried out, again and again. And then, in the deep waters—deeper than she was ever allowed to go—she saw someone struggling to stay afloat, their arms flailing and head just bobbing above water. As she grew closer, she could see it was her mother. She was trying to scream for help, but only frenzied gurgles came out. Mary looked behind her and saw the vacant lifeguard chairs and watched as the other people began to leave for the night.

"Help us! You have to help my mom!" But she was too far away from the shore now, and the people were just black dots disappearing into the summer night. Now they were all alone, the two of them, and Mary could feel the water getting deeper and deeper until it was up to her neck.

"Mary! Mary! You have to help me! Please!" Her mother could barely stay afloat.

Mary dog-paddled over to her. She could barely see the shore now. "I'm coming!"

Her mother tried to reach out to her. "Give me your hand, Mary! Just give me your hand and pull me out!" Mary did as she was told, and her mother grabbed her hand and began pulling her down into the water. She screamed, and her mouth was filled with filthy, foul-tasting water. As she sank deeper, Mary looked down and saw that her mother was now old, her pupils cloudy white with cataracts. Down, down she was being pulled into a whirlpool of foulness and black water. Up above, she could see the starry night sky growing distant, the celestial flickers dwindling, then gone. Enveloped in icy blackness, she could hold her breath no longer, and when she opened her mouth to scream, the cold black water filled her mouth, then her throat, then her lungs—

As she came out of the blackness, Mary was back in her mother's bedroom again, bathed in the orange light that emanated from the lamp on the bedside table. The strange being stood in the corner, immersed in darkness but still very present. The windows were closed, yet it seemed to be snowing in the room. Mary could see the puffs of her breath. Her right hand felt trapped inside a tight warmth. She looked down and saw her right hand forcing its way into her mother's toothless mouth, moving as if beyond her control, as if she were watching some distant nightmare from afar. Her hand moved over the dry tongue and ignored her mother's futile attempts to bite down with toothless gums. Still further, her hand went in, now forcing its way down into her mother's throat, and as her mother gagged, Mary began to cry.

"Please don't make me do this! Please make it stop!"

But the small figure in the darkness simply watched silently as the old woman on the bed struggled and squirmed. It seemed the more Mary tried to resist, the harder her fist forced its way down her mother's throat.

Her mother stared up at her, tears streaming down her cheeks, and tried to scream.

The strange children on the record continued to sing their song, but now it seemed to be playing too fast. The chorus looped and looped and looped as snowflakes continued to fall inside the room.

"I'm so sorry," Mary cried.

As she watched the life drift from her mother, Mary could not help but cry as all the years of memories washed down her mother's face in seconds. As those white pupils gazed up at her, then at the ceiling, she knew her mother was gone. The figure in the room still watched from the darkness, and as the strange flakes fell, Mary felt numb as she watched her hand withdraw slowly from her mother's mouth. She could see blood, saliva, and bite marks on her hand, but felt nothing, as if watching herself from a distance in a dream. Strange whispers echoed in her head, taunting her, some strange language that spoke forward and backward at the same time, in layered whispers. She heard all of this above the record's music, which was now spinning faster. The singers' voices were now almost comically high-pitched, skipping over and over again. The figure, still concealed in the darkness, stood and watched as the windows suddenly blew open, filling the room with frigid air and snow. Mary felt herself turn slowly toward the window, her eyes focused on the white void of the storm swirling about before her. In the snowy abyss, she saw her mother again: younger, smiling, her arms reaching out. *Come to me, child.* The words did not match her lips, like the old dubbed Italian horror films she had watched back in college. *Come to me, child.* And just like that, the room and everything in it faded from her view, wiped clean as if it were all a bad dream. *I'm coming, Mother*, she thought.

CHAPTER THIRTY-THREE

Alice slipped into the hot bath and felt warm for the first time since arriving on the island. That was something she always remembered about growing up here: the long, cold winters in the poorly insulated houses. Everything was old here, she thought. She was tired of it before she had even arrived. She had grown to love the dry heat of Southern California: the long, sunny days and the sunsets over the ocean. L.A. was modern, hot, crowded, and fake, and she loved every minute of it. This place felt so far away from everything, and it seemed to her that it had hardly changed at all. As she soaked in the ancient claw bathtub, Alice found she still could not get warm. The whole house was drafty, and no matter how hot she ran the water, she remained chilled to the bone. She felt a cold draft on the back of her neck, but when she looked, all the windows were closed.

As she turned up the hot water again, Alice heard the creaking and moaning of the old pipes in the wall, as if struggling not to freeze in the dropping temperature. She had already swiped comforters from three of the guest beds and made her bed into a virtual igloo. She could not imagine how Sarah endured the winters here, or how anyone could willingly stay in a place so devoid of culture, people, and life. But here they were, living a life she cared nothing about. She thought about the islanders, then thought again of Sarah.

What did she mean when she said she hadn't called? Alice thought. *Was she lying? Or drunk?* When Alice received the call, she recognized her sister's voice. But when she played the messages for Sarah, it was clearly someone else. Someone...younger. Was someone playing a trick on her? she thought. But no one really knew about their relationship. She told the men she took to bed that Sarah was just "my little sis who lives on an island in the middle of fucking nowhere." And there was never anything more than that. The lights in the room flickered. *Shit*, she thought. *Please don't go out for the night.* She had forgotten to charge her phone, and the battery was low. Outside, above the wind, she could hear the strange sound of static coming from the loudspeakers. Sarah had mentioned something to her about them malfunctioning the past few days, but she had hardly been listening. It almost sounded like a voice was counting down. As the lights flickered again, she realized this was going to be the new normal until she left the island. The lights went out again, and this time they did not come back on.

Alice sighed. "Shit." The temperature in the room began to drop, as if someone had opened a window. "Sarah!" She sat up in the tub, splashing water on the floor. "Sarah, I can't see shit!" *Has she gone to bed already?* she thought. *It's so early.* Alice leaned over the side of the tub and felt around on the floor for her phone. When she found it, she lit the phone screen and saw that it read 3:00. Then the phone died. *There's no way I could have been in here for that long,* she thought. She sat in the darkness for some time as the countdown over the speakers continued. Her bathwater grew cold again, but as she turned on the faucet, even colder water came out. *Fuck it, I'm getting out.* But when she began to rise, she heard what sounded like wet footsteps approaching in the darkness of the bathroom.

"Sarah, is that you?" she asked.

Alice could not tell which direction the steps were coming from. No light from outside shone through the lone window. *There's someone else in here with me.* She sat back down in the tub. *I can run for the door.* She laughed. *That's what Sarah would do. Stop being a child.* Suddenly, the faucet turned on by itself in the dark. She could feel the coldness spreading all around her.

"Sarah, quit fucking around!" she snapped. But as she said it, the footsteps came faster toward the tub, and suddenly she heard what she thought was the sound of someone sticking something into the water. She tried to stand but found that she could not move. The water had gone from cold to frigid in mere seconds, and suddenly the whispering no longer sounded as if it were coming from the loudspeakers but from inside the room. She tried to scream but found that she could not. As she sank deeper into a different kind of darkness, she saw for a moment the face of someone from long ago, a face without a name, watching her drift away into the frozen blackness.

CHAPTER THIRTY-FOUR

Mark was happy to leave the radio tower behind him. He had not destroyed the painting—only turned it around to face the wall—but as he drove, he wished that he had. He had not meant to paint the boat—could not remember doing it—and now its image followed him no matter how fast he sped on his snowmobile. The wind and snow were nearly blinding, but he knew the forest paths well enough to speed through even the most treacherous parts of it. No one had replied to his calls from the walkie-talkie, and something besides the storm had left him feeling worried. Old memories crept up on him, and he drove even faster. The night had raised too many questions, so he was going to the place where he usually found his answers. He hoped Mary would still be awake at this hour, but if not, he would have to wake her. If she felt the same things he was feeling right now, then she was probably already awake.

As he rode on, he heard the static from the speakers start up again. *It's as if someone's at the radio tower*, he thought. *But I'm the only one who has keys to the place.* Then music started to play slowly and faintly, growing over the noise of the storm. It took him mere seconds to identify the song: Ave Maria. It was beautiful, but he had not selected it, and part of him wanted to turn around and find out exactly who had. But he was too far away now. The other islanders would undoubtedly think it was him, drunk and stupid and blasting music over the loudspeakers in the middle of the night. It was loud, loud enough to wake the entire island. The snow seemed to be coming down in thick, blinding blankets of white, so heavy that Mark had trouble seeing at times. He could just make out the white-coated shapes of trees and barely missed hitting a few of them. Truthfully, he wanted to be home, someplace warm with a tumbler of bourbon, watching this mess from a safe distance. As he approached a crossroads in the woods, he caught something from the corner of his eye, flashing near where the forest spilled out into the streets. For a moment, he considered going on, but felt compelled to see exactly what this night would bring.

He maneuvered his vehicle into the thicker part of the woods, closer to where the light appeared. It flashed briefly, then disappeared, then reappeared. It seemed the closer he got, the more the distance between them grew, until suddenly the bright light seemed to change course and head directly toward him. Mark felt his heart pound and gripped the handlebars tightly.

"I'm not afraid of whatever you are, you sonofabitch," he muttered to himself. Now the light was directly in front of him, headed straight at him, and fast. As their game of chicken began, he clenched his teeth, ready for whatever shape death would take. Then light suddenly dodged out of his way, and Mark heard a loud "What the fuck?" He recognized the voice. It was Luke.

He pulled over and removed his goggles. Luke's snowmobile had skidded off the trail and into a ditch. He stepped off and surveyed it. "Goddamnit." He looked over at Mark and shook his head. "Well, that's twice now you've caused me to get into an accident today. That's gotta be somebody's personal best."

"What the hell are you doing out here at this hour?" Mark yelled over the wind.

"My job. What the hell are *you* doing out here at this hour?" Luke attempted to pull his vehicle from the ditch but found that he couldn't. "Great. Fucking wonderful."

Mark shook his head. "I was on my way to Mary's place."

Luke was only half-listening, still pulling on his machine. "Oh yeah? She expecting you?"

"No."

Luke gave up, exasperated. "Look, Mark, I'm sure you're drunk just like everyone else on this island is right now, but I'm trying to keep things from falling apart."

"I'm not drunk, you little prick. Something's happened, and I need to talk to Mary."

Luke stood still for a moment. "What happened?"

"That doesn't matter."

"Did something happen, Mark? I'm going to find out, one way or another. You might as well tell me."

But Mark wasn't listening anymore. The headlight from his snowmobile had caught something moving through the forest. He pointed past Luke. "Shut up. Look out there."

Luke turned around. "I don't see anything."

"Just shut your goddamn mouth and look!"

Luke looked again, and then he too saw something moving in the farthest reaches of the light. Within the heavy wind, he could hear no footsteps. He took out his flashlight. "Is there someone out there? Hello?" The two of them looked at each other, then stepped tentatively into the forest.

"Who the hell would be out walking around outside in this?" Mark asked.

"*We're* out walking around in this." Luke waved the beam of his flashlight around. They were further in the woods now, and the glow from Mark's headlight was becoming more and more dim. Both of their feet were half frozen, and Mark could feel the wind ripping right through his jacket.

Luke scanned the forest. "They had to be around here."

Mark pointed at the ground. "Look."

Luke looked down and saw the footprints Mark was pointing at. "Well, at least we know we're not crazy." With Luke's headlamp on, they followed the tracks as best they could in the snow.

"They're close, wherever they are," Luke added. "The way this snow's coming down, these will be gone in minutes."

They both yelled out their "Hello"s and "Anybody there?"s to no avail. The wind stung their faces, and the snow carried along with it stung their eyes. Up ahead, they could hear the breaking of branches on the ground, the sound of it getting closer. Luke pointed to an area of darkness just beyond the reach of their flashlights. "Over there!"

They ran into the darkness, the beams of their flashlights strobing this way and that, until they came upon a figure's outline in their beams. Luke shined his light on it. From behind, he could already see that the figure was completely naked, their long hair going down close to the waist. The figure did not seem to respond to their voices or the probing of their flashlights.

Luke's feet were frozen. He shivered as he watched the bare figure walk through the snow. "Who is that out there?"

The figure stopped in its tracks, then slowly turned towards them. As she turned around, they could see the clear signs of exposure on Mary's bare skin: both feet from the ankle down were black and blue with frostbite. She wasn't shivering and seemed completely unaware of the elements.

Luke took off his jacket and wrapped it around her. "Mark, stay here with her. I've got a thermal blanket on my snowmobile. She must be in shock, and she doesn't have a chance if we don't get her out of here. Put your jacket under her feet." Mark did as he was told, and as he supported her, he could feel her cold body through his jacket. Luke could see the sickly blackened, blistered flesh of advanced frostbite working its way up from her feet to her ankle. He already knew that she would have to lose both. "Jesus, Mary," he muttered under his breath.

Luke was already running back to his snowmobile and shouted, "Just keep her warm; I'll be right back!"

Mark held Mary close in his arms, and her glazed eyes tried to focus on him. He tried to smile. He had no idea how long she had been out in this or why.

"It's going to be ok," was all he could say, even though he knew that to be a lie. Her eyes finally focused, and she looked at him.

"Mark," her voice sounded ancient. "What did you do with the father?"

Mark stared at her. "What father?"

"The man on the boat. The father and his daughter."

"Mary, he drowned. We tried to save him, but he drowned. They both drowned. Don't you remember?"

"But you went back, Mark. My mother said you went back. What did you find, Mark? You found something. I know you found something."

Mark said nothing, just looked at her in horror. "We didn't find anything. You know, we didn't find anything, Mary. Everybody knows that."

Mary shook her head slowly. "No, Mark, I know you all found the father. I know Frank made you go back. What was it, Mark? What did you bury in the quarry? Who did you bury in the quarry?"

Mark said nothing. Off in the darkness of the forest, he could see the light from Luke's snowmobile approaching slowly, navigating through the untrodden woods with caution. Mary grabbed his face with her icy hands.

"You have to tell them, Mark. You have to tell them what happened, or we're all going to die on this island."

She grew more agitated now, tears rolling down her frozen cheeks. Mark placed his hand over her mouth. "Shhh, it's going to be ok," he said. Then he placed his other hand over her nose and pressed as hard as he could. He struggled to grasp it with his missing ring finger. "I'm sorry, Mary," he grunted as he pressed harder. With the little strength she had left, Mary tried to pull his hand away, but the last of her strength ebbed, and all she could do was watch him smother the last breaths of her life. And then she was gone.

Mark and Mary's bodies were illuminated by Luke's lights and then just as quickly fell back into darkness, and Mark had trouble readjusting his eyes in the dark. Luke came scrambling through the woods with a blanket in his hands. A few times, he slipped in the darkness, his eyes focused on them and not on the path.

"I've got the blanket," he shouted. "How is she?"

Mark stood there, holding Mary's body close against him. He wanted to vomit. His memory was poisoned, now and forever. Or maybe it had always been that way, ever since that day. But holding her body close sold the scene to Luke, and right now, that was the only thing that mattered. Self-preservation. *Damn them all, and damn this island*, he thought. Luke was getting closer now, his headlamp shining on them.

"Is she ok?" he shouted again.

"She's dead," Mark said, without looking up.

"Jesus Christ," Luke ran his hands through his frozen hair. "Jesus Christ, Jesus fucking Christ." He knelt next to her. "If only we'd found her sooner. Fuck, I should have brought the blanket as soon I saw someone…"

"Shut up," Mark said, and laid Mary's head gently down on the snow beneath her. "Just shut up." As he stood, he continued to look at her body. "She was dead anyway. There was nothing we could have done. Must've been out here for hours."

Luke fought back tears and tried to hide them with anger. "What the fuck was she doing walking out here? I mean, who does that? Was she drunk like everyone else on this fucking island? Was she high?"

Mark exhaled slowly, letting the frozen tendrils from his breath rise slowly above his head like a broken halo in the light from the snowmobile. "I don't know."

Luke took the blanket and gently placed it over Mary's body. The two stared down at it for some time without words as the snow came down and began to bury it.

"Her mom's home alone," Luke said. "I'm gonna go there first, then I'll come back for the body."

"With what? I thought you crashed your car."

"I did. I don't know. I'll find something. I'll go there to check on her, and then I'm gonna' have to tell the others. Lines are down right now. No phone calls coming in or out, at least for tonight."

Mark nodded and said nothing. Luke looked at him. "You coming?"

"Coming where?"

"With me. I've got a lot of ground to cover tonight. I'd appreciate all the help I can get."

Mark sighed. "Yeah, yeah. We should ride back to her mom's house. You're right."

"How will we find her body when we come back?"

They looked around. Mark walked to one of the low-hanging branches of a pine tree, broke a branch off with little effort, and stuck it in the ground like a stake. "Let's go."

Chapter Thirty-Five

Out across the ice, Sarah heard a familiar voice calling her name. She was back in the forest of pine and couldn't tell if it was night or day. The path where she took her daily jog was gone now, as were the lamp posts that lit up the path at night. All remnants of island life were gone, and the island felt untamed. Through the thicket of the trees, she could still hear the voice calling her name. She made her way through the thick patches of pine and needles, and the earth beneath her felt strange and unnatural. When she looked down, the ground beneath her was covered with the bloodied, skinless bodies of deer, squirrels, and other animals mutilated beyond recognition. The air grew thick with flies, and their maddening chorus was deafening. She ran back into the darkness of the forest, nearly slipping several times on the slick, bloodied forest floor all around her. As she ran in the direction of the lakeshore, she could hear her name being called once more. It was clearer this time. "I'm coming," she tried to call back, but no words left her mouth. Finally, she reached a break in the forest that gave way to rocks and then the lake. The surface was completely covered in ice, and the white light was blinding. The carcasses and flies were now safely behind her, but she found no comfort in the sight of the endless expanse of frozen lake. From here, she could not see the mainland on the other side. The lake seemed to extend into eternity in every direction. Someone called her name once more.

Out on the lake, she could just make out a figure, and as the whiteness of the world came into focus, she could finally see that it was Alice. But now she wasn't calling her name; she was screaming. In the air around her were hundreds—thousands—of seagulls, all hovering above her, clawing at her, pecking her. She stood there naked, covered in blood, cuts, and gashes, alone and screaming for Sarah. Sarah ran to the edge where ice met rock. She tried to place her foot onto the ice but could not. She felt weighed down, as if there were magnets in her boots. Her sister was still screaming in agony Sarah had never heard before. The screams were angry, directed at Sarah—hateful, painful screams and curses, almost primal in their fury. Sarah cried that she was sorry over and over again, but her mouth would not open. She could only watch as her sister's body was slowly torn apart by the gulls until there was nothing left but a skeleton, still standing, and screaming at Sarah. And then Sarah opened her mouth to scream, and scream she did.

Sarah's screaming had awoken her, and it took mere moments to realize that she was at home, in her bed. But something was different. Something was wrong. The room was cold. No, not cold. Freezing. Unbearable. She jumped out of bed, threw a hoodie on, and closed the window, which was halfway open. She reached out and felt the radiator. Ice cold. The heat had gone out. Sarah's heart raced. *Alice must be freezing to death!* She threw on a pair of pajama pants and slipper socks. *If she wasn't furious about being here before, she definitely will be now,* Sarah thought. She stepped out into the hallway, pulled some extra blankets from the linen closet, and made her way down the hallway. The air was so frigid that she could see her breath. The whole house was quiet. Even the wind seemed muted, the storm outside still visibly raging but silent behind the safety of windows and doors.

From underneath Alice's door, Sarah could feel an icy breeze. *Is her window open, too?* Sarah knocked gently on the door. No response. She knocked again, louder this time.

"Alice?" There was still no reply from inside. Sarah sighed, then opened the door slowly. If Alice was asleep, she did not want to awaken her to a frigid house. She would cover Alice with the extra blanket, then leave as quickly and quietly as she could. A strange, unsettling feeling came over her as she twisted the knob. The house felt too still, as if she were the last semblance of life in a cold, indifferent world. As the door creaked open, Sarah saw that Alice's bed was empty. None of the windows were open. She stepped into the room and felt the cold wetness on the carpet dampening her socks. The room was freezing, and Sarah could see her breath in clouds above her head. Outside, the silent storm raged on, and all she could see beyond the cold glass of the window was blank whiteness. On the other side of the room, the bathroom light was on, the door slightly ajar.

"Alice?" Again, there was no reply. She touched the side of the bed where Alice had been sleeping and felt nothing but coldness. Up on the wall, she saw that the clock was frozen at 3:00 am, just like all the others. It's possible that Alice couldn't sleep. The time difference alone would be enough to justify that. But Sarah couldn't escape the dreadful feeling that something was wrong. As she walked slowly to the bathroom door and knocked once again, the feeling grew heavier in the pit of her stomach as if it were poisoning her very soul. She knocked again. Nothing. And then she pushed the door open.

She could not recall how long she stared at the scene before her or if any scream had escaped from her mouth as the mad rush of horror flooded her mind. Logic and reason were gone, lost out there in the silent storm somewhere, never to be seen again. Encased in ice was her sister, still in the tub, a look of horror frozen on her face. Her eyes were wide open, frozen in mid-scream. Both her hands were reaching out, only the fingertips visible just above the surface of the ice. She had died in terror, in absolute agony, and all Sarah could do was stare. As her senses slowly came back together, she grabbed the closest thing she could find—a plunger—and began to hammer the wooden end into the ice. It splintered and broke after the first few strikes, and Sarah collapsed on the floor and sobbed. With the last member of her family taken from her, she had never felt more alone—and more vulnerable—in her life. As the ghostly whispers began again over the loudspeakers outside, she knew it was only a matter of time before it came back for her, too.

She closed the bedroom door behind her, vowing to never open it again. There was no signal on her phone, and she knew that service would be out all over the island. With as much strength as she could muster, Sarah limped downstairs. She favored her right ankle, which was still very swollen. It could take some weight, and the horror of what had just happened made her forget the pain. Downstairs, she turned on the ham radio and heard nothing but static crackle.

She grabbed the microphone, her voice trembling as she spoke: "Hello? Luke? Luke, are you there?" She sank her head onto her free hand. She was exhausted now and heartbroken. And she was terrified beyond anything that she had ever felt before.

Someone had to answer. She knew the others almost always left their radios on in case of an emergency. Then she remembered the hotel party and wondered if anyone had thought to turn that one on or whether they could even hear. She suddenly understood what Luke had meant about trying to keep the others safe. The microphone was ice-cold to the touch, but Sarah gripped it tightly, as if it were her last chance to cry out for rescue from a fading world.

"Hello, is there anyone out there who can hear me?" Her eyes welled up, and she could not stop the tears that were rolling down her cheeks. "Can anyone please hear me?" Static. Nothing. But as she started to get back up, she heard what she thought was a voice on the other end and quickly sat down again.

"Hello, is someone there?"

Muffled whispers rose above the static until one became clearer. "I can hear you."

Sarah listened, confused. It was the voice of a little girl. And then again, the voice spoke: "I can hear you."

Sarah began to tremble. "Who is this?" There was no response. She gripped the microphone more tightly. "Who is this?" But on the other end, all she could hear was the sound of waves, echoing and crashing against rocks. Then there was nothing but static and her own voice echoing back to her.

The power was still not back on, and Sarah could feel the room—the whole house—getting even colder. Her cell phone was minutes away from dying, not that she had any signal anyway. Her throat was raw from crying, but when she lifted a glass to the faucet, no water came out. *It's Frozen,* she thought. *Fucking frozen.* As she stood there in darkness, the room was once again illuminated by quick flashes of lightning. Sarah walked to the window, felt the wind coming through the smallest crevices around the frame. She felt years away from the mainland or from anyone. She knew she was at the opposite end of the island from everyone else, but she also knew that she could not stay here.

Something is happening, she thought. *Something I don't understand, and I'm not going to stick around for whatever it is to happen to me next.* Sarah hobbled over to the closet and dug out the warmest coat she could find, along with every other piece of winter clothing she could find: a hat, a scarf, and a pair of leather gloves slightly too large for her small hands. She knew where she had to go: to the one person on the island who would understand all of this: Mary. She lived closer than the others, who were now undoubtedly drunk at the hotel. *I can't stay here,* she thought. *But Mary will know what to do.*

As Sarah opened the front door, the cold, wet darkness of the storm exploded into the room. In the dull glow of the storm, she could see mountains of snowdrifts before her. Walking through them would be difficult, even more so with her injured ankle. The car was now sunk beneath the surface of the lake, and every other vehicle was at the other end of the island. She could walk towards town and try to find a snowmobile, a golf cart, or even a pair of skis. But that was in the opposite direction, and even the distance between her and Mary's house was daunting. It could take hours, maybe more. She closed the door behind her and ventured out into the storm, leaving the house—and her sister—behind her. Her left ankle ached, but she found she could still put a little weight on it for now. As she stepped onto the white stretch where the road had been, Sarah stared ahead into the darkness. Fumbling in her oversized gloves, she turned the flashlight on. *The fastest way between two points is a straight line. Mark said that when he was drunk and taking a piss in the snow*, she recalled. The road curved around through the trees and the hills. Sarah knew it would be faster to trek directly through the woods. It was not the safest option; trees and branches could come down in the wind. But in the storm, it could take her at least an hour to make the trip, and she knew she was running out of time. Into the mad whirlwind of the storm, she disappeared. The low, dim light of her flashlight dimmed, then was gone. The indentations of her footprints were erased by snow and wind just as quickly as she had made them.

Chapter Thirty-Six

The Sandy Stone Hotel sat quietly in the storm. Its windows glowed a strange shade of orange as the candles inside projected strange shadows. A relic of the island's past, it had endured storms of every season and was now content to let this storm have its way with her. Near the entrance, stealthy snow drifts had buried the parked cars and snowmobiles. A tree had fallen across the road, the sound of its impact muffled by the constant howl of the storm. No one inside the hotel could discern the difference between thunder and wind, nor did they care. They had taken great care to block out the troubles of the storm.

Inside, Amy had lit a fire in the giant stone fireplace that looked out upon the large lounge area. They sat in wicker chairs or stood and talked. All night, they had enjoyed their cocktails and played their music. When the lights had gone out, they lit candles, gathered around the fireplace, and continued drinking until they no longer remembered there was a storm outside. Amy sat at the piano and played off-key, but no one seemed to care, singing along with the songs.

Dan had filled a few pages with work notes until the drinks hit him and he could no longer write. Now he simply enjoyed the company and felt completely removed from the rest of the world. The mainland itself felt light-years away. His eyes scanned the old paintings on the walls, all the people and places from the island's very beginning. He felt warm and dizzy and knew the following morning would be rough. The Mayor fell back into the seat next to him, and Dan heard the loud crunch of the wicker. He held another full bottle—recently opened—and poured some into Dan's still unfinished drink.

"Just topping you off, sir," the mayor laughed.

Dan nodded, and they toasted each other as they both took a sip. "Well," Dad said, "at least I won't have to drive home tonight."

The mayor laughed. "And even if you tried, you wouldn't get very far. Nah, right now you're at the safest place on the island. Some of Sandy Stone's finest here, for sure."

"So, we're actually not supposed to be here right now?"

"Well," the Mayor pondered this. "Yes and no. Mostly no, but the yes part I think justifies the no part."

Dan stared at him blankly.

"What I mean is, we haven't asked permission from the owner to stay here. But seeing as there's a storm of this magnitude, we all know the owner would have wanted us to look after the place in case something happens."

Dan laughed. "And if something happens because we're here? What then?"

The mayor nodded. "Don't you worry about that. This isn't our first rodeo, and it certainly won't be the last. Every shop and hotel owner knows the risk when they leave the island for the winter. We're more or less a collective group of caretakers, and good ones at that."

Dan squinted in the dim firelight. "I see."

"Besides, by the time they come back, you'll be long gone. Nothing to worry about tonight. Just relax and enjoy the good company. It's all you can do, really."

"I was wondering if you could tell me something more about the island, something you wouldn't tell an average tourist? I haven't lived here nearly as long as you."

"Like what?"

"Well, I mean, every town has its fair share of weird, crazy, or tragic stories. I know mine sure as hell did. You know, the shit that only the locals talk about. Like a strange urban legend or a creepy ghost story?"

The mayor sat back in his chair and said nothing for some time. He finished the last of his drink. "I'm on the board of the Sandy Stone Historical Society..." He let the sentence hang there for a moment, then he looked over at Dan. "You know, for the longest time, this island's been a vacation spot for people all over Ohio. But it wasn't always that way."

"What was it before?"

"Well, back in Prohibition days, it was a bootleggers' paradise, the midway point between Canada and the US. Lots of booze is brought over here illegally. Lots of booze hidden here," he laughed. "Probably some are still hidden. You know, there's an old Catholic church that burned down in the '90s. There was never much interest in rebuilding it, but underneath it were the cellars where they hid all the booze."

Dan sat back and felt himself relax in the warmth of the fireplace. "And down there in those cellars, someone died? Or was he locked inside? Or murdered?"

The mayor poured himself another drink. He cleared his throat and scratched the back of his head. "Nah, no one's ever been murdered here, at least not in my time. But those cellars went back further than just Prohibition. They were there since the War of 1812. This island was a temporary holding place for British prisoners until their transport could be arranged and they were sent to the mainland. It was usually where negotiations were made for their release."

Dan smiled. "And someone died there, right?"

The mayor shrugged. "People die everywhere. Even on this island. I'm sure a few did."

"And that's all? No tragic deaths? No accidents? I don't mean to sound grim. But I just read an article about Yosemite, and you'd be shocked how many stories they have about backpackers going missing and turning up dead."

The mayor hesitated. "Well, that's a major national park. We're just a small island. In all my life, I've only ever lived through one tragedy."

"Just one?"

"One's enough. More than enough, trust me."

"What happened?"

"It was summertime—our peak season—one of those hot, humid days when the sky seemed perfectly clear. Then, out of nowhere, a massive thunderstorm hit even before the sirens could go off. Next thing we knew, we got a call about two little girls stranded on a dinghy boat. Couldn't have been older than 10 and 12."

"What happened to them?"

"Well, the coast guard already had their hands full because dozens of people were stranded everywhere. So a few of us had to go out on our own to get them."

"You went with them?"

"I didn't. A few other people here took one of the larger speedboats and went to find them. It was a miracle that they did. They were terrified but still alive. Another fifteen minutes and their boat would have gone completely under."

"So, they were rescued?"

The mayor finished his drink. "Well, by the time they got out there, there was another boat nearby, with two people onboard. A father and his little girl. Probably about 10? Don't know who they were. Just tourists, out for a boat ride like everyone else."

"Did they rescue them too?"

The mayor looked down at the floor. His eyes seemed to water. "The waves were treacherous, and they nearly capsized a few times. If they had stayed out there any longer, they would have gone under. Once they got the two girls aboard, they had to make a choice. They could risk everyone by going after them or return home, call for help, and hope that someone would come. The girls' father was with them, and he wanted to go back. None of them felt right about it. But then what do you do? Everyone always thinks that if they were in those circumstances, they'd be brave and do the right thing. But being there and having to make those decisions, there's a gravity there, a weight—I don't know what to call it, but we all felt it that day."

Dan said nothing for a while. "So, the other two—the father and daughter—they drowned?"

The mayor nodded slowly.

"Why didn't someone go back for them?"

The Mayor started to reply, but then noticed how quiet the room had become. The others were listening to the story, too. An air of solemnity settled over the room.

Amy put her hands on her hips. "I think that's enough story time for tonight, Mr. Mayor."

The Mayor smiled sadly. "I was just sharing our history."

Amy looked over at Dan. "Listen, there are some stories we prefer to keep to ourselves. It was a tragic day. Nobody likes talking about it. Nobody likes hearing about it. Those wounds took ages for our community to heal, and we'd prefer not to have them reopened."

Dan threw his hands up. "I get it." Then, to the Mayor, "I'm sorry if I was prying. But I appreciate you sharing, of course."

Amy stared at him. "Nobody here wants to remember that. This place has always been about good times and happy memories. It's a place that people want to come back to. People leave their miserable, unhappy places and come here to Sandy Stone. That's what it's always been.

Dan looked up and smiled. "This place is just like any other place. It can be just as tragic or unhappy as it wants to be. Nobody has a right to whitewash it. Not even the people who know it best."

For a moment, they all stood there looking at Dan, then at each other. The room had grown cold, and the candles began to flicker. The Mayor's hand shook slightly as he poured himself yet another drink. "Will someone close that goddamn window?"

Dan picked up a candle and walked over to Amy. "I'm going to go find out where that draft is coming from. It's fucking freezing in here. In the meantime, how about if we just put this thing to rest? Play something nice for us on the piano."

She looked at him with narrowed eyes. "What's something nice?"

He smiled, and she could see his teeth glitter in the candlelight. "How about something Christmassy?"

Amy shook her head and sat down at the piano. She paused for a moment, mentally scanning all the Christmas songs she knew. A somber mood had settled over the group, and she didn't feel like playing anything cheerful.

The storm had not subsided in the least, but the roar of the fireplace and limitless supply of booze kept them warm. She began to play *In the Bleak Midwinter*. A few people continued talking, but then grew silent as she played, her dark silhouette moving like ink against the glowing fire. A few people began singing along, while others sat silently and listened. Everyone tried to ignore the fact that the room was growing colder and several candles had been blown out by the draft Dan could not find. There was a general sense of unease that had been building since The Mayor told his story. And then suddenly, someone screamed.

It had not come from within the lounge where most of them sat. It was distant, yet still within the confines of the hotel. Everyone looked around as the candles flickered violently. Amy stopped playing, and they all listened. The scream had been a woman's, loud and painful. The sound of the wind grew louder outside, roaring against the old building and shaking it hard with its ice-cold grip.

Dan looked around at the dimly lit faces in candlelight. "Who's missing?"

"Should we take a roll call?" someone asked from the darkness.

The Mayor stood, swayed for a moment, and then fell back into his chair. "I don't even know who's in our group."

"It sounded like it came from upstairs," Amy said, trembling a bit.

Now, everyone was silent. They could hear only the angry hissing from the steam radiators, from places unknown in the dark room. It was even colder now, and the strange draft continued to grow stronger. The slow flickering of the candles became more frenzied until, one by one, they were extinguished, each blown out by quick gusts. One at a time, their flames disappeared into shadowy darkness, until only the lonely glow of the fireplace remained. And then came another scream.

This one was a man's voice. Quick and sudden, full of pain, and then it stopped, and the room was silent again. Someone in the room began to cry. The Mayor sat up in his chair and could barely make out the others in the fading glimmer from the fire. A few people had taken out their cellphones and were using their flashlights to look around. Then they heard a low monotone moan. It grew louder, coming from every direction in the room.

"It's pipes," The Mayor muttered, his glass shaking in his hand. "The pipes are freezing."

The moan slowly grew to a low roar, then a metallic grinding shriek all around them.

"Pipes don't freeze that fast," Amy said.

The interior of the hotel sounded as if its innards were grinding all around them, breaking apart at the seams. They could hear cracks forming on the walls, and bits of debris began to fall onto their heads.

"It's so cold," someone said.

The Mayor felt his heart begin pounding faster. This quiet, safe room full of friends and neighbors had turned into something else. There was something present that he could not comprehend, a smell or sound that seemed both familiar and alien to him. In the growing darkness, he could hear a few of the others whispering. He looked over at the piano in the last of the flickering firelight, and Amy was gone. He could see the clock on the wall still read 3:00; The hands had stopped moving. The glow from the fire was fading, and as The Mayor looked at the fireplace, he could see that snow was falling through the chimney. The room went completely dark, and no one spoke, not even a whisper. The Mayor suddenly felt as if he were all alone, not just in that room, but on the whole island. He felt millions of years away from his home on the mainland, and his longing to return had never been stronger. He wanted to cry out, to scream out his late wife's name. But instead, he waited silently with the others. In the darkness, he heard someone crying. After a few moments, their wailing became muffled and then gone.

He stood there, motionless, for what seemed like ages. All he could hear was the pounding of blood in his head and the wind outside, which had not dissipated at all since the night had begun. Alone in the dark, the Mayor realized that he did not know this place. The room suddenly stank of dead fish or something rotten. Tired of the silence, he took a deep breath and called out, "Is everyone ok?"

The scream he heard then was not one but all of them at once, screaming such as he had never heard before. It was anguished, miserable, and hateful. And it was all around him. He could hear movement now, quick footsteps, almost a mad scampering. He heard things being knocked over and something glass falling to the floor and shattering. He wanted to cry out, but did not want to give away his location in the darkness. The Mayor suddenly recalled as a young boy reading about the damned souls in hell, suffering for eternity in endless lakes of fire. Beasts that men had no names for, people burned alive and torn apart throughout eternity, and he had always imagined their screams. That was what it sounded like now. He kept a hand over his mouth to cover his whimpering, and as he searched desperately for any prayer he could possibly remember, all he could manage was, "I'm sorry. I'm so sorry."

Then he could feel their cold hands all around him, grabbing at his clothes. Then a hand grabbed his hair and pulled—pulled hard. Someone grabbed his hand and bit into it. The Mayor screamed as more invisible hands dragged him down onto the floor. He tried to break away, but could see nothing and only felt the weight of them holding him down. They were beating him now, clawing at him and screaming. He felt his flesh being torn and felt the warmth of his blood running down his body. As he began to grow numb from the pain, he hoped it would be over quickly. Then he felt two fingers with long fingernails probing his face until they found his eye sockets.

"Please, God," was all he could mutter.

The fingers crunched down hard, and the Mayor screamed along with the others in horror, pain, and madness.

Chapter Thirty-Seven

Sarah stumbled her way through the dense pine forest, now caked with a thick layer of snow. Her flashlight revealed very little along the path, and though she knew every inch of the island, she felt as if she were lost in a dream. There were quick glimpses of familiar spots, but they were laid out in such a way that was unreal to her. Lightning flashed, giving her quick glimpses of the woods. All around her, she could see fallen tree limbs across her path, and she almost wished she had stuck to the streets instead.

Several times, she tripped over stones or branches hidden under the snow. *If something happens to me out here*, she thought, *I'm as good as fucked.* She had worn what she could find, but the cold dampness still made its way through her clothes, and she could feel her toes going numb. The skin on her face burned where her scarf did not cover, and the snow stung her eyes. *How the hell did I do this as a kid?* she thought. She had walked through this forest a thousand times and knew every inch of it, but it now seemed alien and dangerous. She felt unwelcome there.

Through her scarf, she caught the scent of chimney smoke. *I must be getting close*, she thought. But through the thickness of the woods, she could not see any lights or other signs of life. She thought about calling out, but then thought better of it. *I don't know what's in these woods with me.* As she stumbled forward, Sarah looked ahead into the darkness. Through the trees, she could barely make out a faint outline of light. *That could be a window*, Sarah thought. *It's definitely something.*

As Sarah quickened her pace, she no longer looked down at the path, focusing instead on the dim orange glow. She felt more than just her toes going numb, and as she began to run, she no longer used her flashlight to guide the way. *That's definitely a window*, she thought. *I'm close now.* But as her spirits rose, she stumbled over a tree branch and went tumbling down a steep incline, feeling every cold, hard object batter her body until she finally reached the bottom. She had lost sight of the orange glow and was sprawled out in the darkness. *Move*, she thought. *Move.* She cautiously moved her fingers, then her toes. Slowly, she stood up, and her ankle ached. *At least I can put weight on it.* But as she stepped forward, her good ankle broke through a thin layer of ice over a stream, and she went knee-deep into it. She pulled it out quickly and felt the sharp icy pain envelop her whole leg. She had dropped the flashlight during her fall and could not find it in the dark. *Please*, she thought. *Please let me get out of here alive.*

CHAPTER THIRTY-EIGHT

Mark and Luke stood in silence, looking at Gabriella's withered, shriveled body lying on the bed. Her mouth gaped wide open, and the two men had no words for what they saw in front of them. Luke slowly walked over to the side of the bed and put his shaking hand to the side of her ice-cold neck. He felt no pulse and was almost relieved. Her vacant, blank eyes looked up at the ceiling. Luke quickly closed them, then looked at Mark, who had removed his hat like an embarrassed church congregant who had forgotten the words of a common prayer. The room was frigid, even with all the windows closed. Snow everywhere, and they both assumed that at some point the storm had blown open a window and found its way into the room. But it was quiet now, and they could only hear the old master clock downstairs ticking away the seconds of early morning. Tic, tic, tic...

Luke took out his walkie-talkie. "Luke to Mayor, over." Static. "Luke to Mayor, over."

He shook his head. "He's probably ignoring me." He forced a laugh, and his misplaced levity in the somber moment made him feel ashamed.

"How did she die?" was all Mark could say.

Luke glanced back down at the body, the mouth frozen open in eternal agony. "I don't know. Not naturally, if that's what you're asking." He thought of Mary wandering out in the forest and felt sick. *Did she find her mother's body and just fucking snap?* he wondered. *Or did she snap first, and then this happened?* He tried to brush these unpleasant thoughts away. "The Mayor would know, but he's probably stone drunk right now, just like everyone else on the goddamn island."

"I could use a drink myself."

Luke nodded in agreement. "After we get this mess sorted, I think I'll have one with you." He took the sheets from the foot of the bed and covered the still body. He thought of Sarah and wanted desperately to ride out to her place and warn her. But his responsibility for now was here. "I can't get through to anyone, not in the storm anyway. Once it passes, we'll probably have to phone the base from home."

Mark said nothing.

"Mark? I need you with me on this." Mark nodded silently. Luke continued, "We may not be able to reach anyone in this weather, but that doesn't mean we should stop trying."

Mark sighed. "So, what do we do now?"

Luke shook his head. "I don't know. I have half a mind to head over to the hotel, grab the goddamn Mayor by his throat, and drag him here. We need a physician's signature."

"What if we wait until morning and wait for the storm to pass?"

"Yeah, I'm not doing that. I'm not going to bed tonight knowing we have two corpses, one a potential homicide. If Boss wasn't pissed about me trashing his car. I'll be a fucking corpse in the ground, too, if he finds out. Besides, the others have a right to know. I'd imagine news of this will sober them up pretty quick."

Mark nodded again. "We should get going. That storm's not letting up."

As they were about to head out of the room, they heard a door slam downstairs.

Luke looked at Mark. "Could just be the storm."

Mark groaned. "After everything else, I doubt it."

Footsteps followed on the wooden floor downstairs. The two of them froze, and Luke felt his heartbeat so loud that he almost asked Mark if he could hear it too. The footsteps stopped just beneath them. Whoever it was, they were near the bottom of the stairs.

Mark looked at Luke. "Do you have your gun on you?"

"Since when do I carry my gun anywhere on this goddamn island?" he whispered back.

Mark looked around. "Is there anything in this room we could use?"

"Use for what?"

"A weapon, you jackass."

They both looked around frantically, scanning the room. On the desk next to the bed was a large metal picture frame, and Luke grabbed it quickly, shrugging off Mark's disapproving glare. Mark tiptoed over to the window, reached up, and pulled down the curtain rod. They both stood for a moment, waiting in silence.

Footsteps were now slowly ascending the stairs. Luke hid behind the door, and Mark positioned himself on the other side. The footsteps had reached the landing now and were coming closer. The two men looked at each other and nodded. Had he not already seen the two corpses, Luke would have laughed at the absurdity of the moment, but he could not dismiss the possibility that whoever had done this might have come back. He waited in silence, the frame held high over his head, and suddenly realized just how vulnerable the island was during the wintertime. They had never had any reason to let their guard down. The world's anger and violence had always seemed millions of miles away from here. *But maybe we're just like every other place,* he thought. *Nowhere in this goddamn world can you escape from it.*

The footsteps were getting closer now, coming slowly towards them. Luke gripped the picture frame hard, ready to strike whatever came through that door. He'd have one shot. So would Mark. The door slowly creaked open. Just as he nearly swung down, Luke recognized the familiar figure walking through the door.

"Sarah!" Luke shouted. She turned around and screamed as well, and Mark dropped the curtain rod. Sarah hugged Luke, who held his arms out, still in shock and unsure of what was going on. "What the hell are you doing here?"

Sarah sobbed as she clung tightly to him. "Alice is dead."

"What?! How?"

She trembled violently in his arms, then pulled away and saw Mark. Behind him, she saw the draped outline of a lifeless body beneath the white sheets on the bed.

Mark took her by the shoulders and tried to comfort her. "Sarah, what happened? What happened to Alice?"

Sarah just stared at the bed. "Who is that?"

Luke glanced at Mark. "Let's get her downstairs."

From the fridge, Mark pulled out a bottle of Riesling and a bag of pita bread. He poured Sarah a generous glass, then poured himself an even more generous one. Luke shook his head when offered one. He was looking around the room, searching for anything amiss, but there were no signs of a break-in. The three of them sat silently for a while in the flickering light of the fire. Luke had also lit some candles he found in a kitchen drawer, but no matter what they did, they could not get warm.

Sarah stared wordlessly into the fire. She had finally stopped crying now. She had lost everyone she had ever loved. Her father and sister were gone forever. Now she was the last remaining of her kin, her family's bloodlines holding on by a thread.

She wiped her eyes. Dawn was still hours away, but the storm was still as strong as ever, holding its stubborn grip on the island and refusing to relent. They could all feel it gaining strength. The house moaned, and somewhere outside in the darkness, they heard something crash and break. None of them went to the window to see what it was. "I feel like when the sun comes up—if it comes up—this whole island will be gone, and there'll just be this house left behind."

Mark and Luke exchanged a glance but said nothing. Her glass of wine sat untouched in front of her.

Luke sighed. "Jack still hasn't turned on the generator yet."

"Don't you know how to do that?"

"I forgot."

"You told everyone you did."

"I know. I lied."

"Isn't that part of your job description?"

"Evidently."

Sarah said nothing, just nodded and stared into the fire. She began quietly breaking up pieces of pita, dividing them between the three of them. Luke stopped pacing and knelt on the floor next to Sarah.

"Sarah, why did you come to see Mary?" he asked her.

"Something happened." She swallowed. "Something's been happening."

Luke paused, searching for the right words, trying not to rush her. "I know. We're trying to figure out what it is."

She shook her head. "You don't understand. Alice...someone called her. Someone called her pretending to be me and told her to come here. Before I woke up and found her body, I had a dream. We were kids again. She was out in the lake—dying—but I couldn't leave the shore. I couldn't leave because I was afraid. I've always been afraid to. She was screaming, trying to tell me something, but I couldn't hear her." Sarah stared into the fire, then closed her eyes. "The boat," she whispered.

Mark swallowed. "What did you say?"

"She was saying, 'the boat'."

Mark took another swig of wine, finishing it. "What boat?"

Sarah turned away from the fire and looked at him. "You *know* what boat, Mark."

The three of them were silent for a while. Mark cleared his throat. "That was a long time ago, Sarah."

She looked at Luke. "I came here because I had to tell Mary. I had to ask her if she saw anything, or felt anything, or knew anything that was going on. If anyone on this island did, it would be her."

Luke felt a pang of disappointment. "I wish you'd radioed me first. I would have come as soon as I could." Sarah said nothing. "We can go back there now if you want. We can take care of her body."

"I'm not going back there now."

Luke looked over at Mark and saw the golden reflection of the fire in his glasses. "We should get back to the hotel. Tell the others."

"All of us?"

"All of us."

"Now wait just a goddamn second. Sarah just trekked through that storm and nearly died of hypothermia. You can't drag her back out there again."

"Then what do you propose? Leave her here alone? We've got three dead bodies on this island now without a whole lot of explanation. So, I think that's a seriously bad idea."

"She stays here, where it's warm. I'll stay with her."

"I'd say there's strength in numbers."

"There's one snowmobile. There's three of us. How do you make that work?"

Sarah stood, lost in thought, removed from their conversation. "She had a car."

Luke turned to look at her. "Who? Who had a car?"

"Mary. She has a car in the garage." Sarah looked at Luke. "I don't want to stay here. I feel like all I've done all night is wait, and I'm tired of sitting around waiting for whatever the fuck is out there. Let's go find the others."

Luke squinted at her. "What car?"

"That Beetle she always takes out for the 4th of July parade." The two men stared blankly at Sarah. Her eyes widened impatiently. "The goddamn yellow Beetle!"

They spent nearly twenty minutes looking for the keys. Dumping drawers out onto the floor, emptying jars, and going through pockets. Finally, they tried the garage and found them in the glove box. Mark laughed and muttered, "No one ever keeps anything locked up on this island."

Luke took the key. "That might change after tonight."

The three of them climbed into the old vintage Beetle. It was cold, but less so without the wind upon them. Luke took a deep breath. "Cross your fingers." He cautiously turned the key. Nothing. He exhaled a long, tired sigh. "Because, of course. It's only been sitting here all goddamn winter." They sat in silence for a few minutes.

Mark slapped the back of Luke's head. "What about the snowmobile?"

"Can you fucking tell me anything without swatting my head like I'm a five-year-old? And what about the snowmobile?"

"We can jump-start it."

Luke sighed. "Why do I feel like you've done this before?"

"Because I have. Look, you and I will push the car outside. Sarah, can you pull the snowmobile up alongside it?"

"Yeah, where did you guys park it?"

"Out in the front. We'll meet you outside."

Luke and Mark put the car in neutral and pushed it outside. The force of the wind seemed to be pushing against them, and they slipped more than a few times. Once they made it outside, they sat on the ground, catching their breath as the flakes began piling on top of them.

Mark took out a cigarette. "Well, at least we'll be driving there in style."

"If this works."

They heard the sound of the snowmobile getting louder and watched as Sarah pulled up next to them. Luke found jumper cables in the garage, opened the hood of the car, and connected them to both vehicles.

Mark got into the car. Luke brushed off the windshield and looked in at him: "Start it on my signal." He turned to signal Sarah as well. "You ready?"

She nodded, "Yes."

As one engine started up, so did the other, reluctantly. The three of them whooped and got back into the car, with Luke behind the wheel. "This may not handle very well on the roads, but hopefully we'll get there fast."

Sarah looked out the window at the storm. "I don't think we'll be running into anyone else on these roads tonight." Her comment chilled them as they slowly made their way onto the main street leading to the hotel.

Chapter Thirty-Nine

Susan woke to the sound of branches clawing at her window. She sat up in the darkness and realized the power had gone out. She groped for her phone. Still no texts or calls from Adam. Nothing from Jack either, but she was less concerned about that. The world felt quiet without the power on, and she wondered why Tigger had stopped barking outside. Her cellphone read 3:00 am, and she lay in bed struggling to return to sleep. *Too late to start watching something and too early to get up.* Outside, she could still hear the wind screaming. Somewhere off in the distance, a metal trash can was rolling back and forth, back and forth. Susan thought about Jack and Bill out there on the ice with the winds roaring around them. She had expected them back before midnight, imagined Jack walking through the door with Bill not far behind, tail tucked firmly between his legs, not looking at her or admitting defeat, and pouring himself a drink. Bill would be happy to be back home, realize what a fool his father was, and climb the stairs to his room, where his warm bed was waiting for him. But that had not happened.

The house felt even darker and emptier now. It seemed strange that most of the other houses on the street were empty. Susan closed her eyes, knowing all the houses in Cleveland and Toledo, and Sandusky were full. People were tucked in their warm beds, listening to the wind whistle and howl outside their windows. She felt millions of years away from that world.

She thought about Adam and imagined herself dressing in the dark and marching through the snow and wind to get to him. She had done it before, but never in weather like this. He'd most likely be asleep and probably annoyed that she had come unannounced and disturbed his sleep. This night made her feel like a needy child, but she resolved to stay put until someone reached out for her. She had wanted to enjoy the rare solitude, but now found herself restless and uncertain which would come first, sleep or dawn. As she closed her eyes and hoped for sleep, the sound of shattering glass downstairs suddenly made that impossible.

She got out of bed and felt the cold wooden floorboards beneath her bare feet. She threw on her nightgown and slippers, then stood still, waiting for any further sounds. *The storm is blowing the whole world around*, she thought.

It could easily just be a branch or something else. But the crash had startled her, and now she wished she were not all alone on the block. She wished there were lights on in the other houses, someone she could call. *You idiot*, she thought to herself. *If no one can get off this island, then no one can get onto it either.* She crept to the bedroom door, slowly opened it, and listened. *But if something bad happens on the island*, she thought, *no one can come to help you either.* Susan pushed the door open wider and stepped into the hallway. The floorboards betrayed her every step, and she winced each time she heard them creak. She could feel a cold draft rise above the heat of the furnace, making its presence known to her. *If someone is out there*, she thought, *any weapon we have is out in the garage outside.* She thought about anything else she could use: a kitchen knife, a hammer, his nail gun? But all those things were out of reach, and if there were someone downstairs, they would be between her and her weapon of choice.

The staircase was carpeted, and she used stealth as she made her way downstairs, unarmed but alert. If it were an intruder, she would have to act fast. *How vulnerable we are,* she thought. She stopped in her tracks again and listened. The storm sounded louder now, and as she peeked into the kitchen, she saw shards of glass on the floor, with snow blowing in and covering the floor. She jumped out from behind the corner into the kitchen. There was no tree branch, no burglar going through drawers or shoving a knife in her face.

But there was something there. Almost concealed within the darkness, she saw a small round object on the floor. She knelt and reached out her hand. A snowball? Her fingers clasped around it. It was a baseball. She stood back up and stared at it, then at the window. The wind wouldn't have blown this in. She stood there, looking at the hole in the window facing the backyard. Someone must have thrown it. Susan wrapped herself tighter in her robe. It was frigid outside, and she thought again of Bill and Jack. They wouldn't have stayed out in this weather. This storm could kill. She felt a rush of emotions overwhelm her. *Please don't be out on that ice right now. Please come home. Please be safe.*

Lightning flashed outside. *What kind of a winter storm is this?* she thought. Thunder and lightning and snow, as if the weather had gone mad and let loose all its madness in one storm. The room was repeatedly illuminated by sudden flashes of lightning. She walked closer to the window and thought she caught a quick glimpse of two figures in the backyard. Broken glass crunched beneath her feet, but she was no longer concerned with the damage to the kitchen. Out in the darkness of the backyard, something waited. *Why wasn't Tigger barking? Surely, he would have heard or seen someone?* In the cupboard closest to the window, she searched for the flashlight and found it buried under a pile of expired coupons.

Outside, the shuddering beam from her flashlight scanned the blank wall of snow. The wind seemed to pull it in every direction, and Susan could not focus on any object. More snow spilled through the broken window, and the room felt frigid. She was tired. The window couldn't be fixed until at least the next day, and by then the whole house would be freezing. At that moment, she missed her husband very much. It had been a while since she had missed him. His absence felt almost tangible to her now. Her mind snapped away from these thoughts as her flashlight suddenly caught something in the darkness and snow.

Something was moving, and Susan could tell that it was not the low-hanging branches of a tree. The movement had purpose; it seemed to move away from the light every time she flashed it in that general direction. *Was it Tigger? How cruel am I?* She thought. *How could I leave him out there? What kind of person would do that?* She thought she heard the whimpering of a dog. *He must be freezing to death out there. If Bill comes home and finds him like that, he'll never forgive me.*

Without bothering to put on a coat, she rushed outside. "Tigger? Tigger, are you out here?" She had tied his leash to the pole; she was certain of that. Again, she heard whimpering. "I'm here, boy! I'm so sorry!"

There was no response. She slammed the back door open and was met with a heavy blow of wind and snow. It bit mercilessly into her exposed flesh. *How can anyone be out here in this? Should I call Luke?* She lifted her flashlight, but the beam was immediately consumed by a wall of snow too powerful to penetrate. If someone were out there, she wouldn't be able to see them. The streetlights were out as well, and all the neighbors' houses were hidden in darkness. It felt as if her beam of light was the last beacon, the last trace, of humanity the world would ever know. And then she thought she heard the crunching of snow. She heard it even above the roaring of the wind, and the beam trembled with her hand in the cold.

"Hello? Is anybody there?"

Again, there was no response. She walked further from the house out into the yard. Her hair and robe blew madly about as she reached out her hand to find the pole where she had tied Tigger. She finally located the cold steel pole and felt it covered with snow and ice.

"Tigger?"

She knelt, scanning the ground. Her beam caught a mound of snow where the leash had been tied. "Oh God, Tigger." She brushed aside the snow and felt the cold fur, the frigid, lifeless body of Tigger. She knelt in the snow for some time and wept. *They'll ask me why I didn't bring him in. I don't know what I'll tell them.* She stopped as she heard more footsteps, closer now.

"Who's there? Jack? Bill? Is that you?"

The crunching stopped. As she lifted the beam, she could just make out the outline of a figure in the snow. It seemed tiny, about the size of a child. "Bill? Is that you?" The figure came closer now, almost within reach of the beam of light. Susan wished she had brought a knife out with her. The house felt very far away, and her cold legs felt very heavy beneath her. Then she heard what she thought was a whisper and listened more closely.

"Mother," the voice whispered.

She walked towards the sound. "Bill? Is that you?"

"Mother," it said again, softly.

Bill can't talk, she thought. *But could it be him?* All reason left her. "I'm here, Billy! Mommy's here!" She walked deeper into the darkness until her beam suddenly revealed the figure in the shadows.

Susan did not scream. Her mind was too busy trying to comprehend what she was looking at...

Through the blur of snow, she could see an obscene, toothy smile extending from ear to ear. His face was black and blue, and the pupils were gone, replaced by orbs of glassy white. That blankness looked directly at her. His winter clothes were torn, with red stains all over. It took only a moment for her to register that whatever this thing was, it was not her son.

"Billy? Billy, what happened to you?"

The boy said nothing. He stepped closer, hands outstretched. In the beam of her light, she could just make out his outline. As he came closer, she could see that he did not leave any footprints behind him in the snow. And then he stopped in his tracks.

"Billy?! she screamed. She screamed, though she knew he could not hear her. They looked at each other in silence in the darkness for a moment, and then the boy ran off into the snowy dark.

Undressed as she was, she ran after him, trying to find a trace of footsteps but seeing none as she squinted through the storm. *Where could he be going?* she thought. *And why is he alone? Where's Jack? Damn him*, she thought. She would deal with that later. *Where was he running to?* When she passed a block, she saw the small outline of him at the end of the street. She tried to sign him in the dark. Again, he stood there, playing a game of sorts, and she was in no mood for it. She ran after him, nearly slipping several times on the slick, snow-covered surface of the street. The wind blew hard several times and nearly knocked her over, but Billy seemed to gain ground no matter the elements. *If this was some trick of Jack's to get me out on the ice with them, I will kill them and bury them there,* she thought. Then she realized where he was headed as they both approached it: Carpenter High School, closed and dead for the season. Just like everything else.

Billy ran up the steps, his outline nearly lost in the heavy snowfall. Susan could feel her toes go numb, but she ran anyway. She had come too far and would not turn back. Her anger pushed her onward. She watched him run up the large front stairs of the school and open the door, then disappear inside. *Why is it unlocked?* she thought. *They must have forgotten to lock it.* As she reached the bottom of the steps, she stopped to catch her breath. She looked around, and it felt horrible being alone there at that moment, in that town, on that island. She trudged up the thick layers of snow on the stairs, then opened the door and struggled with the force of the cold wind. As she stepped in, the door behind her slammed shut.

Inside was warm, heated throughout, so the pipes didn't burst. *At least this place had the good sense to have a backup generator,* she thought. Susan heard her footsteps echo down the empty hallways as she walked, using her cellphone light to guide her. Small red EXIT lights gave her a poor view of the hall. She had just been there weeks before for Billy's Christmas play. It had gone on for three hours that night, and Adam had not shown up like he said he would. She clenched her fists as she marched down the hallway.

"Billy!?" Her voice echoed through the whole building, then she stopped and shivered. She was alone. *Where was Billy?* She thought. Why was he doing this? She screamed again, louder this time: "Billy?! Where are you?!" She could hear the panic in her own voice. She had wished someone had stayed here during the winter, a janitor or someone. But that would be Jack, who would take care of this school if it were closed. And she didn't know where he was. "Jack?!" Susan shouted, and again her scream echoed into the dark maze of hallways that seemed to echo right back to her, delayed. She stepped back against the wall and felt the bulge of the light switch on it. She reached behind her quickly and flipped it, then felt the strong pang of relief when the lights came on, illuminating the vacant hallways with the outdated green and yellow walls and dusty glass cases of trophies. The school was small but not too small. The island fit grades 1-12 there, although even during the school season, the place felt empty. But

Susan wished it had been full now. Then she stopped as she heard the faint static of the school announcement speakers. Subtle static rose and fell like waves. Over the static, a low voice whispered over the speaker system. A boy's voice: "Mother."

Susan stopped. Billy had never spoken. Billy could not speak. *Another boy on the island?* she thought. It was a prank. She wanted it to be. *It had to be,* she thought.

Again, the speaker spoke: "Mother." The boy's voice echoed through the empty classrooms, the hallways, and the strange, dark corners of the school where few went. It echoed in her mind. Her heart pounded as she quieted her footsteps. And then the overhead lights began to flicker. She could not calm her heart and all its rabid fury, so much so that she felt it beat in her head—pound, *pound, pound—until* all she could hear was her ascending pulse. The lights began to flicker, but to her they seemed to do so in unusual patterns. Subtle at first. She couldn't place it. Then she realized the lights were flashing to the beat of her heart. She stopped in her tracks, then tried to slow her breathing and slow her heart rate, but it only beat faster, and so did the lights in a frenzied unity. The static on the speakers grew louder, and the sound of the waves became clear to her: it was her breathing. She could hear it echo through the speakers. The lights pounded with her heart, as if the entire school building was now in sync with her body.

Susan stepped forward slowly and felt something cold and liquid at her feet. She looked down and saw water trickling down the hallway, veined streams of it flowing down to her, down the stairs. Ahead, she could hear water rushing. *A burst pipe?* she thought. She walked down the hall and, from a distance, could see water leaking from one of the student lockers. It gushed from the top three slits, gushing foul-smelling filthy water that spilled out onto the floor and flooded the hallway. The lights flashed in union with her beating heart, obscuring her view. *Flash-Flash-Flash.* The speaker spewed out her quick, frenzied breathing as the locker door began to open. A great rush of filthy water exploded from the locker, creating a putrid river down the hallway. Susan turned to run as the water spilled her way, but as it gushed all around her, the strength of the water knocked her off her feet and onto her back, hitting her head hard on the wet terrazzo floor.

She awoke confined, her body unable to move, and for a moment, she thought she was paralyzed. But she was outside, and as her vision focused, she found that she was upright. Upright and trapped. She was tied to something cold—the flagpost outside the school, she guessed quickly—and she could feel something tug at her neck, quick, painful tugs that cut off her air supply more than once. With every gust of wind, the rope around her neck wrapped tighter and choked her. The flagpole rope was tied tightly around her neck, and with each gust of wind that threatened to tear the flag away, it constricted around her throat. A quick gust of wind, a quick, painful choke. A prolonged, angry wind, just a longer choke that blurred her vision. Far ahead in the street, she saw two young figures staring at her, both with dead, blank eyes. One of them was Billy. He looked at her as she choked and said nothing. She tried to call out his name, but the rope was too tight, and the small squeak she emitted was lost in the fury of the wind. The other figure with him had long hair. It was a girl, but Susan knew of no girl on the island now. *Adam, where was Adam? Someone call Adam. Billy, call Adam.* But Billy was right there watching her bound figure choke and twist in the winds of the storm. Watching with such detachment that Susan wanted to cry. And as she tried to call out for him again, a powerful rush of wind ripped the flagpole, and the two young figures on the street watched as the rope snapped Susan's neck, and watched the wind blow her lifeless body, limbs flailing like some absurd comedy. They watched her like that for some time.

CHAPTER FORTY

Mark, Luke, and Sarah stared for some time at the flickering red glow in the windows of the hotel. There were no shadows or movement inside. The hotel stood defiant against the storm. Sarah reached into her pocket and felt the hard outline of the butcher knife she had brought. It had given her the confidence to make the trek across the island, but now she felt that it might as well have been a toy. Whatever was on this island with them was not afraid of weapons.

Mark was the first to break the long silence. "How many of them are in there?"

Luke shrugged. "I think about ten of them said they were going. Maybe more?"

Mark scanned the exterior, noting all the dark windows. He looked down at his wrist and realized he had forgotten his watch. "What time is it?"

"My watch is dead. It has to be well after 3." Sarah said. "It's really late."

"Or really early. Dawn should be coming soon."

Mark looked back and forth at them. "Well, what the hell are we waiting for? It's not like they won't welcome us in."

Luke sighed. "They won't like any news that spoils their little party. Not that I care, really." He looked at Sarah. "You ready?"

She nodded, and the three of them warily approached the quiet hotel.

From the hallway, they could smell smoke from an unseen fireplace. Just beneath the smell was something fouler. With the main door closed behind them, there was only silence inside: no voices, no laughter, no clinking of glasses, no footsteps but their own.

"Maybe they're all asleep?" Mark whispered.

Luke shook his head. "I don't think so. Would they be upstairs?"

Sarah swallowed hard. "No, they'd be in the reception room." Sarah pointed ahead. "It's down the hall, to the left. Through the swinging doors."

Sarah shone her flashlight over the old wallpaper, an outdated design from the 60s. It looked ugly and unwelcoming in the unforgiving shine of her flashlight. She raised her beam to the clock, whose hands had stopped. "3:00," Sarah whispered.

"What did you say?" Luke asked, still looking ahead into the dark hallway.

"The clock. It's stopped at 3:00, just like all the others. Mark, what time does your cellphone say?"

"It's nearly 4:30."

As they approached the doors to the reception room, they could see one of them swinging back and forth, as if pushed by an invisible hand. An icy draft chilled them, and Mark hugged himself. "Jesus, it feels like a window is open."

Luke shook his head. "Why are we whispering? Hello?!"

Mark's light scanned the doors to the reception room. "Maybe they all crashed for the night?"

Sarah shook her head. "No. They're in there."

As they approached the swinging door, Luke reached out and grabbed it. Inside, they could just barely make out a red glow from the dying fire. The smell of smoke and burning wood—and something else—was much stronger now. They slowly entered the room, collectively holding their breaths.

Luke covered Sarah's mouth as she screamed. In the hellish red glow of the fire, they stood, surrounded by bodies and blood. It was impossible to see how the violence had begun or where it had ended. They had stepped into the midst of human ruin and destruction of flesh and blood. Luke turned to Mark. "Get her out of here!" he shouted.

"No," she whispered.

Mark grabbed Sarah by the arm. "Come on," he said grimly.

"No!" She screamed, louder than she had intended. "Whatever this thing is, it took my sister. And Mary and her mom. I'm not leaving."

Mark scanned the room with his flashlight. He winced in disgust every time he came across another body, each one more mutilated than the rest. "Jesus Christ, who would do this? Who *could* do this?"

In the beam of light, Sarah suddenly saw their fingers, all covered in blood. "They did. They did it to each other."

"Or someone made them do it," Luke shuddered.

Sarah shushed him. "Shhh... There's someone else in here."

Luke looked over at her, blinding her with his headlamp. "What? Where?"

Sarah pointed in the direction of the fireplace, where they could just see the silhouette of a figure. It sat still at first, as if it were part of the furniture. But they could see tiny movements and hear soft rasping breaths. The three of them slowly approached, weapons drawn.

"Who are you?" Luke asked. There was no answer. He motioned for the others to follow him as he approached the fireplace. Sitting in a chair was the Mayor, or what had once been the Mayor. He was covered in bites, claw marks, and strange wounds, his eyes swollen shut. His breathing was labored and gurgling, as if his chest were full of water.

"Jesus," Luke said. "Mark, get the first aid kit from the snowmobile."

"But..."

"Just fucking do it!"

Mark nodded and raced out of the room, while Sarah reached out to touch the Mayor's hand. He trembled. "Who is that?" he asked, painfully.

"It's Sarah." She was no longer afraid of what she saw in that room as she looked upon the man who had been her friend and neighbor for so long, dying before her.

"Sarah," he said slowly. He coughed, and Sarah could see blood leaking from his mouth. "Sarah, the bartender, who never serves me after 3."

Sarah tried to smile but had no will to do so. Instead, she held his hand tightly. "You're safe now."

Luke tried to wipe some of the blood from his face. "What the hell happened here?! Can you tell us what happened? Please?"

The Mayor ignored him and continued to look at Sarah, his eyes nearly swollen shut. "We were just trying to help you and your sister."

Sarah shook her head, bewildered. "What are you talking about?"

"On the boat. In the storm. We had to choose between you and them. They were so afraid. We thought we had lost them in the storm."

Luke looked at Sarah. "What the hell is he talking about?"

Sarah held the Mayor's hand even tighter. "But they did die in the storm. They did."

The Mayor shook his head. "No... The father washed up on the beach. We found him. He was mad with grief. He tried to get us to go back out with him and said his daughter was still out there somewhere. Mark tried to stop him."

Sarah grabbed his face gently and held it. "But you weren't even on the boat. How do you know that? Did my dad tell you?"

"No. *She* did." His voice fell, and he exhaled his final breath.

Mark came back into the room, carrying the kit. "How is he?!"

Sarah wiped the tears from her cheeks. "He's dead."

As they looked at the motionless body sitting in the chair before them, they suddenly heard loud static from the loudspeakers, and music began to play. It was The Righteous Brothers' "*Ebb Tide*," a slow, scratchy version Sarah almost didn't recognize.

Luke stood. "Who's playing that song?" He looked at Mark. "Who's at the control tower?"

Mark said nothing, shaking his head in confusion.

"I know who played that song." Sarah stood up and looked at Mark. "And so do you."

. "We have to go. Now," Luke said. He grabbed Sarah's hand as she still held the Mayor's. "Now, Sarah."

She pulled away from Luke. "Go where, Luke? Where do you expect me to go? I'm stuck here on this island. I've always been stuck on this island. And now we all are; do you understand that?" She turned toward Mark. "What happened out on the lake that day?"

"Sarah, you already know what happened..."

"There's something else that you and Dad never told me." In the dull haze from their beams, they looked at each other.

Mark swallowed. "We had to choose between you and them. It was the most difficult decision I've ever had to make. But I'd do it a thousand times over because we saved you."

Sarah stared at him. "Did someone come back? Did one of them make it back alive?"

"No, I told you already. By the time we got back to shore, they were gone. We couldn't go back out, or we'd have all died. We wanted to—your dad wanted to—but if we'd all died, then what the fuck was the point?"

Sarah nodded as she processed this. "Is that why Dad jumped off the cliff?"

"Look, we all suffered from that. No one walked away from that day the same. Hell, you couldn't even leave the island after that..."

The music blared louder now, making itself known above the howling of the storm. Off in the distance, they could see flashes of lightning out over the lake and hear distant booms of thunder.

"Whatever it is," Sarah said, "It knows we're here."

Luke was covering his eyes. "Can we please get out of this fucking room?"

Mark nodded. "I'm with him."

They stumbled out of the room, trying to avoid looking down but also trying not to trip and fall over the bodies around them. They could hear awful, moist, squishing sounds underneath their feet, like walking through mud. Sarah now found herself grateful that the music was playing so loudly to drown out those sounds.

They scrambled through the darkness of the lobby, unable to see the blood-stained footprints they left behind. They could no longer see The Mayor's limp body in the chair, his blank face painted orange by the dying fire. They could not see that all the clocks on the island now proclaimed 3:00, and the invisible eye of whatever was watching them waited.

Chapter Fourty-One

Even with all the doors and windows shut, they could feel the cold seeping into the hotel. Sarah stood and waited for a minute until she realized that Luke had no plan.

"What do we do now?!" She asked. Her teeth were chattering.

Luke sighed. "I don't know."

Mark shone his flashlight at the clock, forgetting it had stopped hours ago. "We have our snowmobile here," he said. "One's all we need. We can take it out on the ice. Make it across to the mainland. We can get a signal there once we get across the lake to Marblehead."

Luke looked at Mark, not caring if his headlamp blinded him, which it did. "You're forgetting one thing." They both looked at Sarah.

Sarah nodded. "No, Mark is right. One of you should take the snowmobile to the mainland. Call for help. You'll get there faster without me."

Luke walked over to her. "I'm not leaving you alone here with whatever the hell is going on. Absolutely out of the fucking question."

Sarah pushed his headlight away from her eyes. "Let's try it."

Luke stared at her. "Try what?"

"The three of us. Let's try to get off this island."

"The car will never make it across. It's too heavy."

"The Beetle's too heavy," she said. "But the snowmobile's not. There's at least one outside. I say we take it and go."

"Are you sure you'll be ok?"

"No, but you're right. Leaving one of us behind just leaves that person to die. I don't know who's still alive on this island, and I don't know where this thing is, but I think we have a better chance of surviving if we stay together."

Mark scoffed. "Yeah, just like all of them in there, right? That worked out really well for them."

Luke grabbed Mark by his coat. "Look, whatever chance we have of surviving, it's gonna' be off this island. Now I can get us to the mainland, but I'll need your help. I'm gonna need you on board with us here. And if you're not, then you can stay behind."

Mark stood there a moment, staring at Luke, who seemed to have grown years older in a matter of hours. He looked exhausted. For the first time in ages, he was glad that Luke was here on the island and grateful that one of them still had the sense to lead. But he wouldn't let Luke know that. He pushed him away. "Fine," he snapped.

Luke glanced at Sarah, who stood there shivering. "Are you sure you can really do this?"

Sarah tried to smile. "I'll be ok. It's just one trip."

Luke didn't blink. "Are you sure?"

Sarah nodded. "I can do it."

Luke stepped back and looked at them both. "Alright. Let's get the hell off this island."

Chapter Forty-Two

Sarah felt her heart racing as they made their way through the dense, snow-covered underbrush of the forest. Already she could feel her extremities growing numb, and she wondered if she would survive the night, whether she would ever feel warm again. She was sandwiched between Mark and Luke on the snowmobile, but that did not stop the frigid wind from biting her face. She had not willingly left the island for over ten years. But now she hoped this nightmare would be enough to overcome her fears and that her fragile psyche would understand once the island was left behind them.

Luke was taking the fastest trek possible off the island. They would cut through the forest, make their way through the abandoned amusement park, and then find the trail that went directly to the lake. They were on a downslope now, and even with the thick snow and the weight of three passengers, the snowmobile did not put up much of a fight. Sarah held onto Luke. She did not know what they would do once they reached the mainland. She did not know what they would say to the police or to anyone who might take them in. She did not know what to do with her sister's body or all the other bodies they had left behind. What she did know was that once she arrived on the mainland, she intended to never come back to this island again. That thought made her feel both sad and free. But all that was so far away now.

"What the fuck is that?" Luke stopped the snowmobile dead in its tracks. Sarah squinted her eyes into the darkness ahead.

"What is it?" she asked. She wiped the snow from her eyes, and suddenly everything seemed very bright. Not daylight bright, but something else.

Luke turned around and looked at Mark. "Do you see that?"

Mark nodded. "Yeah, I see it."

Sarah looked up and saw it, too. The amusement park lights were on. All of them. Over the shrill howl of the wind, they began to hear the eerie sound of the carousel's organ music playing. They smelled popcorn and cotton candy as the wind cupped the scent in its icy, invisible hand and carried it to them. It made Sarah's stomach churn.

Mark swallowed. "Maybe somebody from the hotel came and turned it on?"

Sarah stared straight ahead. "I doubt it."

Luke shook his head. "Well, if we don't go through it, we'll have to double back through the woods and around the quarry. We'll lose at least an hour if we do that."

"It knew we had to come this way," Sarah said, almost in a whisper.

Mark tapped Luke's shoulder. "I unlocked the gate earlier when Sarah and I went through. It'll be open."

Luke looked at them and said nothing.

"Like you said," Sarah said. "It's the fastest way through."

Luke started up the machine again, and they continued forward to the gate. As they approached, they could just make out the lights from the roller coaster. Above the music, they could hear all the machines and rides running. Through the snow, they could see the empty rollercoaster cars speeding up and down over the wooden tracks and heard the clank-clank of metal wheels on wood. Sarah looked over to her left and saw the merry-go-round spinning faster than she had ever seen. The speed of everything was exaggerated and unsafe. The coaster appeared dangerously close to going off the rails at any moment. The merry-go-round cars spun furiously in the wind. Sarah had never seen such a sight. It was a mockery of their beloved park. It felt blasphemous.

Mark looked around, both hands on his head: "Where the fuck is that music coming from?" It was loud and cacophonous, as if mocking their plight, a cheerful organ song played on fast forward.

Luke looked around, then identified the source. "Over there!" he shouted, pointing. Off in the distance was the carousel, which seemed to spin so fast they could hardly make out the revolving horses.

Sarah tried to focus and could just make out the form of what looked like a small child on the ride. Her heart began to race, matching the carousel's speed. It was a bright, obscene onslaught of colors and music. But she could barely see it, riding on one of the horses. It was a child.

Luke stood alongside Sarah. "Is that... is that a kid?"

Sarah remained silent. As she watched, she caught quick glimpses of the child and could see long hair flowing and a dress ripping in the wind. The carousel's speed was beyond safe for anyone, yet the child held onto the pole effortlessly. And through the snow, lights, and movement, she could see something else: The child was looking at them.

"She knows we're here," Sarah said, almost in a trance.

"Who?" Luke could feel his heart racing as well. Something told him to get on the snowmobile and flee as far away from this place as possible. But he couldn't leave the other two behind. "Sarah, who is that?"

Sarah looked past Luke at Mark. "Ask him."

Luke looked at Mark. "Who is that? Do you know who it is?"

Mark glared back at them. "What the hell are you looking at me for? How should I know who the fuck that is?"

Then the music suddenly stopped, along with the carousel. The child now sat motionless, facing them. Sarah peered through the dim, flashing lights of the amusement park but could not make out the features of the face.

"We need to go," Sarah said, without taking her eyes off the girl.

"The exit is behind the carousel," Luke said. "We'll have to backtrack out through the forest."

Mark swallowed. "I'm not going anywhere near that fucking thing."

And then they saw it: the child was no longer sitting on the back of the plaster horse, watching them without motion. It was moving towards them, fast. It had to be running, but Sarah could see no feet. She grabbed Luke's arm, squeezing it tightly. "Luke..."

"Everybody get on the snowmobile. Now!"

As they turned to rush toward it, the lights in the amusement park all shut off, and they were cast in total darkness.

Sarah clutched Luke's arm. "I can't see a goddamn thing." They were all following the small, shaky light from Luke's headlamp, struggling through the snow towards their ride. They hadn't realized they had moved so far away from it.

Luke looked around in panicked frustration. "Where the hell is it?" As he struggled to locate the machine, Sarah listened fearfully for any sounds that might not be theirs: any small, fast footsteps. The distance between them and the carousel was at least twenty yards, but after what she had seen tonight, she no longer trusted that things such as distance, time, and space had any meaning here.

"Luke, where the hell is it?" she screamed.

"It's got to be close!"

"Hurry!"

The three of them fumbled desperately through the snow and wind. Over the loudspeakers, they heard the storm sirens going off once again.

Mark looked up. "It's a little late for that..."

"It's trying to distract us," Sarah said grimly.

The sirens continued to grow louder and deafening, and Mark and Sarah placed both hands over their ears to block them out. Luke's beam finally caught the outline of the snowmobile. "I found it!" He grabbed both their arms, shoving them toward it. "Get on!" he yelled, loud enough for them to hear him over the siren. Sarah held onto Mark this time, who held onto Luke for dear life. As Luke started up the engine, Sarah swore she felt something like ice touch the back of her neck. Luke reversed the machine, turned on the headlights, and sped out the same way they had come. The only thing that mattered now was leaving the island, and by any means necessary.

Part Five

The Child

BAYNAM BOOKS PRESS

CHAPTER FORTY-THREE

20 YEARS EARLIER

Cleveland, Ohio

"She's not angry all the time," Lucy's father explained. The therapist nodded, watching as Lucy refused to play with the toys on the floor or look at any of the children's magazines. Instead, she gazed out the window at the low summer clouds slowly crawling across the Cleveland skyline.

The therapist sat back in her chair, watching him, then watching Lucy. She took a few notes, careful not to seem disinterested. "No outbursts at home? No...difficult moments with Lucy at home?"

Charles shook his head. "She's quiet a lot at home. It's like pulling teeth getting her to talk. But outbursts? No. Nothing like what she has at school. She doesn't talk to me the way she talks to her teachers, that's for sure."

Dr. Ash nodded. "You said earlier that you had already withdrawn her from one school this year. And both you and her school counselor said that before she lost her mother—your wife—that her grades were consistently good, and she got along well with her classmates."

Charles sighed as he fumbled with his pen, bending the plastic cap further and further. "Yeah, I mean, she was always shy. But shyness was never a problem. I'd take shyness over this any day."

"Does she say anything to you about her mother or to her teachers?" Dr. Ash asked.

Again, he shook his head. "No. No, I think I tried in the beginning, but really, I'm just afraid to push the issue. It seems like, as long as she's around me, she's under control."

Dr. Ash nodded as she added another note to her pad. "Separation anxiety is common after losing a parent. It's not altogether uncommon for her to want to be around you."

"But I've had to go pick her up early from school over a dozen times already. She can't keep missing school, and I can't keep leaving work to get her. And I try not to be angry with her, because I'm not. Because I understand. I can't even take the time to process how I feel. I have to be strong and "on" all the time for her."

Dr. Ash let his last words hang in the air, let them sink in. She looked over at Lucy and smiled. "She knows we're watching her."

Charles nodded. "She always knows. She just doesn't want to give you the satisfaction."

"Since the passing of your wife, has she...been outside of the house much, the two of you?"

"What do you mean?"

"Have you taken her out, like, to the movies, or for a walk, or anything like that?"

Charles shrugged. "We've stopped for ice cream a few times. I asked her if she wanted a puppy, and she said no. I think I might just get her one anyway."

Dr. Ash took off her glasses. "If I may, your wife passed away in that house?"

Charles finally looked away from the window. "She did. Lucy was the first one to find her."

"I can't even begin to imagine what she felt. But is she in that same house now, all the time?"

Charles nodded. He bent the plastic pen tip back until it snapped. "We both are."

Dr. Ash clicked her tongue. "Then it sounds to me like it might do you both some good to get away from there for a little while. Maybe take a trip? Is there some place you both really like to go?"

"All the places we went, we went with Angela. It might be too much for Lucy. It might...trigger something. Or maybe that's just me being paranoid. I don't know."

"What about...someplace you two haven't been before? Someplace that would be new to both of you. A place that you could call your own, without any painful memories attached?"

Charles sighed and leaned his head back. "That sounds great. Only I used most of my vacation time already, trying to help Lucy."

Dr. Ash sat back in her chair and looked up at the array of family photos decorating the wall. One of them caught her eye. It was of herself, her husband, and their son, together on a golf cart on one of the Lake Erie islands. *Which one was it?* she thought. In the background, she could just make out the summit of a rollercoaster. *Of course*, she remembered.

"There's an island off the coast of Sandusky. It's very family-friendly, and it's not far at all. My family and I love it because it feels like you're getting away, but you're really not that far at all from home."

Charles looked up from his broken pen. "What's it called?"

"Sandy Stone."

Charles sat behind Lucy on a pink and gold horse made of wood and plaster as they spun around to the music-box tinkle of *"Let the Sunshine In."* The day had been cooler, but the amusement park seemed to absorb every last ray of sunlight, and Lucy's ice cream cone melted down her hand. The air was thick and sweet with the smell of popcorn, hot dogs, and cotton candy, and everywhere Charles looked, there were swarms of people. He held onto Lucy tightly, as if she could be flung from the horse, rotating up and down to the slightly out-of-tune music. Lucy clutched the horse with her free hand. The ride seemed like it would never end, and he noticed the look of discomfort on his daughter's face.

"It's almost over, baby," he said, though he did not know that to be true. All over the island were droves of people from every corner of Ohio and beyond. He was starting to wonder how so many people could fit on such a small island. "Looks like most of Ohio is here, huh?" He smiled, but she simply nodded in silence. Finally, the horses and music began to slow down. As the two of them vacated the ride, he took Lucy by her hand and led her down the rusty metal ramp.

"What would you like to do next?" he asked. She shrugged and took another bite of what was left of her cone, which had oozed its way down her arm. "Come on, let's get you cleaned up." He grabbed some napkins from a nearby vendor and wiped her arm down. Lucy stared at a ride where the carts looked like little boats that spun around and around.

"Do you want to go on that?" he asked encouragingly.

She shook her head. "When we were up on the Ferris wheel, I could see the lake."

"I know, darling. We were really high. You could see the whole island."

"I saw people out on the lake."

Charles nodded his head. "Probably. It's a beautiful day to be out on the water."

Lucy nodded. "It is." She turned and looked at him. "Can we go out on the water, too?"

Charles had never been out on a boat by himself, but he did not tell Lucy this. This moment, with the two of them rocking peacefully on benevolent waves, seemed too perfect to shatter. The two of them sat quietly, enjoying the breeze coming off the lake, the peaceful calm of being far from the shore. Lucy had not spoken much since they had been out on the water, but she smiled more and seemed more animated. It had taken him this long to finally find a place where she could be at peace, and he wanted the moment to last as long as it could. He had rented the boat for the whole day and intended to milk every second of it as long as Lucy was happy. And she finally seemed to be.

"When we get back later tonight," he said while paddling, "we can get some dinner at that hot dog stand everyone keeps talking about. And then I was thinking we could stop by that old theater. They're showing Jurassic Park tonight."

"We have Jurassic Park at home, Dad."

"Yeah, well, we do. But it's not the same as watching it in the theater. That's the way films are meant to be seen, you know?"

She nodded. "Okay."

Charles watched the flickering light from the water calm and mesmerize his daughter. It had been ages since he had seen her so peaceful, so calm. He smiled.

"You know," he said as he rowed. "This whole lake freezes during the wintertime. If it gets cold enough, you can even walk out onto the ice."

Lucy dipped her hand into the cool water. "But isn't that dangerous? Couldn't you fall through?"

"If it gets cold enough, people come out onto the lake and go ice fishing. I've even been told you can drive your car on it." He laughed. "Not that I'd ever do that."

"I'd like to do that. To walk on the lake when it's frozen."

Charles shook his head. "It's still dangerous, and you're still too young for anything like that. Lucy frowned, and Charles worried that this might spoil the mood. He had worked so hard to get her to this point. "Maybe when you're older, I'll take you out, if you still want to?"

Lucy continued to frown. "When?"

Charles sighed. He did not want to disappoint her, but he also didn't want to go out onto the lake when it was frozen. "I'll take you for a birthday trip. A big birthday." *Something far off*, he thought. "How about...your 30th birthday?"

She turned to look at him. "30? But that's 20 years away."

Charles shrugged. "Yes, but you'll be older, and I won't have to worry about you because then we'll both be adults. And you'll appreciate it more."

"My birthday comes right after Christmas. Will it be a Christmas or birthday present?"

He smiled. "It can be both."

And then her face lightened, and she smiled as well. "Do you promise?"

Charles nodded. He knew she never forgot a promise, and she would not forget this one and would hold him to it. But he hoped by then she would lose interest, and he could avoid the frozen lake altogether. They rowed on in silence, content with the arrangement they had made.

From the corner of her eye, Lucy saw another boat floating not far from them. She leaned over to watch it, and inside, she could see two little girls. "Look, Dad. There's some girls on that boat way out here."

Charles looked over and smiled. "I see them. Let's wave." He did so, and so did Lucy. As she waved, she looked back at her father questioningly.

"Do you think their mom and dad let them come out here all by themselves?"

Charles shrugged. "I'm sure they've been out here a million times. They wouldn't let children take these things out unless they knew how to use them."

Lucy nodded. "Yeah, I guess so," she agreed.

The two girls in the boat waved back at them, and Lucy smiled.

"See?" her father said. "They're fine."

The waves had grown rougher, and Charles could feel his arms tiring from rowing so much. "Getting a little choppy out here," he said. And then they heard the rumble of thunder off in the distance. They both turned and, to their dismay, saw the black clouds coming in from the north. The wind had picked up, and several of the higher waves began splashing into their boat.

"Will we be safe out here?" Lucy asked nervously.

Charles felt sick. He was angry with himself for not checking the weather beforehand and for spacing out when he should have been paying attention. "We'll be fine, baby. But we really should start heading back. We don't want to get soaked out here." He smiled at her, and she nodded.

"Can we come back out again tomorrow?" she asked.

"Of course."

His arms were already aching from the trip out, and now he battled against the wind and current. As hard as he tried to paddle, they did not seem to be moving. Lucy watched the other girls in their boat. They, too, had seen the storm coming in, and it appeared they were trying to paddle back as well.

"Will those girls be okay, Dad?" Lucy asked.

"I'm sure they'll be okay. They're probably better at this sort of thing than we are."

They could hear the rumble of thunder growing louder and felt the first droplets of rain. Yet the shore was still so far away, they could just barely make it out. Charles wished he had not lost track of where they were. The world around them was becoming dark, and Charles could smell moisture in the air. A quick streak of lightning flashed over the lake, not far from where they were. His arms grew more and more tired as he paddled. He knew that if his wife were still alive, she would never have forgiven him for bringing Lucy out so far. She was all he had left. He looked at her and tried to smile as she grew more and more frightened by the approaching storm.

"Lucy," he said as he paddled, "I love you very much."

Part Six

Absolution

Chapter Forty-Four

J ust over the landscape of tortured ice, a flickering gray light crept slowly up from the darkness, beginning the slow divide between night and dawn. In this dull whiteness, objects began to re-form from nothingness, trees reappeared from their black slumber, and houses materialized on streets wiped clean from the storm.

The three of them stared out at the barren, ice-riddled lake that twisted as if the water beneath it was trying to break through and gasp for air. Sarah could see the vast expanse of ice, seemingly endless past the snow, which obscured much of their view. The mainland on the other side of the lake had disappeared in the wintry haze of the storm. Sarah held tightly onto Luke. She could feel her wet clothes beneath her winter gear and shivered violently as her fever rose. Her hands shook, and she hoped Luke would not notice. The exhaustion and fever had taken control of her senses. Several times, she had thought about trying to call Alice. The thought of it made her want to both cry and vomit at once. If she were ever going to be in front of a warm fireplace again, it would have to be back on the mainland. Sarah hoped all this would distract her and dull her senses once they tried to cross the ice. Already, she could feel her heart pounding as they looked out over the great white expanse.

"How long to get across?" she asked.

Luke shook his head and looked through his binoculars out over the ice. "In this? With the three of us on the snowmobile?" He hissed through his teeth and watched a cloud of moisture rise above him. "Maybe an hour?"

Mark looked down at the machine. "You got enough gas in this thing to make it all the way across?"

Luke glanced down and saw that the fuel gauge was near empty. "Maybe not all the way. But hopefully most of the way." He turned and looked at them. "At some point, we may have to get out and just fucking run." He looked at Sarah, who nodded, then at Mark, who shrugged.

"I'm not staying on this fucking island with that thing. I'll hopscotch across that lake if I have to."

Sarah held on tighter to Luke. "I don't think she's going to let us leave."

Luke turned around again. "Alright, I feel like you two are holding out on me. First the Mayor with his bullshit, and now this girl or whatever it was. I can't help feeling like

I'm the only one left out of this thing." He surveyed his surroundings. "I mean, not that I want to wind up dead too, but considering everything that's been going on."

Sarah looked up, her eyes frightened and sad. Suddenly, the sirens began to blare again. "We don't have any more time," she said.

Luke reached out and grabbed her hand. "Can you make it?" he asked urgently. Sarah said nothing. "I'll be there with you the whole way. Won't we, Mark?" Mark nodded. "We won't leave you behind, Sarah." She clasped his hand tightly.

"Then let's go. Drive as fast as you can."

"I will. Just keep your eyes closed."

They began their descent down the snowy slope that led to the ice-covered lake. Sarah closed her eyes, clenching them tightly shut. In the darkness, she could feel them speeding up, gaining momentum. Once again, she felt her fingertips going numb, the icy cold making its way through her thin gloves. The world spun without reason, and everything was a blur. And as all logic disappeared, so did any sadness she thought she might have felt about leaving her home forever. These thoughts were interrupted as Luke slammed on the brakes and let out a loud "Jesus!" The snowmobile skidded over the slick earth, and Sarah could not tell if they had even reached the lake yet. She was terrified to open her eyes but forced herself to.

They had not quite reached the lake but were mere yards away from it. Sarah could see now what had made Luke stop. Up ahead, out on the lake, there were dozens of them, if not more. From a distance, they almost looked like icy scarecrows, standing strong against the winds. But through the gusts of snow, she could see that they were something else.

"What the hell are those?" Mark barked, his glasses fogged over from the flakes.

Luke squinted. "It looks like...people. Or statues of people on the ice." He took out his binoculars. Through them, he could see up close the frozen, tortured expressions of what he now realized were the remaining residents. They were frozen in various poses, and all appeared to be reaching out in pain or terror, as if pleading for help. Was it meant to be a blockade? He could easily maneuver around them. "It's the rest of the islanders," he said shakily.

Sarah took the binoculars from him and looked at them. "Are they alive? Why are they all just standing there?"

Luke shook his head. "I don't think they're alive, Sarah."

Mark waved off the binoculars. "Maybe it's a warning."

"Yeah," Sarah agreed. "But a warning of what? For us to stay on the island or leave?"

Luke took a deep breath and felt the frigid air fill his lungs. "Well, we know what happens if we stay. Our best bet right now is to get out of here, like we planned." He looked at Sarah. "Ok?" She nodded. "Good," he said. "Then let's get the fuck off this island."

Luke started up the engine. Sarah closed her eyes and felt the rough transition of the mobile leaving land and moving over the ice that surrounded the island like an arctic moat. Sarah could feel her heart race, her legs going numb, and the all-too-familiar trembling of her body. It was another panic attack coming on. Already she was finding it hard to breathe, and the tighter she closed her eyes, the more her mind was aware that she was getting farther and farther from the island. Her fever and the dizziness she had felt growing were now muted by the terrible darkness that threatened to swallow her whole, like a giant mouth that had always been surrounding the island, waiting for her. And now she was willfully jumping in, arms outstretched. She opened her eyes to see how far they were from the island and found they were still so close that she could almost touch it.

She could still go back. Maybe, if she turned back now, everything would be as it had been before the storm fell upon the island. Alice would still be alive, waiting for her with a hot cup of coffee and a snarky remark. The Mayor would be there too, sipping a glass of whiskey. The months would pass and get warmer, and after the great thaw, everyone would return, and the island would come alive again. She would see the orange glow of the July sun setting on the horizon over the sparkling water as the boats bobbed gently upon the calm waves. When she was younger, she would watch the sun go down as the moon rose to take its place. The blue sky would darken to indigo and then fill with stars, with the sound of crickets chirping and fireflies flashing like Christmas lights all over the island. But now she was leaving it all behind, leaving behind the safety of her home. She couldn't breathe. She gasped for air, as if she were sinking beneath the ice into frozen depths unknown.

"I have to go back," she gasped, barely audible. Neither of them heard her. "Please stop. Please take me back." It felt like something out of a nightmare. To call out, but not have anyone hear her. She had dreamt of this before but had told no one. She had even refrained from writing about it in her dream journal. She didn't want to die out here, but each second away from the island felt like someone was wringing the life from her body the way one twists water from a rag. She shook Luke's shoulders and screamed with all the air she had left in her lungs. "Luke, take me back!"

Mark finally heard her. "Luke, stop the snowmobile!" he shouted.

Luke didn't turn around. "We can make it!"

Sarah felt her head spinning as nausea overtook her. She knew it would be only a matter of minutes before she blacked out. It felt as if her chest was collapsing into itself. Mark shook his head. "We have to take her back."

"We already know what's going to happen to us if we go back."

Sarah could feel her grip loosening on Luke as the world spun around her. She felt the blood rushing in her ears and heard the sounds of the storm slowly fading out. And then all was blackness, and her unconscious body slid off the mobile.

Luke felt her body disappear from behind him, and the absence of warmth that had been there a minute ago. He yelled, "Grab her!" But she was already beyond their reach, and her body fell limply onto the ice. Luke slammed on the brakes and made such a sharp turn that he nearly fell off. As they spun around the rough, jagged ice, they could see the outline of her body on the ice. Luke pulled up alongside her and jumped off before the snowmobile came to a full stop. He knelt at her side and held her face in his hands. Still warm. Very warm. Burning to the touch.

"Sarah, can you hear me?" Luke turned toward Mark. "She's got a high fever. "

Mark looked back towards the vastness of the expanse between them and the mainland they could not yet see. "She'll never make it across the ice. Even if we make it halfway there, we'll still have to walk the rest of it."

"Then I'll fucking carry her!" Luke yelled, and his voice carried farther than he would have liked. The sirens had stopped, and all was quiet except for the howling of the wind across the frozen surface of the lake.

Mark looked at him sadly. It was the first warm look Luke could ever recall Mark giving him. "We'll never make it to the other side alive."

Luke looked down at Sarah. Her eyes were fluttering, and she was mumbling something. "I'm not going to leave her here." The words choked out of Luke's mouth. "She's my responsibility. All of you are my responsibility, and I've let most of you die. I'm not leaving anyone behind, Mark."

"Mark's right." Sarah's voice was a whisper, and her eyes were barely open. "You'll get to the other side faster without me. You can call for help then. I'll only slow you down."

"If something happened to you here, I'd never forgive myself."

"You have a better chance of making it without me. Trust me."

Luke knelt next to Sarah and whispered into her ear, "I love you. I have always loved you. I will always love you." He had waited his whole life to say it. And now that he had, he walked back to the snowmobile, his heart heavy with the weight of the words he wished he had said years ago.

Mark held her hand. "I'll stay here with her. You go." Luke looked at them as if he barely recognized them. "Go! Now!" Mark instructed him.

Luke turned the snowmobile back around and continued his trek across the ice, alone.

Chapter Forty-Five

"You can open your eyes now," Mark told Sarah. He was trying not to scream, but found he had no other way for her to hear him over the storm. He held her close to him. As her eyes fluttered open, the world still spun, but she recognized her surroundings. The familiar line of ice, immediately followed by an expanse of pine trees covered in snow. The sky was lighter now, and she could see the island starting to come back to life. The darkness of night dissolved into pure white, a frenzy of snow and wind she had never known before. She was warmer now, and she knew that something wasn't right.

"Here," Mark said, reaching out to her. "Take my hand."

She grabbed it, and he pulled her up over the ice bank back onto land. She could feel herself breathe again and felt the pounding of her heart begin to slow. But she was still far from calm. Because of her, they were back on the island again.

She looked up at Mark: "I'm sorry," was all she could manage to say.

Mark held her, but she felt no warmth from his embrace. "It's okay, Sarah. I'm not going to leave you."

Sarah looked out at Luke on the lake. "Can he make it?"

Mark continued to watch Luke for some time. "He's going to have to." He finally met Sarah's gaze. "Trust me, he has a better chance without us."

Even with his snow goggles, Luke's eyes stung. The ice beneath him was anything but smooth, and several times he hit invisible drifts so hard that he nearly capsized. He checked the fuel gauge and saw the needle hovering dangerously near E. *Please, just enough*, he thought. *Just get me far enough*. He imagined the vehicle slowly running out of gas, coming to a stop with the mainland just in sight, and prayed for a burst of adrenaline to carry him the rest of the way on foot. He would insist on going back with them, of course. They would return to the island prepared, and he would bring Sarah back with him. And Mark, of course. They would have to give Sarah something to sedate her for the trip next time.

Just ahead, he could see the first of the frozen figures, demonic ice sculptures frozen in their wretched pain. The ice was too thick to reveal who they were; the thought of all those he had cared for made him sick. One of the figures was holding the hand of what must have been a child, as if they were trying to protect them. Luke thought again of the little girl on the carousel at the amusement park.

The island grew smaller in his mirror as he approached the field of frozen scarecrows before him. He passed another one that was on its knees, one hand over its eyes, the other reaching out in a futile attempt to protect itself. It appeared that most of the islanders were out here. It had all happened so fast that most of them probably never knew what was happening. *Better for them*, Luke thought.

The ice was becoming more uneven now. Giant snowdrifts sprang up out of nowhere, often concealing treacherous, jagged ice. In his mirror, the island was still within sight, while the gauge still flirted with E. *Still so much farther to go*, he thought. *Just get me a little bit farther.*

The snowmobile suddenly shook beneath Luke. He felt he was no longer in control, and it was simply guiding him across the ice with an unknown destination. *At least it's getting lighter now*, he thought. He almost laughed as he realized the false comfort the light brought and how vulnerable they had always been on that island. He doubted if light or dark made any difference to this thing. The ice was increasingly uneven, and surrounded by the small army of ice figures was a large snow slope. It was the only way through this patch; going around it would mean backtracking and wasting what precious little gas he had left. Luke felt a sudden surge of adrenaline. *Fuck it*, he thought.

As he maneuvered up the slope, he quickly discovered that it was much steeper than he had anticipated. As he cranked the machine up to full speed, he felt himself going airborne and felt his body slowly slipping away from the machine beneath him. For a few moments, it felt as if he were floating weightlessly in a white abyss, cold and endless, until he came tumbling back down onto the ice, and he rolled down the other side of the slope. He rolled over and heard the loud crash of the snowmobile, catching quick glimpses of the broken pieces spinning across the ice. Once his body hit the bottom of the slope, all the noise around him stopped. When his head finally stopped spinning and he realized nothing was broken, he got to his feet to continue toward the mainland.

"Give me the binoculars!" Sarah yelled to Mark. From their vantage point, they had seen the crash and the snowmobile go airborne. The binoculars shook in her hands, and for a moment she had difficulty focusing them on anything. Everything looked white, and Luke seemed to be lost amongst the ice. But then she spotted him, struggling to stand up.

"Shit," she nearly whispered.

Mark hovered close by. "What is it? What do you see?"

"The snowmobile's wrecked."

"Can he still drive it?"

She shook her head. "I doubt it." She could see the debris from the snowmobile scattered all around Luke. It was a miracle that he was even able to get up. She watched as Luke pulled himself slowly to his feet and limped over to the machine. He appeared to inspect it, tried the engine, and shook his head. "It's not starting," Sarah said. "He's going to have to go the rest of the way on foot." As she refocused the lenses, she could see that he was limping quite a bit. He attempted to run but stopped almost immediately, favoring his right leg. He continued walking, but not very fast. *Hurry, Luke*, she thought. The lake looked even larger with him out there on it, and Sarah could not see the mainland through the snow. She knew that eventually he, too, would be out of her sight as he got closer to the other side.

Then something caught her eye. A movement in her vision, but it wasn't Luke. Sarah wasn't sure if it was her exhaustion or her fever, but it almost appeared as if the ice figures were starting to move. Her vision blurred again, and Sarah quickly tried to readjust the lenses and focus back on Luke. The binoculars came back into focus. She could see them clearly now, and her heart began to race. She had been right: the ice figures were indeed moving. They were moving towards Luke, following him.

Luke knew the moment he put weight on his ankle that it wasn't broken. A bad sprain, maybe, but it could still bear his weight. But he knew the trek to the mainland would take him much longer now, perhaps the better part of the day. The prospect of not reaching land until nightfall was disheartening. He had hated the idea of leaving Sarah and Mark behind. He did not want them to see another nightfall on that island. And so he limped on, hoping that the other two could see him. He turned around and waved to let them know that he was alright. But as he turned around, the ice figures seemed to be closer now. There were even more of them, surrounding him. He assumed it to be the after-effects of the crash and shrugged it off. All that mattered now was getting to the other side. Above the roaring of the wind, Luke heard something he thought was a scream. Distant, but it seemed to rise above the wind—a voice, calling his name. It sounded like a woman's voice, and then a man's, and then both together.

He could hear it more clearly now. It was Mark and Sarah calling his name. He turned around again, and through the snow, he could just make them out. They were flailing their arms frantically, pointing at something. *Maybe they think I'm hurt from the crash?* he wondered. *Maybe they want me to come back?* He waved to them again. "I'm ok!" he shouted. But he doubted they would be able to hear him. And then he heard a heavy, scraping sound nearby. It was close, as if someone was dragging something across the ice. As he turned around to continue his trek, Luke realized he was completely surrounded by the ice figures. Their stationary menace had become mobile.

They moved slowly, and had his ankle not been injured, Luke could have easily run past them. He could see their faces beneath the layer of ice and imagined they had been dead for some time. Yet there they were, limbs moving, and approaching him with malicious intent. He realized his gun was back in the snowmobile, and even if he had it, he doubted it would be of much use.

He would have to run and hope his ankle could withstand the pain. The distance between him and the mainland seemed infinite. Luke thought of Sarah, unable to leave the island. He thought of the storm that seemed ready to swallow up the entirety of the world. He wondered if it would move onto other places beyond the island, tearing away all living things until there was nothing left but a winter without end. With this final thought, he began to run, and as he did so, he could clearly see the ice figures moving towards him. His ankle throbbed with pain each time he placed weight upon it.

As he ran past the first of the ice figures, he saw no semblance of humanity beneath the layer of ice. Only the limbs and semblance of a head made it appear somewhat human. Up close, their lack of features made them much more menacing, and they moved much faster than he had anticipated. He ran past the first few without turning to see if they were following him. In his peripheral vision, he saw more of them closing in, but he continued looking straight ahead, toward the bleak white wall of oblivion. But as he ran on, the weariness from the long night began to catch up with him. He could feel himself tiring, feel his heart struggle from the exertion, and cursed himself for being out of shape. He thought of Sarah watching him from afar, watching her last shred of hope sputter and dwindle. *Some hero I am*, he thought.

Then he felt something grab onto the loose fabric of his jacket, something that pulled so hard he was almost forced backwards. He lurched forward and pulled himself free, and as he did, he heard dozens more footsteps behind him, moving faster. There was no doubt in his mind that he was going to have to walk part of the way across, but he was very far from an Olympic athlete, and the frigid air made it difficult to breathe. His lungs were already on fire, though he did his best to block out the pain.

And then finally, he made it past them. Up ahead, the going seemed clearer. There was nothing between him and the other side but the snow drifts and ice that he prayed were strong enough to support his weight. *I can do this*, he thought. *I can make it*. He thought about all the times he had been across the lake via boat or ferry. Thousands, maybe more. But he had never been so far out on it when it was frozen over. The lake seemed alien to him, almost unreal.

Sarah. He winced as he ran on. The moment he'd said he would go alone, he knew that he might never see her again. Now, as he ran farther and farther away from the island, completely out of her view, he wished he had told her he had stayed on the island just to be close to her. That he had wanted nothing more than the two of them to be together, watching the seasons come and go. But the urgency of the moment had overtaken him, and he realized that he had left her without even saying goodbye. He hadn't been to church in years and hadn't prayed in nearly as long, but now, as he ran, he spoke out loud to God: "If I don't make it, please protect Sarah." Suddenly, he felt something cold grab hold of his ankle. Down onto the cold, hard surface of the ice, he fell face first, and the whole world went black.

Sarah gripped her binoculars hard as she watched Luke fall. "Shit," she whispered.

Mark watched alongside her, unable to make much out through the snow. "What is it? What happened?"

"He fell. He fell and he's not getting up." Sarah adjusted the lens again. Luke seemed to be struggling against something. It looked almost as if his foot was stuck in the ice, and he was trying to pull it free. As she watched, she saw the group of ice figures slowly making their way towards him.

"Shit," she said again. "Get up, Luke. Get the fuck up!"

Luke looked down in disbelief as a strange tentacle of ice gripped his foot. As hard as he tried, he could not free himself. Through the snowy wind, he could see the silhouetted figures approaching him, their images blurred by the snow. He had a sudden vision of a coyote chewing off its foot to free itself from a trap, and he almost laughed. He had no such sharp object to cut his leg free, and even if he had, he'd doubt that he'd get very far. He tried to smash away the ice with his free foot, but it felt like stone and would not give him up.

As he watched the figures growing nearer, their arms outstretched, he began kicking harder. "Let me go, you fuck!" he yelled. But as much as he tried to pull away, the ice seemed to only tighten its grip. He could feel the coldness traveling up his leg. As he looked up again, he realized they had surrounded him.

Luke hoped Mark was making sure that Sarah was not watching. He had always wondered what profound thoughts he might have at the moment of his death, if he would see some kind of divine light, or feel some kind of interconnectedness with the universe. He would finally understand what it was all about, and his soul would drift away and join all the others who were waiting for him in some place of eternal light, warmth, and love. But he experienced none of this now, and as he watched the ice figures approaching him, the only profound thought he had was, I'm *fucked.*

Mark would not allow Sarah to watch what was happening out on the ice. He had grabbed the binoculars away from her, and she fought him for them, then sobbed and buried her face in his chest. He, too, looked away. Mercifully, they could not hear Luke's screams through the howling of the wind. Mark held her tightly even when the strong gusts of wind coming over the lake threatened to knock them both over. Sarah clung onto Mark, still crying.

"It's just us now," she sobbed. "He's gone."

"Yeah. But we're going to be ok. I promise."

"I'm so sorry I made you stay here with me." She pulled away and looked up at him. "So, what do we do now?"

Mark looked back at the island and remained silent for some time.

"What is it?" she asked him.

He stood there watching the trees bend against the wind, staring past them deep into something she could not see. "We need to go to the quarry."

"The quarry? Why?"

Finally, he looked at her and reached out to feel her forehead. It was hot to the touch. "Your fever's getting worse."

"That doesn't matter now."

"Let's get to the quarry. I'll explain on the way." He noticed how pale she was and that she was shivering. "We obviously can't take the snowmobile. Can you make it there on foot?"

Sarah could feel that her clothes were sopping wet under her jacket. "I don't have much of a choice. Let's go."

Chapter Forty-Six

20 Years Earlier

A few hours had passed since the storm had come and gone, and the streets bore witness to the reckless fury it had brought down upon the island. The streets were covered with fallen trees and their limbs. Power lines spewing sparks still dangled in what was left of the breeze, and yellow police tape draped the trees and streets like Christmas tinsel. But it was far from quiet; everywhere there was the sound of chainsaws and police sirens—the cacophony of cleanup. Neighbors stood outside talking and assessing the damage. The island would most likely need to be closed to tourists for a week, some said, which would hurt the pockets of many on the island.

As the cloud cover began to dissipate, a low sun emerged for the final hours of daylight, casting a strange orange glow over the island. It was bright but strange, and the trees that were still standing cast long, eerie shadows as they swayed in the strong breeze. The sky had cleared, but the fear from the storm remained strong in the air. In the distance, one could still see the tail end of the darkness making its way across the lake, the storm clouds still flashing. Most of the power was out on the island, and once the sun set behind the horizon of the lake, there was a strong possibility that they would fall asleep and wake up still in darkness.

From the shore, the three men looked out over the lake, their boat bobbing back and forth. Frank looked through his binoculars, watching the search boats, including a Coast Guard boat. The three of them were hidden by the shroud of cliffs that faced the north side of the island. They stood in the shadow of the rock that eclipsed the last of the dying red sun. They were all exhausted, and Frank could feel his legs shaking under the weight of his body. All he wanted was to be back at home with his two daughters, whom Gabriella had graciously agreed to watch until he returned home. But he knew he would not sleep tonight—and might not sleep ever again—if he didn't go back out on the lake to search for them. They had already been back out several times and, like the others, had found nothing.

Before them, the waves were rough, unfriendly to most boats. There was still a gale warning, and they had been advised not to venture out far from the island. The waves were higher than Frank had ever seen here before, and the beaches on all sides of the island would be closed to the public. The ferries will not be running tonight. Those on the island would have to stay the night, whether they wanted to or not.

There was something foul in the air, even stronger than the mess a storm stirs up. Leaking septic tanks? An overflowing sewer? All possible, Frank thought, but this smelled even fouler. It seemed to be coming from the lake itself. The sky above them had cleared, and the scythe moon had revealed itself along with the stars that dotted the transition from day to night. On any other night, it would have been a beautiful sight. Frank clenched and unclenched his fists restlessly.

"We're going out again," he decided abruptly.

Mark, who was kneeling beside him, staring out across the lake, looked up at him. He picked up a large stone and tossed it into the water, watching it splash and then sink instantly. "What the hell do you think we're going to find that we didn't before?"

"I'm not going back home until somebody finds something," Frank replied.

Mark spat on the stony beach. "You saw those waves. We almost flipped over twice. You want to go back out there again? You want your daughters to wake up tomorrow morning without a dad?"

That was enough for Frank, who pulled Mark up by his coat. "We have as much goddamn right to be out there as the others. If they're still out there somewhere, I'm not going to just leave them to die."

Jack pushed himself between the two, separating them. "Enough, the both of you. This is stupid. Frank, Mark's right. Those waves could capsize us, too, and what good would that be to anybody, your family? Mine too. I think enough bad shit has already happened today, don't you?"

Frank dusted off his jacket. "You really want to go to bed tonight with that on your conscience?"

Mark shook his head. "Listen, it wasn't our fault. It wasn't anybody's fault. We did everything we could." He leaned in closer to Frank. "Listen. No one will blame you for this, ok? We tried. Everybody knows that. They've got the Coast Guard out there now. Let them handle it. They have the training and all the equipment. We're just three slobs on a little fucking boat."

Frank walked into the water towards their boat. Mark ran after him. "Frank, don't be stupid. It's crazy to keep going out there. We got damn lucky the first few, but if the three of us..."

"Then stay here!" Frank shouted. He began to push their boat further out into the water. He did not look back or ask for their help. Mark threw his arms up in defeat and began walking away.

"What the hell is that?" Jack yelled from behind them. "Look out there, in the water!"

From a distance, it looked like a large tree branch, bobbing unnaturally in the rough tide, just a shadowed speck floating across the glittering water. But as they looked closer, they could see the silhouette of what appeared to be a figure, the head, arm, and shoulder of someone holding on. The waves were indifferent to the passenger aboard the object, and as each wave picked it up, another would throw it back down into the water again. Frank turned to the others. "I'm going back out there; you two can stay here if you want." Mark climbed into the boat but said nothing as they looked ahead at the object, which was still a good distance from the shore. Going against the tide would make their trip more difficult. As Jack began to step in, Frank stopped him.

"It's best you stay here, Jack. Three of us will make it too heavy, and you can help pull us in when we get back."

"Do you want me to go call for help?" Jack looked restless, unsure if he wanted to follow Frank's order. He was used to being the one in charge.

"No, just wait here until we come back. We may need your help."

Jack decided he could live with that logic and watched as they pushed the boat deeper into the water. Frank started the motor up, and the boat fought against the waves as they made their way toward the object.

As they approached, they saw what appeared to be a middle-aged man, soaked from head to toe, and clinging to a wooden board. They steadied their boat near him, but the waves carried them up and down, making it difficult to get close without crashing into him. Frank pulled out a life preserver and tossed it to the man. "Grab it!" he yelled. But the man held tightly onto the board and did not even look at the preserver or up at their boat. He clung to the plank of wood as if it were the last object on earth, floating over dark oblivion.

Mark looked over Frank's shoulder. "A few more of these waves and he's done for."

"I know." Frank looked around the boat for anything—rope, a fishing pole—but there was nothing. "Get ready to pull me back in!" he shouted, not waiting for a reply. He jumped off, and before Mark could respond, he was submerged in the rough waters.

As Frank resurfaced, he found himself near the life preserver. He grabbed it and began to swim toward the plank. "Hey!" he yelled at the man, who still did not respond. Frank kicked hard, wishing he had taken his shoes off before he jumped in. But there was no time. The man seemed only half alive, and with his hair plastered to his face, Frank could not tell his age. He clung onto the board as the waves threatened to part them with each rise and fall.

Frank fought against the waves as he neared the plank. In his hand, he clutched the rope from the life preserver, knowing even before he reached the man that it would be difficult to bring him back. He seemed to be in no condition to swim if he fell off. As Frank struggled to keep his head above water, he screamed, "Listen to me! I'm going to take you back to the boat!" Frank thought he saw the man glance his way briefly, then turn away. "Take my hand and I'll bring you back!" he yelled.

Frank reached out and felt the hard surface of the board, clasped it, and then pulled himself forward. With his other hand, he tossed the life preserver onto the board, then swam around to the other side where the man was hanging on for dear life and placed his arms carefully around him. Surprisingly, the man did not struggle as Frank pried him away from the plank. The weight of them dipped the board briefly underwater, and more waves threatened to submerge it completely. Mark waited on the boat, ready to pull them both in. It was all he could do just to stand upright as the boat rocked violently back and forth. Frank slipped his arm through the life preserver, his other arm clutching tightly to the man's waist. The man did not fight him, his body floating limply like a ragdoll in the water.

Once he saw Frank was ready, Mark pulled hard on the rope and began dragging it through the water. The slack was heavy, and he was already tired from their earlier rescue. As he pulled the two men back into the boat, the last red glow of the sun sank beneath the waves and disappeared. Night would be upon them soon.

On the beach, Jack could only watch as the boat returned to shore. As they grew closer, he waded out until he was nearly thigh deep to help pull them back to shore. Though he had seen them pull the man onboard, Jack could see only Mark and Frank and assumed he must be resting on the bottom of the boat. Alive, he hoped. Mark and Frank jumped out, and the three of them pushed the boat through the water until they heard it scraping rocks on the bottom and could push no more. Jack and Mark lifted the man out, his limbs hanging limply.

"Is he alive?" Jack asked, watching as they gently placed him on the beach.

Frank nodded. "He was still holding on when I got to him. He's in shock, but he's alive."

The man lay still on the wet stones as the three looked down at him. "No sign of the girl?" Jack asked. The other two said nothing, just shook their heads. Frank knelt next to the man and felt his wrist for a pulse. The man took slow, shallow breaths. Frank looked up at the other two. "We need to get him to a hospital," he said. As he spoke the words, the man slowly opened his eyes.

"Where am I?" he asked hoarsely.

Frank looked down at him. "You're ok. We got you back to the beach. Just take it easy. We're going to get you some help. What's your name?"

Charles looked to both sides. "Charles. My name is Charles. Where's my daughter? Where's Lucy?"

Frank shook his head. "We found you out there alone. You're lucky to be alive."

Charles sat up. His breathing was agitated. "What do you mean, alone? Lucy was out there with me! She was on the boat with me!" He suddenly seemed to regain his strength. "Lucy!" He shouted, his voice desperate.

Frank tried to calm him. "Just take it easy. You've really been through it. Just take it easy." He put his hand on the man's shoulder, but Charles shook it off."

"Don't touch me!" Charles rolled onto his knees, then leaned his head forward into the sand as if in some sort of strange prayer. He moaned briefly and coughed. It looked as if he were waking from some terrible nightmare. Charles pulled himself up to his feet. He looked to be about middle-aged, balding a bit, but strongly built. His legs shook under his weight, and he walked a crooked line toward the water's edge. He began wading back into the water and screamed out toward the horizon: "Lucy! Lucy, where are you?!" The three men stood behind him, watching him scream at the lake. A large wave threatened to knock him down, but again he screamed, "Lucy, baby, I'm coming!" He looked around, dazed, until he spotted the empty boat on the beach. He stumbled his way over to it and began pushing it back into the water.

Jack and Mark ran after him. "You can't go back out there!" Mark shouted. "We just risked our lives to bring you back here!"

Charles gestured frantically at the lake. "My daughter's out there!" he cried.

Frank approached. "Look, Charles, you have to listen to us. We searched out there for hours. They're still out there looking for her now. They won't stop until they find her. But in the meantime, we need to get you some help." As they began pulling him back to shore, he fought against them and slapped them away.

"I'm not leaving here without my daughter!"

Mark grabbed his arm harder this time. "Look, man, if you go back out there, you're dead. We risked our lives to get you back here. Like he said, they're out there looking for your daughter now."

Charles shook them off again, with more power this time. He turned around suddenly and looked at them. "I remember you now. You're the ones that left us out there." His eyes narrowed.

Frank stepped back, sensing the escalation. "What are you talking about?"

"You left us out there. My daughter and I. We were in the boat. You saw us. I know you did. I know you heard us."

Mark stepped up alongside Frank. "Look, we can talk about that later. Right now, we need you to come with us."

Charles took a step closer to them. "You heard us. I know you heard us. I know you saw my daughter. She was only twelve."

Frank threw his hands up. "We couldn't go back for you. If we had taken you on board, we would have all sunk and died." His chest hurt from his heart pounding, and daylight was slipping away. "It was the most difficult decision I ever had to make. But there were children on the other boat, too. They didn't have any adults there to help them. What choice did we have?"

Charles moved closer. "Your children. They were your children, weren't they?" Frank said nothing. Charles scanned over them. "Look at you, look at all of you. Murderers. Just looking out for yourselves." He lunged forward and jumped at Frank, and the two of them went tumbling into the shallow water. Charles rained blows upon Frank, who tried to cover his face. "You murdered my daughter. You murdered us."

Jack attempted to separate them, but the man pushed him back into the water. As he got to his feet, he stepped on a razor-shaped rock, which sliced deep into his flesh. He screamed out in pain and fell back into the water. Mark grabbed Charles' arm and attempted to rip him away, but Charles turned and landed a sharp blow on his cheek, hard enough for him to be spun around and momentarily dazed. He had not expected that much force behind the strike.

As Frank tried to roll out from underneath him, Charles grabbed his throat with both hands and shoved his head under the water. Frank's arms were tired, and he did not have enough fight left in him to pry the man's frenzied grip from his neck. He thought of his daughters and how he held them tightly when they were back on the boat. He didn't want to let them out of his sight, and now he wished he hadn't. He knew they were waiting for him back at the house, counting on him to come home. *Is this how it ends for me?* he thought. *Maybe it is. Maybe this is what I deserve.* The world was growing dark around him, the water ready to rush into his lungs at any moment. Then, suddenly, the grip was gone, and Frank saw the shaky silhouette of Charles collapse into the water beside him.

Frank burst out of the water, gasping for air. Mark pulled him up, and Frank saw in his hand a sharp, jagged rock with what looked like blood on it. Next to him, Charles floated face down in the water, his limp body carried gently on the waves. The water slowly turned inky crimson around him.

Mark looked at Frank, who was still clutching at his sore neck. "Are you ok?" Frank nodded silently, watching the floating body.

"Quick, help me." Frank grabbed onto the body and began dragging it back to shore. He turned Charles over and saw the blood gushing from his temple. Behind him, Mark looked at the rock for some time before throwing it as far as he could back into the lake. As Frank continued dragging the body to land, Mark grabbed Charles' other arm and helped Frank lift him from the water until only his legs were still submerged. They set him gently down on the rocks, the blood from his wound spilling out upon the smooth sandstone.

Frank took off his shirt to cover Charles' wound. Mark stood, watching them and shaking his head. "I tried to get him off you. I just wanted to stop him, that's all." Frank felt Charles' wrist for a pulse, then his neck. He leaned down to listen for a breath. Charles was ice-cold from the water, and Frank knew he would never be warm again.

Mark stepped back. "Is he alive? Is he ok?" He rubbed his hands together nervously. "The poor guy, I must have hit him really hard. He must be out cold." Mark laughed a little. "Gonna wake up with one hell of a headache."

Frank did not look up at him. "He's dead, Mark."

Jack limped over to them and fell onto the sand. "Is he gonna' make it?"

Frank shook his head and took his shirt from Charles' wound. It was red and soaked in blood. He attempted to rinse it in the waves, to no avail.

Mark ran his hands through his hair. "Jesus, I didn't mean to kill him." He looked at Jack. "You saw the whole thing, right? I mean, Jesus, Frank, he was going to kill you. You woulda died."

Jack nodded. "He's right, Frank. That guy wasn't going to stop. He was out of his mind. Mark did what he had to do to stop him."

Frank looked at his bloodied shirt, then stuffed it into his pocket. He sat there for some time, watching the crescent moon rise over the lake. His daughters were waiting for him. He knew they would not fall asleep until he returned home. Out across the lake, he could still see the search boats, looking for the bodies. He should call them in and tell them they only had to look for one body now.

After a long silence, Frank finally stood up. "We can't just leave him here."

Mark looked back out over the lake. "What if we just pushed him back into the water, like we never found him?" He nodded, agreeing with his own plan. "Then, when they find him, they'll think he just hit his head on a rock or something."

Frank shook his head. "We need to get the sheriff down here. He'll understand when we explain what happened."

Mark grabbed Frank by the shirt. "Don't be an idiot. I'm not going to jail for this."

Jack tried to separate them but fell back down again. "He's right. It was self-defense. We have witnesses. Everyone will understand."

Mark let go of Frank. "I'm not going to jail. We can just push him back out onto the lake, like I said."

"He'll just wash up again by morning," Frank yelled back. "He'll wash up, and someone else will find him. How do you think it'll look if they find out we did this and tried to cover it up?"

Mark paced back and forth on the beach. "I've been drinking, Frank. You don't think they'll test for that? I have pot in my system. You don't think they'll test for that? You don't think that'll show up? A drunk, drugged-up hippie bashes in a man's skull. You know exactly how they feel about my reputation on this island, Frank. If word gets out about this, they'll want a scapegoat. The Sheriff already doesn't like me. He won't mind throwing me under the bus."

Frank shook his head. "It's not right. We have to tell them."

Mark continued pleading his case. "If you tell anybody, then I'm as good as fucked. I saved your life. You owe me one and you know it!"

Frank looked at Jack, who nodded. "He's right, Frank. He saved you. It was my fucking fault. If I hadn't cut my foot, I would have been able to help Mark."

Frank looked at them both, then down at the man's body. "So, what are we going to do with him?"

Mark looked around as if he could find some tangible answer waiting on the beach with them. The temperature had begun to drop, and they were cold as they stood there, the three of them, damp. "Why not toss him back in the water, like I said?"

"No, Mark, he'll wash up, and they'll see it wasn't an accident. Think about it... Everyone is out searching the water right now. If we leave him, someone is bound to find him sooner or later."

Mark threw his arms up in frustration. "Well, we can't just leave him here on the beach."

"No, we can't," Frank agreed grimly.

They all watched as Charles' limbs gently lifted with the waves, his arms and legs slowly rising and falling again, as if the water was using him as a ghoulish puppet. Off in the distance, they could see searchlights from the boats appear and disappear behind the waves. As stars filled the sky, they were shrouded in darkness.

"I know where we can take him," Jack said suddenly.

Their path was lit only by the occasional flashing of fireflies as they carried the body down the steep, rocky slope of the quarry. Frank realized just how quiet it was tonight, how completely alone they were on this part of the island. Jack, with his injured foot, had limped back the other way to town, promising to touch base with them when they returned. How many times had he brought his daughters here to play and hide? The dynamite-blasted rocks had created caves and caverns. There were so many that they eventually had to ban the public from entering and getting stuck or trapped within the granite basins. Frank hated the idea of defiling a place that had meant so much to his family. All of those memories here would seem poisoned now. As he and Mark reached the apex of the quarry, he realized just how large the chasm was. It was Jack who had remembered that it was to be filled with water this summer, submerging most of it.

Suddenly, they both stopped in their tracks. "Where?" Frank asked.

Mark looked around. They did not have flashlights with them, so there was only the light from the moon and stars to guide them. Thankfully, they would have been completely invisible to anyone who might be watching from miles in any direction. In the dim glow of moonlight, they found a pile of rocks that seemed to create a tomb of sorts. Mark pointed at it. "How about there?"

Frank could just barely make it out. "Is there an opening?"

"Let's find out."

The two of them placed the body gently down at the foot of the giant rockpile and searched for an opening. The loose rocks were treacherous, and neither of them wanted a broken bone from a misstep.

"Over here," Mark said in almost a whisper.

Frank crawled over the rocks to where Mark stood. Mark clicked his lighter and shone it into an open chasm of darkness. Mark nodded: "This might work."

Inside was a small cave of sorts, a narrow tunnel that twisted and turned downwards. Mark looked at Frank and said, "We can put him down there, then pile some rocks on top so he won't rise to the surface when they fill this place up with water? What do you think?"

Frank nodded. "It looks deep enough. But how do we know nobody's gonna find him before they bring in the water?"

"It's all private property anyway. They'll fill this all up at the end of the month."

Frank sighed heavily. He was tired. "Alright, then." They climbed down to retrieve the body, then struggled to carry it back up again. They stopped frequently to be sure of their footing as they hoisted the body up to the entrance. Once there, they slowly pushed the man's body in. Mark carefully maneuvered the limp body down into the crooked crevice until he was certain it was at the bottom.

"There," Mark said. "Now let's get some rocks to cover him and weigh him down." The two of them scoured the ground for loose stones. After rolling a few of the larger ones down, they were satisfied. As they left the site, both said nothing. They heard crickets and frogs croaking in the distance, along with their own breathing. When they eventually parted ways, neither of them said anything to the other. They just looked at each other and then walked away, each to his own house. As he walked home, Frank picked his way around all of the fallen trees. It was late, but a few houses still had their lights on.

Later that night, Sarah awoke and looked out her window. She saw her father standing shirtless outside in the backyard, tossing his shirt into the fire pit. She wondered why her father would have built a fire so late, all by himself. *Maybe he was going to have friends over?* She thought. But he was all alone, and he looked sad. She watched him quietly as he stared into the fire, watching its flames transform the wood into ash until there was nothing left. Once the fire had died out, he came back into the house and went to bed, but did not sleep. The next morning at breakfast, he did not mention it. Sarah did not want her father to know that she had spied on him, so she too said nothing, and the night was soon forgotten. She had seen the bruises on his face and had pretended not to notice. But after that night, the whole world somehow seemed different, and her father seemed different too. She would think about this for years to come, up until the night her father was found in the water, dead. Afterwards, she always wished that she had asked him what troubled him so much and why he had looked into that fire with the greatest sadness she had ever seen.

CHAPTER FORTY-SEVEN

Sarah said nothing as she and Mark came upon the clearing of the quarry's chasm. Its gaping expanse seemed just as wide now as it had when she was a child. The thought of someone's body buried amongst all the memories she had in that place made her feel sick. She couldn't bring herself to look at Mark. "Do you remember where it is?"

Mark scanned the site quietly. It looked the same as before, blasted rock upon rock, only now it was covered in snow. "It's been a while," he whispered. "I can't tell from here. We'll have to go down there."

She didn't return his gaze. "Come on."

They climbed slowly down the steep wall. The snow provided some padding but also concealed the treacherous holes and jagged rocks beneath. They took their time, knowing they could be just one misstep away from a broken ankle, or worse. The wind had not subsided, making their descent even more difficult. Several times,

Mark offered Sarah his hand, which she refused. In her feverish delirium, her mind went to strange places. She remembered playing with Alice here in the quarry as children and laughed aloud.

Mark looked at her but said nothing. His chest felt heavy, and his breathing was labored. He had never told anyone that story, and the weight of those words left his body and soul exhausted but purged of it. Free after all these years. He thought that if he did somehow manage to survive this, prison was better than anything he could deserve. He had been living in one all these years anyway, and he was tired now. He let Sarah lead the way down to the base of the quarry.

Sarah had known every pile of rocks in the quarry before filling it up with water. Afterwards, they would sneak in after the sun went down and swim with their friends or with the boys from school. She felt almost ghoulish now, knowing she had swum in water where the dead lay. Then she thought of all the people who swam in the lake and how many bodies lay at the bottom from all the shipwrecks her father had told her about. She imagined a layer of human skulls on the floor of the lake, their vacant eyes watching, their jagged arms reaching up, ready to pull her down—

"Fuck," Mark said loudly to himself. His voice did not echo, even within the walls of the quarry. He was cold and stamped his feet as he looked around.

Sarah looked straight ahead, into nothing. The quarry blurred before her eyes; she could no longer distinguish it from the rest of the island. The rushing memories that swam in her head had been poisoned, and the island no longer felt the same. The island of her childhood, with warm summers spent running across hot pavement and the smell of tar and cotton candy in the air and daylight that never seemed to end, had vanished like a dream, disappearing in the morning mist. This island, the one where she stood now, was haunted with lies, with murder, and with ghosts. It was something from a nightmare now, one that had returned to claim all of them and drag them down under the ice.

"Why didn't he tell me?" she asked, her vision slowly coming back into focus. She was burning up and could feel herself swaying where she stood.

"Come on, Sarah. You know why." Mark couldn't meet her gaze. "The same reason he couldn't go to the police or tell anyone else what happened."

"All those years, he never said anything. Not to me. Not to Alice. Not to anyone. But you knew, Mark. Who else? Who else knew?"

Mark sighed. "Jack knew. Wherever the hell he is now, he knew."

"He's probably dead. Out on the lake, with the others."

"We were all going to take it to our graves. Honestly, Sarah, we never spoke of it to each other again."

They walked on for a bit in silence as Mark scanned the various piles of rocks caked in snow. Then Sarah continued: "My father took your ugly little secret to the grave with him. He kept his secret well, Mark. But you know the thing about ugly secrets? If you don't tell someone, then they'll eat you up inside for the rest of your life."

"I don't disagree with you there."

"But the thing is, Mark," she continued, "all this time I thought it was the guilt he felt about leaving that man and his daughter behind. I always wished that he had gone back to look for them. I dreamt about it for years. I always thought it was so strange that he never went back out there. But he did go back. It was your ugly little secret that made him jump off that cliff. He wasn't an ugly man inside until you made him that way."

Mark sighed. "I was just trying to help him. I didn't want anybody to get hurt; that's the honest truth. I didn't want your father to go back out there. I had a bad feeling about the whole thing. But you know how your dad was.

We made a pact, and he was always a man of his word. He kept it. We all kept it until now."

"This thing that's back, she wants us all dead. Do you think she gives a fuck about good intentions or pacts, Mark?" Sarah stopped to face him. "You and I both know we're the last ones left. When she comes for us, Mark, you can tell her that story too."

Mark forced a laugh. "I think she already knows. That's why she's here."

Sarah nodded. "And if, by some miracle, you and I live through this, then you can tell the police your story too."

Mark said nothing as Sarah walked on without him. She looked around at the rock mounds, as if she alone knew the spot where the body lay hidden.

"Did you forget where you put him?" She asked.

"It's been a long time, Sarah." Mark took off his hat, and he suddenly looked very old. "Honestly, I've never been back here since that night."

"Well, they only drained it a few years ago. It can't have changed too much. We'll find it." The wind showed no signs of subsiding, and a gust nearly knocked Sarah from her feet. Snow devils were spinning around the chasm, whirling and twisting and taunting them, then disintegrating back into the storm.

"Let's hope we find him before she finds us," Mark said.

"And what happens if and when we do find it?"

Mark shook his head. "I don't know."

A snow devil swirled before them, moving against the wind. It spun around them for a few moments, then moved slowly back and forth between them. It was different from the others and remained in place. They stopped in their tracks to watch this strange phenomenon, watch it dance around them with its invisible feet. Then it began to move slowly in a straight path towards a pile of rocks that was stacked very high. As it reached the surface of the pile, it finally dissipated, and Mark looked over at Sarah.

"Well, I guess that's as close to a sign as we can hope to get."

Sarah started to run. "Come on!" she shouted. They moved as quickly as they could through the thick, wet snow. Sarah could no longer feel her toes, but no longer cared. She could feel her heart working overtime, and she was exhausted and out of breath. The rock pile was larger than the others, big enough to conceal small caves or hide old secrets.

"Is this it?!" Sarah yelled above the wind.

Mark looked around. "Could be. We'll have to climb. The entrance was further up." They began a slow ascent over dangerous rocks and crevices concealed by snow and ice. As they neared the top, Sarah caught a glimpse of darkness hidden behind a mound of snow. It seemed big enough for an entrance.

"Mark, over here!" Sarah struggled to move the heavy snow aside, scooping it out with her arm. Mark crawled around the mound over to her side.

"Let me see." He peered inside. "This could be it." They both began digging away at the crevice, scooping piles of snow out until Mark was able to stick his head in further. "There's a cavern back there; I can see it. Dig faster!" They dug frantically, and Mark could see that the snow had not filled up the cavern. "I think I can climb in."

"Are you sure?"

"Yeah, it's not big enough for both of us, but I can definitely get in."

"Just be careful. If you fall and get trapped, I can't get in there to help you."

Mark began to crawl inside. He could feel the snow from above trickling into his collar and down the back of his shirt. He felt the cold wetness on his knees and his legs. Mark realized that if he were to find the body, they would have to act fast. If the girl didn't get them, then the elements surely would.

He had no flashlight with him and used the light from his phone to guide him down into the narrow tunnel. Even in the darkness, it seemed somehow familiar to him. He had dreamt about that night many times and felt certain that he could find the way.

Sarah waited outside, scanning the open chasm. Her head pounded, and at times her vision blurred. One pile of rocks would become two, and two swirling snow devils became four. She no longer trusted her senses as the fever took hold of her. The wind transformed into whispers, then back again to wind. At times, it seemed to be calling her name, beckoning her. Then, above the wind, she heard what she thought were sirens. She tried to focus, shaking her head several times and pinching her numb face. The sound grew, rising above the wind.

"Mark," she called down into the crevice. He had descended beyond her line of view. "Hurry!" she cried.

Mark heard the sirens too and felt his heart skip a beat. *She's coming*, he thought. He snaked his way farther into the tunnel. *Either this place got smaller, or I got bigger.* He almost smiled at this thought, but knew that the sirens meant she was close. *How can it be colder in here than it is outside?* he thought. The floor of the cavern was close now, and he could already make out something buried in the snow. He reached the bottom and began to clear away as much snow as he could until he came across what appeared to be a skeletal hand. As he dug around it, he found that much of it was calcified, almost fossilized. Fearful of breaking it apart into brittle pieces if he pulled too hard, he grabbed a loose rock nearby and began chipping away at it. Up against the rear wall of the cavern, he could see what must have been the skull. Mark could no longer feel the sting of the wind but heard its mad howl echoing down the cavern to him as he dug faster.

"Mark, please hurry!" Sarah screamed down into the cavern.

"I found it, but it's stuck!" He yelled back. He felt it loosen, but the skeleton would not budge. "Goddamn you," he whispered, his blows coming down harder, more urgent. He cleared the snow away from the skull, then began to pull it from the body. He used his rock to smash into the neck several times. The cold wetness had sunk past the cotton layer of his gloves, and Mark could no longer feel his fingers. He no longer cared. Outside, the sirens were growing louder. The skull was coming loose but still fighting to stay attached to the rest of the body. "Come on, you bastard," he muttered.

He heard Sarah scream something down to him, but the sound of his work and the sirens drowned her words out. He stopped. "What is it? What did you say?"

"She's coming, Mark! Hurry!"

Sarah could see the small figure moving down the slope of the quarry. She moved along with the wind, as if she were a part of it. Snow devils swirled around her, spinning off in every direction. As stealthily as she could, Sarah crept around the other side of the rocks, where she was out of sight. *Did she see me?* she thought. *Or does she already know where we are?* The onslaught of snow had thickened and made everything hard to see. Her field of vision grew smaller, and she could only see a few yards in front of her. The wind played tricks on her ears, drowning out everything but the storm. The girl had swept through the entire island in a single night, leaving as much damage as the storm she traveled in on. *They never had a chance. Just like the girl and her father never had a chance on that boat.*

Mark came crawling out of the entrance, covered in snow, gasping as his heart strained against the exertion and the elements. "Sarah?"

"I'm over here, Mark. She's in the quarry with us now!"

Mark climbed alongside the rocks until he found Sarah on a small ledge. She stared at him in confusion. "Where the hell is the body?"

Mark reached into his jacket and pulled out a skull. "This was all I could manage to get out."

Sarah gestured desperately. "So, what do we do now?!"

Mark peered out into the abyss of snow and wind. "We wait. There's nothing else left for us to do." He looked down at the skull in his hands and began to sob. Sarah reached out her hand to grab his.

"I'm sorry, Sarah. I'm just so sorry."

A strange column formed, clearing a path through the storm. It was as if a tunnel through the storm itself had opened up invisible walls on both sides, holding back the wind and snow. Through the clearing, they could see a tiny figure making its way towards them. Her hair seemed to flow freely against the force of the wind. The passageway led straight towards them.

Mark turned to Sarah. "I'm climbing down."

She held onto his hand. "Let me come with you."

He shook his head. "No, this is my fault. This has always been my fault. If something happens to me, I want you to be the one who gets away."

Sarah shook her head frantically. "Mark, where the hell will I go?"

He looked past the girl into the storm that followed her. "You're gonna' have to make it back to the mainland. Get off this island, Sarah. Leave it and never come back."

And with that, Mark began his descent down the rocks. He tucked the skull back under his jacket, using his hands to help slowly guide him down. Sarah watched him and then saw the darkened outline of the little girl stop and wait. She didn't know what Mark's plan was, or if he even had a plan. But she knew he was right about leaving the island, and that was what frightened her most. She knew there was no point in searching the island for survivors; there were none. All she could do now was watch as Mark made his way down the rocky slope, as the little girl watched down from below.

Mark had reached the bottom, and as he turned around, he saw the girl approaching him. From her hiding spot, Sarah could see that Mark had pulled the skull from his coat. He knelt, placing the skull at his feet, and then backed away a few steps. For a moment, the girl did not move from her space. Sarah could not make out her face and did not want to. It was blurred by the snow and shrouded by her hair.

Suddenly, the girl bent over and picked up the skull. She examined it, holding it up above her with both hands.

Mark slowly backed away until he could retreat no further, the wall of rocks impeding his escape.

Sarah heard another sound above the wind. It sounded like a faint scratching, but she could not place its source. It grew louder, a dragging sound, like rock being dragged over rock. She looked around, but the rest of the quarry was empty. Yet the sounds continued, as if they were right next to her. Then she realized where the sounds were coming from: inside the cavern of stones. From her hiding spot, she could see the entrance. Down below, she could see the shadowy silhouette of the girl holding the skull and beckoning. *Calling who?* She wondered. And then she saw it...

It crawled slowly out from the mouth of the cavern. From her vantage point, she watched as two skeletal hands reached out, grabbed onto nearby rocks, and began to pull themselves out from the hole. Headless and covered in snow, she saw what was now forming into the remains of a skeleton coming to life. Sarah clamped a hand over her mouth, trying not to scream. She could smell something foul in the air, fouler than dead fish or rotting flesh. She felt her stomach churning, and the urge to vomit was overpowering. The form slowly crawled down the slope of the rock formations, almost spider-like in its movements. It was heading toward them, but Mark did not see it.

The little girl remained in front of him, summoning the rest of her father's body. Sarah removed her hand, screaming, "Mark, look out!" But the thing was upon him even before he had a chance to turn his head; both of its hands locked around his neck.

As he struggled against it, all he could get out was, "Sarah, run!"

Without a moment's hesitation, she began to climb down. She did not take the time to be careful, allowing herself to slide down the slippery edges. When she came to the last rock, she lost her balance and slid down onto the snowy floor of the quarry. She could no longer see Mark, but could hear his screams of pain. With all the strength she had left in her, she began to run.

Mark felt the cold, bony fingers clasped firmly around his neck. As much as he tried to fight against it, he had no more strength left in him. He stared ahead at the girl, whose face was finally revealed to him. It was a young face, but twisted, wasted away by years of rot and hate. Her toothy smile, full of hate, and those pupil-less eyes, staring blankly through him. Her frilly white dress was filthy and torn, and he smelled the stench of decay, the stink of the lake on the hottest day. She walked slowly towards him and reached out her hand. It was small, and he could see bits of bones through the wasted flesh. The more he tried to struggle against the grip that held him, the tighter it became. He could barely breathe, and his chest burned.

The little girl approached him. She was no longer smiling. She reached her hand out to his chest, which was exposed after he had removed the skull from his jacket. She touched it, and without piercing flesh, her hand went inside him, reaching deep, past his ribs, until finally it clasped his heart. It was the coldest, darkest thing he had ever felt. As she stared at him with those dead, lidless eyes, and he at her, he felt the last remnants of warmth being siphoned out of him. All of his extremities went numb, and all the sounds around him were muted and then silenced. As his vision began to fade to black, he found himself sinking into a wet abyss, the darkest waters he had ever known. Up above the surface of the water, he saw a storm and heard the distant, muted booms of thunder. He felt himself sinking deeper, reaching out for help, holding the last gasps of air in his burning lungs. He could just barely make out the shape of a boat, heading away, leaving him here to sink all alone. He had never felt so alone. Even before he sank to the bottom, he knew that he would wait down there until one day his hate would awaken him from his slumber at the bottom of the lake, and he would come back and find those who had left him behind to die.

Mark opened his eyes and watched the little girl sink to the bottom of the lake. Her hands reached out to him, and then she disappeared into the darkest depths of the water, where she would wait. When the last of his breath finally gave out, his lungs filled with the coldest water he had ever known, and then there was nothing.

CHAPTER FORTY-EIGHT

Sarah looked out over the white expanse, and the distance between her and the mainland seemed endless. She was all alone now. Mark was gone, dead most likely. She hoped his death had been quick and painless. She had not wanted him to suffer, even after everything he had told her. She fought back tears. It was midday now, and she knew it would not be until nightfall that she reached the other side, just as Luke had said. She had no snowmobile, no company, and no one to hold her hand as she stepped across the ice. The fever had taken hold of her, and she knew that once she stepped foot off this island, she would never come back again.

She stopped, gasping for air. The trek out to the quarry and back had tapped much of the strength she had left. As she made her way back to the shore, Sarah did not look behind her. She did want to know if the girl was behind her, ready to place her bony hand on her shoulder. *Run to the beach and don't look back*, she repeated to herself over and over again as she ran. Out across the lake, she no longer saw the ice figures that had attacked Luke. Ahead of her, there was nothing but ice, snow, and a treacherous wind that was sure to steal what little fight she had left. Beyond that was a thick, white veil of snow, shrouding the salvation of the mainland. But it was there, on the other side. All she had to do was leave. She closed her eyes, tightened her fists until her nails dug into her palms, and took her first step out onto the ice.

Sarah's fever dulled her senses, and her body was too weak to register the panic that had taken hold of her every time she had tried to leave the island in the past. Still, she trembled as she felt the world spinning and felt the sickness in her stomach grow with rising urgency. Behind her, the sirens were still blaring, taunting her. She moved one foot, then another, staring straight ahead into the white nothingness. Her legs trembled beneath her. She was exhausted, ready to collapse onto any resting place she could find. And she still had so much farther to go...

Sarah had not willingly ventured out onto the lake on her own for what seemed a lifetime now, and the world seemed to expand before her very eyes. It went on forever. *I could become a part of that other place,* she thought. *All I have to do is make it across.* A sudden gust of wind from behind nearly blew her down, and she smelled the familiar foul stench again. She turned and saw not one but two darkened silhouettes standing on the shore, staring out at her. A man and a child. Not moving, just watching. Sarah began to quicken her pace. Her body ached, and as she felt her old fear creeping back upon her, she began to cry.

"Stop it," she told herself. She pictured Alice walking next to her, and suddenly, here she was. She was walking alongside her sister. Alice laughed mockingly at her. "You'll have to speed it up if you want to get out of here alive."

"Shut up," Sarah said aloud. "I can make it."

Alice continued walking alongside her, matching her pace. "Remember the last time we were out here together? Remember those people in the boat, the ones Dad left behind so he could save us? That was our last time out here, sis."

"You're not really here." Sarah was fighting against the wind. The imaginary argument with her sister was at least helping to distract her.

"Why did you stay on this island so long?" Alice demanded. "You're almost in your mid-30s, and you haven't done anything with your life."

"You were the coward who left," Sarah said. "You were the one who packed up your bags and never came back. Not once did you come back to visit Dad's grave. And look where you are now." Sarah looked alongside her again, but Alice was gone. There were no footprints behind her. But the argument had given her the strength she needed. She was farther across now, just a few miles away from the shore. The two figures remained behind, watching her. She wondered if they were confident that she wouldn't get far. *Maybe they expect me to fall on my knees and beg for mercy. Throw my arms up. Well, I'm not going to."* Sarah stopped in her tracks, looking back at them. "You can fucking watch me leave you behind, both of you!" she called to them. But still, the figures did not move.

Sarah's heart pounded, and she knew her body was working overtime. She thought of the daily runs she had made around the island. *Where was that strength now?* she thought. Her hands and feet had grown numb, and her legs felt heavy as sandbags. She swallowed, but her dry throat allowed her no comfort. She would have given anything for a sip of water. She felt her chapped lips sting and tasted the salty blood that followed. She slipped a few times, finding it harder to pull herself back up again. And still, the two behind her watched silently.

The island was getting farther and farther behind her. Sarah knew she at least had the will, if not the physical strength. She felt the sweat trickling down her back turn icy cold. The inside of her shirt was soaked, and she was both hot and cold at once. She hugged herself as she trudged on, snow swirling all around her. As she lifted her arm to shield her face from a fierce onslaught of wind, she caught her foot on an outlying chunk of ice and slipped. She quickly extended her arms to cushion her fall but landed face-first on the slick ice.

The world was quiet around her, and as she slowly opened her eyes, Sarah wondered how such a peaceful world could harbor such horrors. She was soaked through, and her body shook. Try as she might, Sarah found she did not have the strength to push herself back up to her feet. The distance ahead was still so far. Behind her, she knew they watched and waited. Again, she attempted to rise, and again her arms betrayed her. *I'm sorry, Dad,* she thought. She closed her eyes, feeling the cold breeze lull her to sleep, whispering its arctic lullabies in her ear.

"You're not going to get anywhere lying there like that."

It was a man's voice, low but not threatening. Sarah opened her eyes again. She recognized that voice. "Dad?"

She lifted her head but saw nothing. *Am I going insane?* she thought. *Or are hallucinations one of the symptoms of hypothermia?* She let her forehead rest on the ice, cooling her hot flesh. "Daddy, please don't let me die out here." Her voice was barely above a whisper.

"Once you start walking, you'll be alright," the voice said to her. "Just keep your eyes focused ahead and don't look back."

Sarah rolled over onto her back and sat up slowly. A lone ray of light shone down up ahead, and the swirling snow glittered in the brilliant light. She looked out across the barren landscape, and not too far ahead, she glimpsed the outline of the mainland on the other side. She knew it was still far on foot, but it no longer seemed like some unknown place on the other side of the world. And standing a few yards away, she saw a familiar figure shimmering in the light. Even from her distance, she recognized his outline, his hands in his pockets, and the way he always seemed to hunch over a bit when he was talking. It was her father.

Tears swelled in her eyes. She felt she could no longer trust anything that she saw or felt. But this seemed real, and she recognized his voice. "Dad," her voice was raspy.

The shimmering figure said nothing, and she could not tell if it was moving towards or away from her.

"I don't know if I can make it," she said. "It's so far."

"Do you remember our walks around the island when you were young, when you were tired and wanted me to carry you on my back?"

"I remember."

"I always said you could make it, that the walk would make you stronger. It did. It always has."

The figure shimmered. It seemed translucent, yet it had form, and she knew that form was her father. Her whole body ached, and she felt she could no longer tell reality from hallucination. But hearing his voice again, her heart felt the fullest it had in years. She pulled herself back up to her feet and stood watching as the figure began to dissipate into the dying storm.

"See you on the other side, Sarah."

And then it was gone, as if it had never been there at all. But she found herself back on her feet, and more light streamed in from the sky above. The storm was finally nearing its end. Miles away, the faint, unmoving outline of the mainland beckoned to her. As she began to walk, she remembered the two who were watching her from the island. She wondered if they were still there. 'Just keep your eyes ahead and don't look back,' her father had said. But if this was to be the last that she would ever see of the island, she wanted one glimpse, one last goodbye to the only home she had ever known. But as she turned around to look, all she could see was the man and his daughter out on the ice, not far behind her. The sky remained dark above the island, as if the storm had been anchored to it.

Sarah began to run, though her legs ached. She felt the force of the wind behind her, emanating from the island in a vortex aimed primarily at the path she was taking. It rocked her, testing what strength she had left in her legs. As a small slit in the sky above the mainland released another ray of light, Sarah could see the sky above her darkening. She ran on, blocking out the sheer horror and pain she felt with another memory of her father.

"The clouds always look darker when the sun is out, especially after a storm passes." She sat on his knee as they looked out over the lake. The water was still rough, but the storm that had arrived unannounced was now leaving just as abruptly. The retreating storm clouds appeared black, and the sun's glow was blindingly brilliant. "That's the storm fighting against the sun. Even when the clouds block it out, it's still up there above them. It'll always come through." She hugged him as she watched the storm clouds disappear over the horizon of the lake.

The clouds above the mainland were fiery and brilliant, reflecting the rays from the rising sun. It didn't seem so far away now. The fire that she thought she had left behind on the island burned deep within her. Though her lungs ached, she felt stronger, more sure of herself as she ran. She had found a rhythm with her steps. How many times had she run long distances on that island? *I could run laps around it all day*, she thought. And so she imagined this was just another one of her runs, her final run of the island. But as she found her stride, something grabbed her ankle, and again she felt the cold, hard surface of the ice.

She looked behind her and saw a piece of ice that almost looked like a hand gripping her ankle tightly. Not too far behind, she could see the man and his daughter, their faces no longer wasted away. Their forms were complete, and they were only a few yards from her now. They walked hand in hand, staring coldly at her with angry, unblinking eyes. Sarah pulled as hard as she could, but the ice would not release her.

Sarah had lost everyone and everything, and she would not allow them to take anything more from her, not while she had any fight left. She squirmed out of her shoe until her foot was free. The two were almost upon her, and she scrambled up and began to run again. She ignored the stinging pain on her bare right foot until it finally became numb, and the pain faded.

She did not look back again as she ran. The mainland was her focal point, and her eyes remained fixed upon it. Her limbs felt numb and disconnected from her body, as if they were no longer a whole. The wailing from the sirens was growing more distant behind her. As she ran on, she realized it had stopped snowing. Large gaps of clear blue sky emerged from the darkness. Sarah remembered the storm from her childhood, out on the lake with Alice. She remembered how the sky cleared later that day, the bright sunset that had eclipsed the darkness as if there had never been any storm. This storm would pass, too, just as they always did. She could see the outlines of houses popping up one by one along the shoreline, still and quiet, some with lights already on. Her quick, labored breaths misted in front of her.

As she approached the first group of rocks lining the banks of the shore, she felt almost silly to have lived so close without ever venturing over to the other side. The world suddenly expanded and unfolded before her very eyes, and the possibilities seemed infinite. As she reached the beach, she could no longer hear the sirens from back on the island. She turned around and saw that the storm had moved on from the island. Far out across the ice, she could just make out two tiny, dark figures, standing still. They watched her for some time, and then, hands interlocked, turned around and walked back toward the island until they disappeared behind the milky white horizon.

Sarah watched the island silently for a moment. It had taken her so long to get to the other side. The island, her home, looked so distant and far away. She wished she had found the courage years ago to cross this lake, along with the others. To be free. She had been a prisoner for her whole life, a prisoner she had made for herself. Sarah could see her shadow before her as she stood there in a ray of sunlight that broke through the clouds. She smiled as she felt its warmth upon her skin, closed her eyes, and collapsed onto the rocky beach.

CHAPTER FORTY-NINE

In her hospital bed, Sarah drifted into some nameless world between sleep and consciousness. All the sounds of the world were muted and distant to her. Her skin burning from her rising fever, she was unable to open her eyes. She could only sense the presence of someone in the room. Their hushed, concerned voices seemed distant.

In her mind's eye, she could see the outline of the island from above. She saw the rocky outline of Sandy Stone and the calm, peaceful waves breaking upon the rocks and then receding. The waves ebbed and flowed with her breaths. Each wave would recede farther back, then reach out for one more touch of the sand, leaving its print; then it would recede even farther back into the depths. The tides slowed, as did her breathing. As they receded away from the island, she could see Alice standing there along with her father. They were both waving and smiling at her. In the sky of blue glass, there were no storm clouds,-+ no wailing sirens, and no signs of past sins left unforgiven.

She only realized that her hand was still clenched into a fist, and finally she relaxed and let go. The sounds from the outside world grew fainter, and she heard the beeping of her monitor begin to stretch, wail, and flatline. And then there she was, back on her island, the water glittering in the warm summer sun, the trees once again lush after a barren winter. Here in this place, she knew that these waters would never freeze over again, the leaves would never fall, the sun would never set, and all the memories and people she loved would be built like a house for her to call home for all eternity.

She saw herself once again as a child back on Sandy Stone, hidden away within the rocks of the quarry, hiding from her father on that summer afternoon. *Sarah! Sarah!* He was calling her name. He looked so distant, just a shimmering figure in the low summer sun. But this time, Sarah did not stay hidden for long. This time, she ran out laughing, running up next to him, giving him a playful push, his smile full of relief. As she walked alongside him, her legs grew heavy, and she found that she could no longer walk.

"I'm tired, Daddy," she said. Her father smiled and picked her up. As he carried her, she looked back over his shoulder, leaving the quarry behind her until it was out of sight.

"You can sleep now, Sarah," he said.

And then she closed her eyes.

For nearly 20 years, the island lay quiet. From the mainland, the sight of it still brought shudders, and many parents would not let their children venture out into the lake. Any body of water that shared space with that place was to be feared and avoided. It went unspoken amongst the adults, but children whispered about it at sleepovers, during long nights after their parents had gone to bed. For these 20 years, the island was shunned, then all but forgotten. It became just a giant mass of land that boaters kept a distance from. When a storm would break out over the lake, people would shut their blinds and lock their doors. There was never an explanation for what had happened there, but rumors spread quickly in the small coastal towns that lined Lake Erie. There were stories of one survivor who had made it across to the beach, covered in frostbite, and eventually died from pneumonia in a hospital bed. Eventually. All the businesses left behind on the island were either up for sale or left to decay.

After twenty years, as fewer people remembered and more forgot, the island slowly began to rebuild and reopen. New hotels, along with new restaurants, were built. The island was renamed. No one ever mentioned the name "Sandy Stone" again, nor its dark history. More years passed, and the stories about the island were only whispered around campfires at night. Most people had forgotten about what happened on the island during that storm.

One night, a young girl went missing in the forest of red pines. She had wandered off on her own while her parents prepared dinner inside. As she explored the island, she had drifted off the path and out of the light from the lampposts. Her parents, the police, and some neighbors had all ventured out across the island with flashlights, calling her name. They had searched the amusement park, which, like everything else on the island, had also reopened with a different name. They searched the quarry, which had once again been filled with water. They searched the streets downtown, where all the shops and even the movie theater had been brought back to life but were closed for the night. But they could not find the girl. Just as her parents had begun to lose hope, they saw the sheriff turn the corner with their daughter sitting on his shoulders. As he placed her on the ground, they asked him where he had found her. He explained that he saw her walking on the path that led from the pine forest. They asked her if she was alright, and she did not seem afraid. Their daughter had told them that she had gone into the forest, gotten lost when the sun went down, and could not find her way back. She explained that a beautiful young woman with short hair approached her in the forest. She asked if the little girl was lost. She said yes, and the woman said she would help her find her way back home. She took the girl's hand and led her down a path that followed the edge of the island. The girl was frightened, but when the woman smiled at her, she knew she did not have to be afraid. When the police found her walking alone and she told them about the woman, they jogged down the path to find her and thank her. But they found no one on the path. The girl's parents hugged their daughter and told her that if she were to ever see the woman on the island again, she was to point her out so they could thank her.

"Did you at least get her name?" they asked.

"Yes," their daughter said. "She said her name was Sarah."

At night, the island was quiet again. The last of the fireflies had faded away for the night, and the first early songs of the birds had begun. Across the horizon, the dull blue glow of dawn presented itself. Here on the island where all things still slept peacefully, where the morning waves gently kissed the rocky shores, and the last of the stars readied themselves to fade from the sky, here a woman walks along the path that lines the perimeter of the island, walking past houses and walking past stores, and she walks by them alone. And as the early sun rises and casts its first few rays, she is gone, as if she had never been there at all.

Acknowledgements

I would like to thank Crystal Baynam and the staff at Baynam Books for providing me the opportunity to bring my novel to life. I would also like to thank all my professors and classmates at the Cleveland State University NEOMFA program, especially my thesis panel consisting of Imad Rahman, Christopher Barzak, and Hilary Plum, whose guidance helped provide me with the confidence to see my novel to the end. Additionally, I would love to thank my wife Samantha Lewis, and my sister Nancy and Cathy Lewis, along with so many of my beta-readers including Sara Wagner, Joseph Hoyt and Meghan Wagner. Your notes greatly helped guide my story along. I'd also like to thank all the other individuals that helped me along the way: Cat and Eliot Klein, Ryan Frazier, Stephen Johnson, Dave Omeara, and all the wonderful people of Lakeside, Ohio and Kelly's Island, Ohio who helped inspire this story.

ABOUT THE AUTHOR

Joseph Lewis received his MFA in Creative Writing from the NEOMFA program at Cleveland State University. His work has appeared in several literary magazines, including Coffin Bell, Novel Noctule and Black Works. His work has also been published in Piece by Piece, a horror anthology published by Dark Moon Rises Press. His screenplay, Retribution, won second place in the Ohio Independent Screenplay Contest. A former Peace Corps volunteer, he taught Western Literature and Film Studies at Sichuan University of Arts and Science in China. He is also an active member of the Horror Writers Association. He currently lives in Cleveland, Ohio. Please visit his website at https://jlewis.squarespace.com